KU-440-614

This book belongs to

....

Ten-minute Stories

Miles
KeLLy

First published in 2011 by Miles Kelly Publishing Ltd
Harding's Barn, Bardfield End Green, Thaxted, Essex, CM6 3PX, UK

Copyright © Miles Kelly Publishing Ltd 2011

2 4 6 8 10 9 7 5 3 1

Publishing Director Belinda Gallagher

Creative Director Jo Cowan

Editor Amanda Askew

Senior Designer Joe Jones

Production Manager Elizabeth Collins

Reprographics Anthony Cambray, Stephan Davis

All rights reserved. No part of this publication may be reproduced, stored in a
retrieval system, or transmitted by any means, electronic, mechanical, photocopying,
recording or otherwise, without the prior permission of the copyright holder.

ISBN 978-1-84810-546-1

Printed in China

British Library Cataloguing-in-Publication Data
A catalogue record for this book is available from the British Library

ACKNOWLEDGEMENTS
Artworks are from the Miles Kelly Artwork Bank

Every effort has been made to acknowledge the source and copyright holder of each picture.
Miles Kelly Publishing apologises for any unintentional errors or omissions.

Made with paper from a sustainable forest

www.mileskelly.net
info@mileskelly.net

www.factsforprojects.com

Self-publish your
children's book

buddingpress.co.uk

Contents

Wisdom and Fortune

Craftiness and Cunning

Animal Adventures

Lads and Lasses

Heroic Deeds

Amazing Adventures

Rags and Riches

Love and Friendship

Royal Tales

Enchantment and Sorcery

Wisdom
and Fortune

The Four Clever Brothers

By the Brothers Grimm

A POOR MAN ONCE SAID to his four sons, "Dear children, I have nothing to give you. You must go out into the wide world and try your luck. Begin by learning some craft or another, and see how you can get on."

So the brothers took their walking sticks in their hands, and their little bundles on their shoulders, and after bidding their father goodbye, went out of the gate together. When they had gone some way, they came to four crossways, each leading to a different country.

Then the eldest said, "Here we must part, but on this day in four years time we will come back to this spot, and in the meantime each must try to see what he can do for himself."

So each brother went his way, and as the eldest was hastening on he met a man, who asked him where he was going, and what he wanted.

"I am going to try my luck in the world, and should like to begin by learning some art or trade," answered he.

"Then," said the man, "Come with me, and I will teach you to become the most cunning thief that has ever been."

"No," said the other, "that is not an honest calling, and what can one look to earn but the gallows?"

"Oh!" said the man. "You need not fear the gallows, for I will only teach you to steal what will be fair game. I meddle with nothing but what no one else can get or care anything about."

So the young man agreed to follow his trade, and he soon showed himself so clever, that nothing could escape him that he had once set his mind upon.

The second brother also met a man, who, when he found out what he was setting out upon, asked him what craft he meant to follow.

"I do not know," said he.

"Then come with me, and be a stargazer. It is a noble art, for nothing can be hidden from you, when once you understand the stars." The plan pleased him much,

and he soon became such a skilful stargazer, that when he had served out his time, and wanted to leave his master, he gave him a glass, and said, "With this you can see all that is passing in the sky and on earth, and nothing can be hidden from you."

The third brother met a huntsman, who took him with him, and taught him so well about hunting, that he became very clever in the craft of the woods. When he left his master he gave him a bow, and said, "Whatever you shoot at with this bow you will be sure to hit."

The youngest brother likewise met a man who asked him what he wished to do. "Would not you like," said he, "to be a tailor?"

"Oh, no!" said the young man. "Sitting cross-legged from morning to night, working backwards and forwards with a needle, will never suit me."

"Oh!" answered the man. "That is not my sort of tailoring. Come with me, and you will learn quite another kind of craft from that."

Not knowing what better to do, he came into the plan, and learnt tailoring from the beginning. When he left his master, he gave him a needle, and said, "You can sew anything with this, be it as soft as an egg or as hard as steel, and the joint will be so fine that no seam will be seen."

After the space of four years, at the time agreed upon, the four brothers met at the four crossroads, and having welcomed each other, set off towards their father's home, where they told him all that had

happened to them, and how each had learned some craft.

Then, one day, as they were sitting before the house under a very high tree, the father said, "I should like to try what each of you can do in this way." So he looked up, and said to the second son, "At the top of this tree there is a chaffinch's nest, tell me how many eggs there are in it."

The stargazer took his glass, looked up, and said, "Five."

"Now," said the father to the eldest son, "take away the eggs without letting the bird that is sitting upon them know anything of what you are doing."

So the cunning thief climbed up the tree, and brought back to his father the five eggs from under the bird, and it never saw or felt what he was doing, but kept sitting at its ease.

Then the father took the eggs, and put one on each corner of the table, and the fifth in the middle, and said to the huntsman, "Cut all the eggs in two pieces at one shot." The huntsman took up his bow, and at one shot struck all the five eggs as his father wished.

"Now comes your turn," said he to the young tailor, "sew the eggs and the young birds in them together again, so neatly that the shot shall have done them no harm." Then the tailor took his needle, and sewed the eggs as he was told, and when he had done, the thief was sent to take them back to the nest, and put them under the bird without its knowing it. Then she went on sitting, and hatched them, and in a few days they crawled out, and had only a little red streak across their necks, where the tailor had sewn them together.

"Well done, sons!" said the old man. "You have made good use of your time, and learnt something worth knowing, but I am sure I do not know which ought to have the prize. I wish that a time might soon come for you to turn your skill to some account!"

Not long after this there was a great bustle in the country, for the king's daughter had been carried off by a mighty dragon, and the king mourned over his loss day and night, and made it known that whoever brought her back to him should have her for a wife. Then the four brothers said to each other, "Here is a chance for us, let us try what we can do."

And they agreed to see whether they could not set the princess free. "I will soon find out where she is," said the stargazer, as he looked through his glass, and he soon cried out, "I see her far off, sitting upon a rock in the sea, and I can spy the dragon close by, guarding her."

Then he went to the king, and asked for a ship for himself and his brothers, and they sailed together over the sea, till they came to the right place. There they found the princess sitting, as the stargazer had said, on the rock, and the dragon was lying asleep, with his head upon her lap. "I dare not shoot at him," said the huntsman, "for I should kill the princess also."

"Then I will try my skill," said the thief, and went and stole her away from under the dragon, so quietly that the beast did not know it, but went on snoring.

Then away they hastened with her, full of joy in their boat towards the ship, but soon came the dragon roaring behind them through the air, for it awoke and missed the princess. But when it got over the boat, and wanted to pounce upon them and carry off the princess, the huntsman took up his bow and shot it straight through the heart so that it fell down dead. They were still not safe, for it was such a great beast that in its fall it overset the boat, and they had to swim in the open sea upon a few planks. So the tailor took his needle, and with a few large stitches put some of the planks together, and he sat down upon these, and sailed about and gathered up all pieces of the boat, and then tacked them together so quickly that the boat was soon ready, and they then reached the ship and got home safely.

When they took the princess back to her father, there was great rejoicing, and he said to the four brothers, "One of you shall marry her, but you must settle among yourselves which it is to be." Then there arose a quarrel between them, and the stargazer said, "If I had not found the princess out, all your skill would have been of no use, therefore she ought to be mine."

"Your seeing her would have been of no use," said

the thief, "if I had not taken her away from the dragon, therefore she ought to be mine."

"No, she is mine," said the huntsman, "for if I had not killed the dragon, it would, after all, have torn you and the princess into pieces."

"And if I had not sewn the boat together again," said the tailor, "you would all have been drowned, therefore she is mine."

Then the king said, "Each of you is right, and as all cannot have the young lady, the best way is for neither of you to have her. The truth is, there is somebody she likes a great deal better. But to make up for your loss, I will give each of you half a kingdom." So the brothers agreed that this plan would be much better than either quarrelling or marrying a lady who had no mind to have them. And the king then gave to each half a kingdom, as he had said, and they lived very happily the rest of their days. They took good care of their father, and somebody took better care of the young lady, than to let either the dragon or one of the craftsmen have her again.

I Wonder

By Kate Douglas Wiggin

ONCE UPON A TIME there was a man who had three sons – Peter, Paul, and the least of all, whom they called Youngling. I can't say the man had anything more than these three sons, for he hadn't one penny to rub against another. He told the lads, over and over again, that they must go out into the world and try to earn their bread, for at home there was nothing to be looked for but starving to death.

Now nearby the man's cottage was the king's palace, and, you must know, just against the windows a great oak had sprung up, which was so stout and tall that it took away all the light. The king had said he would give untold treasure to the man who could fell the oak,

but no one was man enough for that, for as soon as one chip of the oak's trunk flew off, two grew in its stead.

A well, too, the king desired, which was to hold water for the whole year, for all his neighbours had wells, but he hadn't any, and that he thought a shame. So the king said he would give both money and goods to anyone who could dig him such a well as would hold water for a whole year round, but no one could do it, for the palace lay high, high up on a hill, and they could only dig a few inches before they came upon rock.

But, as the king had set his heart on having these two things done, he had it given out far and wide, in all the churches of his dominion, that he who could fell the big oak in the king's courtyard, and get him a well that would hold water the whole year round, should have the princess and half the kingdom.

Well! You may easily know there was many a man who came to try his luck, but all their hacking and hewing, all their digging and delving, were of no avail. The oak grew taller and stouter at every stroke, and the rock grew no softer.

So one day the three brothers thought they'd set off and try, too, and their father hadn't a word against it, for, even if they didn't get the princess and half the kingdom, it might happen that they would get a place somewhere with a good master, and that was all he wanted. So when the brothers said they thought of going to the palace, their father said "Yes" at once, and Peter, Paul and Youngling went off from their home.

They had not gone far before they came to a fir wood, and up along one side of it rose a steep hillside, and as they went, they heard something hewing and hacking away up on the hill among the trees.

"I wonder now what it is that is hewing away up yonder?" said Youngling.

"You are always so clever with your wonderings," said Peter and Paul, both at once. "What wonder is it, pray, that a woodcutter should stand and hack up on a hillside?"

"Still, I'd like to see what it is, after all," said Youngling, and up he went.

"Oh, if you're such a child, it'll do you good to go and take a lesson," cried out his brothers after him.

But Youngling didn't care for what they said, he climbed the steep hillside towards where the noise came, and when he reached the place, what do you think he saw?

Why, an axe that stood there hacking and hewing, all by itself, at the trunk of a fir tree.

"Good day," said Youngling. "So you stand here all alone and hew, do you?"

"Yes, here I've stood and hewed and hacked a long, long time, waiting for you, my lad," said the axe.

"Well, here I am at last," said Youngling, as he took the axe, pulled it off its haft, and stuffed both head and haft into his wallet.

So when he climbed down again to his brothers, they began to jeer and laugh at him.

"And now, what funny thing was it you saw up on the hillside?" they said.

"Oh, it was only an axe we heard," said Youngling. When they had gone a bit farther they heard something digging and shovelling.

"I wonder, now," said Youngling, "what it is digging and shovelling up yonder at the top of the rock?"

"Ah, you're always so clever with your wonderings," said Peter and Paul again, "as if you'd never heard a woodpecker hacking and pecking at a hollow tree."

"Well, well," said Youngling, "I think it would be a piece of fun just to see what it really is."

And so off he set to climb the rock, while the others laughed and made fun of him. But he didn't care a bit for that. Up he clambered, and when he got near the top, what do you think he saw? Why, a spade that stood there digging and delving.

"Good day," said Youngling. "So you stand here all alone, and dig and delve?"

"Yes, that's what I do," said the spade, "and that's what I've done this many a long day, waiting for you, my lad."

"Well, here I am," said Youngling again, as he took the spade and knocked off its handle, and put it into his wallet, and then he climbed down again to his brothers.

"Well, what was it, so strange and rare," said Peter and Paul, "that you saw up there at the top of the rock?"

"Oh," said Youngling, "nothing more than a spade, that was what we heard."

So they went on again a good bit, till they came to a brook. They were thirsty after their long walk, and so they sat beside the brook to have a drink.

"I have a great fancy to see where this brook comes from," said Youngling.

So up alongside the brook he went, in spite of all that his brothers shouted after him. Nothing could stop him. On he went. And as he went up and up, the brook grew smaller and smaller, and at last, a little way farther on, what do you think he saw? Why, a great walnut, and out of that the water trickled.

"Good day," said Youngling again. "So you lie here and trickle, and run down all alone?"

"Yes, I do," said the walnut "and here have I trickled and run this many a long day, waiting for you, my lad."

"Well, here I am," said Youngling, as he took a lump of moss and plugged up the hole, so that the water wouldn't run out. Then he put the walnut into his wallet, and ran down to his brothers.

"Well," said Peter and Paul, "have you found where the water comes from? A rare sight it must have been!"

"Oh, after all, it was only a hole it ran out of," said Youngling, and the others laughed and made game of him again, but Youngling didn't mind that a bit.

So when they had gone a little farther, they came to the king's palace, but as every man in the kingdom had heard that he might win the princess and half the realm, if he could only fell the big oak and dig the king's well, so many had come to try their luck that the oak was now twice as stout and big as it had been at first, for you will remember that two chips grew for every one they hewed out with their axes.

So the king had now laid it down as a punishment that if anyone tried and couldn't fell the oak, he should be put on a barren island, and both his ears were to be clipped off. But the two brothers didn't let themselves be frightened by this threat, they were quite sure they could fell the oak, and Peter, as he was the eldest, was to try his hand first, but it went with him as with all the rest who had hewn at the oak —for every chip

he cut two grew in its place. So the king's men seized him, and clipped off both his ears, and put him out on the island.

Now Paul was to try his luck, but he fared just the same. When he had hewn two or three strokes, they began to see the oak grow, and so the king's men seized him, too, and clipped his ears, and put him out on the island, and they clipped his ears closer, because they said he ought to have taken a lesson from his brother.

So now Youngling was to try.

"If you want to look like a marked sheep, we're quite ready to clip your ears at once, and then you'll save yourself some trouble," said the king, for he was angry with him for his brothers' sake.

"Well, I'd just like to try first," said Youngling, and so he was given permission. Then he took his axe out of his wallet and fitted it to its handle.

"Hew away!" said he to his axe, and away it hewed, making the chips fly again, so that it wasn't long before down came the oak.

When that was done, Youngling pulled out his spade and fitted it to its handle.

"Dig away!" said he to his spade, and so the spade began to dig and delve till the earth and rock flew out in splinters, and he soon had the well deep enough, you may believe.

And when he had got it as big and deep as he chose, Youngling took out his walnut and laid it in one corner of the well, and pulled the plug of moss out.

"Trickle and run," said Youngling, and so the nut trickled and ran till the water gushed out of the hole in a stream, and in a short time the well was full.

So as Youngling had felled the oak that shaded the king's palace, and dug a well in the palace yard, he got the princess and half the kingdom, as the king had said, but it was lucky for Peter and Paul that they had lost their ears, else they might have grown tired of hearing how everyone said each hour of the day, "Well, after all, Youngling wasn't so much out of his mind when he took to wondering."

The Wise Girl

By Katharine Pyle

THERE WAS ONCE A GIRL who was wiser than the king and all his councillors – there never was anything like it. Her father was so proud of her that he boasted about her cleverness at home and abroad. He could not keep his tongue still about it. One day he was boasting to one of his neighbours, and he said, "The girl is so clever that not even the king could ask her a question she couldn't answer, or read her a riddle she couldn't unravel."

Now it so chanced the king was sitting at a window nearby, and he overheard what the girl's father was saying. The next day he sent for the man to come before him.

"I hear you have a daughter who is so clever that no one in the kingdom can equal her, and is that so?" asked the king.

Yes, the man said, it was no more than the truth. Too much could not be said of her wit and cleverness.

That was well, and the king was glad to hear it. He had thirty eggs, they were fresh and good, but it would take a clever person to hatch chickens out of them. He then bade his chancellor get the eggs and give them to the man.

"Take these home to your daughter," said the king, "and bid her hatch them out for me. If she succeeds she shall have a bag of money for her pains, but if she fails you shall be beaten as a vain boaster."

The man was troubled when he heard this. Still his daughter was so clever he was almost sure she could hatch out the eggs. He carried them home to her and told her exactly what the king had said. It did not take the girl long to find out that the eggs had been boiled.

When she told her father, he made a great to-do. That was a pretty trick for the king to have played upon him. Now he would have to take a beating and all the neighbours would hear about it. Would to heaven he had never had a daughter at all if that was what came of it.

The girl, however, told him to be of good cheer. "Go to bed and sleep quietly," said she. "I will think of some way out of the trouble. No harm shall come to you, even if I have to go to the palace myself and take the beating in your place."

The next day the girl gave her father a bag of boiled beans and told him to take them out to a certain place where the king rode by every day. "Wait until you see him coming," said she, "and then begin to sow the beans." At the same time he was to call out so loudly that the king could not help but hear him.

The man took the bag of beans and went out to the field his daughter had spoken of. He waited until he saw the king coming, and then he began to sow the beans, and at the same time to cry aloud, "Come sun, come rain! Heaven grant that these boiled beans may yield me a good crop."

The king was surprised that any one should be so stupid as to think boiled beans would grow and yield a crop. He did not recognize the man, for he had only seen him once, and he stopped his horse to speak to him. "My poor man," said he, "how can you expect boiled beans to grow? Do you not know that is impossible?"

"Whatever the king commands should be possible,"

answered the man, "and if chickens can hatch from boiled eggs why should not boiled beans yield a crop?"

When the king heard this he looked at the man more closely, and then he recognized him as the father of the clever daughter.

"You have indeed a clever daughter," said he. "Take your beans home and bring me back the eggs."

The man was glad when he heard that, and made

haste to obey. He carried the beans home then took the eggs and brought them back to the palace.

After the king had received the eggs he gave the man a handful of flax. "Take this to your daughter," he said, "and bid her make for me a full set of sails for a large ship. If she does this she shall receive half of my kingdom, but if she fails, you shall have a beating."

The man returned home lamenting his hard lot.

"What is the matter?" asked his daughter. "Has the king set another task that I must do?"

Yes, that he had – her father showed her the flax the king had sent her and gave her the message.

"Do not be troubled," said the girl. "No harm shall come to you. Go to bed and tomorrow I will send the king an answer that will satisfy him."

The man believed what his daughter said. He went to bed and slept quietly.

The next day, the girl gave her father a small piece of wood. "Carry this to the king," said she. "Tell him I am ready, but first let him make me a large ship out of this wood so that I may fit the sails to it."

The father did as the girl said, and the king was surprised at the cleverness of the girl.

"That is all very well," said he, "and I will excuse her from this task. Here is a glass mug. Take it home to your clever daughter. Tell her it is my command that she dip out the waters from the seabed so that I can ride over the bottom dry. If she does this, I will take her for my wife, but if she fails you shall be beaten."

The man took the mug and hastened home, weeping aloud and bemoaning his fate.

"Well, and what is it?" asked his daughter. "What does the king demand of me now?"

The man gave her the glass mug and told her what the king had said.

"Do not be troubled," said the girl. "Go to bed and sleep in peace. You shall not be beaten, and soon I shall be reigning as queen over all this land."

He trusted her, so went to bed and dreamed he saw her sitting by the king wearing a crown.

The next morning the girl gave her father a bunch of wool. "Take this to the king," she said. "Tell him that I am willing to dip the sea dry, but first, with this wool, let him stop up all the rivers that flow into the ocean."

The man did exactly as his daughter instructed him. He took the wool to the king and repeated what she had said word for word.

Then the king saw that the girl was indeed a clever one, and he sent for her to come before him.

She came just as she was, in her homespun dress

and her rough shoes and with a cap on her head, but for all her mean clothing, she was as pretty and fine as a flower, and the king was not slow to see it. Still he wanted to make sure for himself that she was as clever as her messages had been.

"Tell me," said he, "what sound can be heard the farthest throughout the world?"

"The thunder that echoes through heaven and earth," answered the girl, "and your own royal commands that go from lip to lip."

The king was so well satisfied with the way the girl answered that he no longer hesitated, he was determined that she should be his queen, and that they should be married at once.

The girl had something to say to this, however. "I am but a poor girl," said she, "and my ways are not your ways. It may well be that you will tire of me and send me back to my father's house to live. Promise that if this should happen, you will allow me to take the thing that has grown most precious to me."

The king was willing to agree to this. Then she and the king were married with the greatest magnificence, and she came to live in the palace.

Now after the girl became queen, she would wear nothing but magnificent robes and jewels and ornaments, for that seemed to her only right and proper for a queen. But the king, who was of a very jealous nature, thought his wife did not care at all for him, but only for the fine things that he could give her.

One day the king and queen were to ride abroad together, and the queen spent so much time in dressing herself that the king was kept waiting, and he became very angry. When she appeared before him, he would not even look at her. "You care nothing for me, but only for the jewels and fine clothes you wear!" he cried. "Take with you those that are the most precious to you, as I promised you, and return to your father's house. I will no longer have a wife who cares only for my possessions and not at all for me."

Very well, the girl was willing to go. "And I will be happier in my father's house than I was when I first met you," said she. Nevertheless she begged that she might spend one more night in the palace, and that she and the king might sup together once again before she returned home.

So he and his wife supped together that evening and when the king was not looking, she put a sleeping potion in the cup and gave it to him to drink. He drank it to the very last drop, suspecting nothing, but soon after he sank down among the cushions in a deep

sleep. Then the queen ordered him to be carried to her father's house and laid in the bed there.

When the king awoke, he was surprised to find himself in the peasant's cottage. The girl came to the bedside, dressed in common clothes.

"What means this?" said the king.

"My dear husband," said the girl, "your promise was that I might carry with me the thing that had become most precious to me in the castle. That is you."

The king could no longer feel angry. They returned to the palace, and from then on, lived together happily.

Hans in Luck

By Joseph Jacobs

SOME MEN ARE BORN to good luck – all they do or try to do comes right and all that falls to them is gain, all their geese are swans and all their cards are trumps. Toss them which way you will, they will always, like poor puss, alight upon their legs, and only move on so much the faster. The world may very likely not always think of them as they think of themselves, but what care they for the world? What can it know about the matter?

One of these lucky beings was neighbour Hans. Seven years he had worked hard for his master. At last he said, "Master, my time is up, I must go home and see my poor mother once more – so pray pay me my

wages and let me go." And the master said, "You have been a faithful servant, Hans, so your pay shall be handsome." He gave him a lump of silver as big as his head.

Hans took out his handkerchief, put the piece of silver into it, threw it over his shoulder, and jogged off on his road homewards. As he went lazily on, dragging one foot after another, a man came in sight, trotting gaily along on a capital horse. "Ah!" said Hans aloud. "What a fine thing it is to ride on horseback! There he sits as easy and happy as if he was at home, in the chair by his fireside, he trips against no stones, saves shoe leather, and gets on he hardly knows how."

Hans did not speak quietly, so the horseman heard it all, and said, "Well, friend, why do you go on

foot then?"

"Ah!" said he, "I have this load to carry. To be sure it is silver, but it is so heavy that I can't hold up my head, and you must know it hurts my shoulder badly."

"What do you say of making an exchange?" said the horseman. "I will give you my horse, and you shall give me the silver, which will save you a great deal of trouble in carrying such a heavy load about with you."

"With all my heart," said Hans, "but as you are so kind to me, I must tell you one thing – you will have a weary task to draw that silver about with you." However, the horseman got off, took the silver, helped Hans up, gave him the bridle into one hand and the whip into the other, and said, "When you want to go very fast, smack your lips loudly together, and cry 'Jip!'"

Hans was delighted as he sat on the horse, drew himself up, squared his elbows, turned out his toes, cracked his whip and rode merrily off, one minute whistling a merry tune, and another singing.

After a time he thought he should like to go a little faster, so he smacked his lips and cried, "Jip!" Away went the horse full gallop, and before Hans knew what he was about, he was thrown off, and lay on his back by the roadside. His horse would have run off, if a shepherd who was coming by, driving a cow, had not

stopped it. Hans soon came to himself, and got upon his legs again, sadly vexed, and said to the shepherd, "This riding is no joke, when a man has the luck to get upon a beast like this that stumbles and flings him off as if it would break his neck. However, I'm off now once and for all, I like your cow now a great deal better than this smart beast that played me this trick, and has spoiled my best coat, you see, in this puddle, which, by the by, smells not very like a nosegay. One can walk along at one's leisure behind that cow – keep good company, and have milk, butter, and cheese, every day, into the bargain. What would I give to have such a prize!"

"Well," said the shepherd, "if you are so fond of her, I will change my cow for your horse, I like to do good to my neighbours, even though I lose by it myself."

"Done!" said Hans, merrily. 'What a noble heart that good man has!' thought he. Then the shepherd jumped upon the horse, wished Hans and the cow good morning, and away he rode.

Hans brushed his coat, wiped his face and hands, rested a while, and then drove off his cow quietly, and thought his bargain a very lucky one. "If I have only a piece of bread (and I shall always be able to get that) I can, whenever I like, eat my butter and cheese with it, and when I am thirsty I can milk my cow and drink the milk. What more can I wish for?"

When he came to an inn, he halted, ate up all his bread, and gave away his last penny for a glass of beer. When he had rested himself he set off again, driving his cow towards his mother's village. But the heat grew greater as soon as noon came on, till at last, as he found himself on a wide heath that would take him more than an hour to cross, he began to feel so hot and parched that his tongue stuck to the roof of his mouth. 'I can find a cure for this,' thought he, 'now I will milk my cow and quench my thirst.' So he tied her to the stump of a tree, and held his leathern cap to milk into, but not a drop was to be had. Who would have thought that this cow, which was to bring him milk and butter and cheese, was all that time utterly dry? Hans had not thought of looking to that.

While he was trying his luck in milking, and managing the matter very clumsily, the uneasy beast began to think him very troublesome, and at last gave him such a kick on the head as knocked him down. And there he lay a long while senseless. Luckily a butcher soon came by, driving a pig in a wheelbarrow.

"What is the matter with you, my man?" said the butcher, as he helped him up. Hans told him what had

happened, how he was dry and wanted to milk his cow, but found the cow was dry too. Then the butcher gave him a flask of ale, saying, "There, drink and refresh yourself, your cow will give you no milk. Don't you see she is old, good for nothing but the slaughterhouse?"

"Alas, alas!" said Hans, "Who would have thought it? What a shame to take my horse and give me only a dry cow! If I kill her, what will she be good for? I hate beef, it is not tender enough for me. If it were a pig now – like that fat gentleman you are driving along at his ease – one could do something with it. It would at any rate make sausages."

"Well," said the butcher, "I don't like to say no, when one is asked to do a neighbourly thing. To please you I will change, and give you my fine fat pig for the cow."

"Heaven reward you for your kindness and self-denial!" said Hans, as he gave the butcher the cow, and taking the pig off the wheelbarrow, drove it away, holding it by the string that was tied to its leg.

So on he jogged, and all seemed now to go right with him – he had met with some misfortunes, to be sure, but he was now well repaid for all. How could it be otherwise with such a travelling companion as he had at last got?

The next man he met was a countryman carrying a

fine white goose. The countryman stopped to ask what was the time. This led to further chat, and Hans told him all his luck, how he had so many good bargains, and how all the world went gay and smiling with him. The

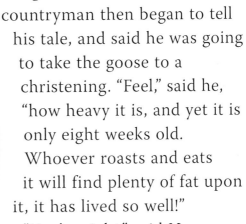

countryman then began to tell his tale, and said he was going to take the goose to a christening. "Feel," said he, "how heavy it is, and yet it is only eight weeks old. Whoever roasts and eats it will find plenty of fat upon it, it has lived so well!"

"You're right," said Hans, as he weighed it in his hand, "but if you talk of fat, my pig is no trifle."

The countryman began to look grave, and shook his head. "Listen!" said he, "My worthy friend, you seem a good sort of fellow, so I can't help doing you a kind turn. Your pig may get you into a scrape. In the village I just came from, the squire has had a pig stolen out of his sty. I was dreadfully afraid when I saw you that you had got the squire's pig. If you have, and they catch you, it will be bad for you. The least they will do will

be to throw you into the horse pond. Can you swim?"

Poor Hans was greatly frightened. "Good man," cried he, "pray get me out of this. I know nothing of where the pig was either bred or born, but he may have been the squire's for all I can tell – you know this country better than I do, take my pig and give me the goose."

"I ought to have something into the bargain," said the countryman, "give a fat goose for a pig, indeed! 'Tis not everyone would do so much for you as that. However, I will not be hard upon you, as you are in trouble." Then he took the string in his hand, and drove off the pig by a side path, while Hans went on the way homewards, free from care. 'After all,' thought he, 'that chap is pretty well taken in. I don't care whose pig it is, but wherever it came from it has been a very good friend to me. I have much the best of the bargain. First there will be a capital roast, then the fat will find me in goose grease for six months, and then there are all the beautiful white feathers. I will put them into my pillow, and then I am sure I shall sleep soundly.'

As he came to the next village, he saw a scissor-grinder with his wheel, working and singing.

Hans stood looking on for a while, and at last said, "You must be well off, master grinder! You seem so happy at your work."

"Yes," said the other, "mine is a golden trade, a good grinder never puts his hand into his pocket without finding money in it – but where did you get that beautiful goose?"

"I did not buy it, I gave a pig for it."

"And where did you get the pig?"

"I gave a cow for it."

"And the cow?"

"I gave a horse for it."

"And the horse?"

"I gave a lump of silver as big as my head for it."

"And the silver?"

"Oh! I worked hard for that seven long years."

"You have done well in the world," said the grinder, "now if you could find money in your pocket whenever you put your hand in it, your fortune would be made."

"Very true – but how is that to be managed?"

"How? Why, you must turn grinder like myself, said the other, you only want a grindstone, the rest will come of itself. Here is one that is but little the worse for wear, I would not ask more than the value of your goose for it – will you buy?"

"I should be the happiest man in the world, if I could have money whenever I put my hand in my pocket – what could I want more? There's the goose."

"Now," said the grinder, as he gave him a common rough stone that lay by his side, "this is a most capital stone, do but work it well enough, and you can make an old nail cut with it."

Hans took the stone, and went his way with a light heart, his eyes sparkled for joy, and he said to himself, 'Surely I must have been born in a lucky hour, everything I could want or wish for comes of itself. People are so kind – they think I do them a favour in letting them make me rich, and giving me bargains.'

At last he could go no farther, for the stone tired him sadly, and he dragged himself to the side of a river, that he might take a drink of water, and rest a while. So he laid the stone carefully by his side on the bank – but, as he stooped down to drink, he forgot it, pushed it a little, and down it rolled, plump into the stream.

For a while he watched it sinking in the deep, clear water, then sprang up and danced for joy, and thanked heaven for its kindness in taking away the heavy stone.

"Nobody was ever so lucky as I." Then he walked on till he reached his mother's house, and told her how easy the road to good luck was.

The Tiger, the Brahman and the Jackal

By Joseph Jacobs

ONCE UPON A TIME a tiger was caught in a trap. He tried in vain to get out through the bars, and rolled and bit with rage and grief when he failed. By chance, a poor Brahman (Indian priest) came walking by.

"Let me out of this cage!" cried the tiger.

"Nay, my friend," replied the Brahman mildly, "you would probably eat me if I did."

"Not at all!" swore the tiger with many oaths. "On the contrary, I should be forever grateful, and serve you as a slave!"

Now when the tiger sobbed and sighed and wept and swore, the holy Brahman's heart softened, and at last he consented to open the door of the cage. Out

popped the tiger, and seizing the poor man, cried, "What a fool you are! What is to prevent me eating you now, for after being cooped up so long I am just terribly hungry!"

In vain the Brahman pleaded for his life, the most he could gain was a promise to abide by the decision of the first three things he chose to question as to the justice of the tiger's action.

So the Brahman first asked a papal-tree what it thought of the matter, but the papal-tree replied coldly, "What have you to complain about? Don't I give shade and shelter to everyone who passes by, and don't they in return tear down my branches to feed their cattle? Don't whimper – be a man!"

Then the Brahman, sad at heart, went further afield till he saw a buffalo turning a well-wheel, but he fared no better from it, for it answered, "You are a fool to expect gratitude! Look at me! Whilst I gave milk they fed me on cotton-seed and oil-cake, but now I am dry they yoke me here and give me refuse as fodder!"

The Brahman, still more sad, asked the road to give him its opinion.

"My dear sir," said the road, "how foolish you are to expect anything else! Here am I, useful to everybody, yet all, rich and poor, great and small, trample on me

as they go past, giving me nothing but the ashes of their pipes and the husks of their grain!"

On this the Brahman turned back sorrowfully, and on the way he met a jackal, who called out, "Why, what's the matter? You look as miserable as a fish out of water!"

The Brahman told him all that had occurred. "How very confusing!" said the jackal. "Would you mind telling me over again, for everything has got so mixed up?"

The Brahman told it all over again, but the jackal shook his head in a distracted sort of way, and still could not understand.

"It's very odd," said he, sadly, "it all seems to go in one ear and out the other! I will go to the place where it all happened then perhaps I'll be able to give a judgment."

Wisdom and Fortune

So they returned to the cage, by which the tiger was waiting for the Brahman, sharpening his teeth and claws.

"You've been away a long time!" growled the savage beast, "but now let us begin our dinner."

'Our dinner!' thought the wretched Brahman, as his knees knocked together with fright, 'what a remarkably delicate way of putting it!'

"Give me five minutes, my lord!" he pleaded, "in order that I may explain matters to the jackal here, who is somewhat slow in his wits."

The tiger consented and the Brahman began the whole story over again, not missing a single detail, and spinning as long a yarn as possible.

"Oh, my poor brain!" cried the jackal, wringing its paws. "Let me see! How did it all begin? You were in the cage, and the tiger came walking by—"

"Pooh!" interrupted the tiger. "What a fool you are! I was in the cage."

"Of course!" cried the jackal, pretending to tremble with fright. "Yes! I was in the cage – no I wasn't. Dear! Dear! Where are my wits? Let me see – the tiger was in the Brahman, and the cage came walking by – no, that's not it, either! Well, don't mind me, but begin your dinner, for I shall never understand!"

"Yes, you shall!" returned the tiger, in a rage at the jackal's stupidity, "I'll make you understand! Look here – I am the tiger—"

"Yes, I understand, my lord!"

"And that is the Brahman—"

"Yes, my lord!"

"And that is the cage—"

"Yes, my lord!"

"And I was in the cage – do you understand?"

"Yes – no – please, my lord—"

"Well?" cried the tiger impatiently.

"Please, my lord! – how did you get in?"

"How! Why in the usual way, of course!"

"Oh, dear me! My head is beginning to whirl again! Please don't be angry, my lord – what is the usual way?"

At this the tiger lost patience, and, jumping into the cage, cried, "This way! Now do you understand how it was?"

"Perfectly!" grinned the jackal, as he swiftly shut the door, "and if you will permit me to say so, I think matters will remain as they were!"

Nail Soup

By Gabriel Djurklou

THERE WAS ONCE A TRAMP who went plodding his way through a forest. The distance between the houses was so great that he had little hope of finding a shelter before the night set in. But all of a sudden he saw some lights between the trees. He then discovered a cottage, where there was a fire burning on the hearth. 'How nice it would be to roast one's self before that fire, and to get a bite of something,' he thought, and so he dragged himself towards the cottage.

Just then an old woman came towards him.

"Good evening!" said the tramp.

"Good evening," said the woman. "Where do you come from?"

"South of the sun, and east of the moon," said the tramp, "and now I am on the way home again, for I have been all over the world with the exception of this parish," he said.

"You must be a great traveller, then," said the woman. "What is your business here?"

"Oh, I want a shelter for the night," he said.

"I thought as much," said the woman, "but you may as well get away from here at once, for my husband is not at home, and my place is not an inn," she said.

"My good woman," said the tramp, "you must not be so cross and hardhearted, for we are both human beings, and should help one another."

"Help one another?" said the woman. "Help? Did you ever hear such a thing? Who'll help me, do you think? I haven't got a morsel in the house! No, you'll have to look for quarters elsewhere," she said.

But the tramp was like the rest of his kind. He did not consider himself beaten at the first rebuff. Although the old woman grumbled and complained as much as she could, he was just as persistent as ever, and went on begging and praying like a starved dog, until at last she gave in, and he got permission to lie on the floor for the night.

That was very kind, and he thanked her for it.

"Better on the floor without sleep, than suffer cold in the forest deep," he said, for he was a merry fellow, this tramp, and was always ready with a rhyme.

When he came into the room he could see that the woman was not so badly off as she had pretended. But she was a greedy and stingy woman of the worst sort, and was always complaining and grumbling.

He now made himself very agreeable, and asked her in his most insinuating manner for something to eat.

"Where am I to get it from?" said the woman. "I haven't tasted a morsel myself the whole day."

But the tramp was a cunning fellow. "Poor old granny, you must be starving," he said. "Well, I suppose I shall have to ask you to have something with me, then."

"Have something with you!" said the woman. "You don't look as if you could ask anyone to have anything! What have you got to offer one, I should like to know?"

"He who far and wide does roam sees many things not known at home, and he who many things has seen has wits about him and senses keen," said the tramp. "Better dead than lose one's head! Lend me a pot, granny!"

The old woman now became very inquisitive, as you may guess, and so she let him have a pot. He filled it with water and put it on the fire, and then he blew with all his might till the fire was burning fiercely all round it. Then he took a four-inch nail from his pocket, turned it three times in his hand and put it into the pot.

The woman stared with all her might. "What's this going to be?" she asked.

"Nail broth," said the tramp.

The old woman had seen and heard a good deal in her time, but making broth with a nail, well, she had never heard the like before.

"That's something for poor people to know," she said, "and I should like to learn how to make it."

If she wanted to learn how to make it she had only to watch him, he said, and went on stirring the broth.

The old woman sat on the ground, her hands clasping her knees, and her eyes following his hand as he stirred the broth.

"This generally makes good broth," he said, "but this time it will very likely be rather thin, for I have been making broth the whole week with the same nail. If one only had a handful of sifted oatmeal to put in, that would make it all right," he said. "But what one has to go without, it's no use thinking more about," and so he stirred the broth again.

"Well, I think I have a scrap of flour somewhere," said the old woman, and went out to fetch some, and it was both good and fine. The tramp began putting the flour into the broth, and went on stirring, while the woman sat staring now at him and then at the pot until her eyes nearly burst their sockets.

"This broth would be good enough for company," he said, putting in one handful of flour after another. "If I had only a bit of salted beef and a few potatoes to put in, it would be fit for gentlefolks, however particular they might be," he said. "But what one has to go without, it's no use thinking more about."

When the old woman really began to think it over, she thought she had some potatoes, and perhaps a bit of beef as well, and these she gave the tramp, who went on stirring, while she sat and stared as hard as ever.

"This will be grand enough for the best in the land," he said.

"Well, I never!" said the woman, "and just fancy – all with a nail!" He was really a wonderful man, this tramp! He could do more than drink a sup and turn the tankard up, he could.

"If one had only a little barley and a drop of milk, we could ask the king himself to have some of it," he said, "for this is what he has every blessed evening – that I know, for I have been in service under the king's cook," he said.

"Dear me! Ask the king to have some! Well, I never!" exclaimed the woman, slapping her knees. She was quite awestruck at the tramp and his grand connections.

"But what one has to go without, it's no use thinking more about."

And then she remembered she had a little barley, and as for milk, well, she wasn't quite out of that, she said, for her best cow had just calved. And then she went to fetch both the one and the other.

The tramp went on stirring, and the woman sat staring, one moment at him and the next at the pot.

Then all at once the tramp took out the nail. "Now

it's ready, and now we'll have a real good feast," he said. "But to this kind of soup the king and the queen always take a dram or two, and one sandwich at least. And then they always have a cloth on the table when they eat," he said. "But what one has to go without, it's no use thinking more about."

But by this time the old woman herself had begun to feel quite grand and fine, I can tell you. And if that was all that was wanted to make it just as the king had it, she thought it would be nice to have it just the same

way for once, and play at being king and queen with the tramp. She went straight to a cupboard and brought out the brandy bottle, dram glasses, butter and cheese, smoked beef and veal, until at last the table looked as if it were decked out for company.

Never in her life had the old woman had such a grand feast, and never had she tasted such broth, and just fancy, made only with a nail! She was in such a good and merry humour at having learnt such an economical way of making broth, that she did not know what to do.

So they ate and drank, and drank and ate, until they become both tired and sleepy.

The tramp was now going to lie down on the floor. But that would never do, thought the old woman. No, that was impossible. "Such a grand person must have a bed to lie in," she said.

He did not need much pressing. "It's just like the sweet Christmastime," he said, "and a nicer woman I never came across. Ah, well! Happy are they who meet with such good people," said he, and he lay down on the bed and went to sleep.

And next morning when he woke, the first thing he

got was coffee and a dram. When he was going, the old woman gave him a bright dollar piece. "And thanks, many thanks, for what you have taught me," she said. "Now I shall live in comfort, since I have learnt how to make broth with a nail."

"Well it isn't very difficult, if one only has something good to add to it," said the tramp as he went on his way.

The woman stood at the door staring after him. "Such people don't grow on every bush," she said.

The Six Soldiers of Fortune

By the Brothers Grimm

THERE WAS ONCE A MAN who was a Jack-of-all-trades, he had served in the war, and had been brave and bold, but at the end of it he was sent about his business, with three farthings and his discharge.

"I am not going to stand this," said he, "wait till I find the right man to help me, and the king shall give me all the treasures of his kingdom before he has done with me."

Then, full of wrath, he went into the forest, and he saw one standing there by six trees that he had rooted up as if they had been stalks of corn. And he said to him, "Will you be my man, and come along with me?"

"Alright," answered he, "I must just take this bit of

wood home to my father and mother." And taking one of the trees, he bound it round the other five, and putting the bundle of sticks on his shoulder, he carried it off, then soon coming back, he went along with his leader, who said, "Two such as we can stand against the whole world."

And when they had gone on a little while, they came to a huntsman who was kneeling on one knee and taking careful aim with his rifle.

"Huntsman," said the leader, "what are you aiming at?"

"Two miles from here," answered he, "there sits a fly on the bough of an oak tree, I mean to put a bullet into its left eye."

"Oh, come along with me," said the leader, "three of us together can stand against the world."

The huntsman was quite willing to go with him, and so they went on till they came to seven windmills, whose sails were going round briskly, and yet there was no wind blowing from any quarter, and not a leaf stirred.

"Well," said the leader, "I cannot think what ails the windmills, turning without wind," and he went on with his followers about two miles farther, and then they came to a man sitting up in a tree, holding one nostril and blowing with the other.

"Now then," said the leader, "what are you doing up there?"

"Two miles from here," answered he, "there are seven windmills, I am blowing, and they are going round."

"Oh, go with me," cried the leader, "four of us together can stand against the world."

So the blower got down and went with them, and after a time they came to a man standing on one leg, and the other had been taken off and was lying near him.

"You seem to have got a handy way of resting yourself," said the leader to the man.

"I am a runner," answered he, "and in order to keep myself from going too fast I have taken off a leg, for when I run with both, I go faster than a bird can fly."

"Oh, go with me," cried the leader, "five of us together may well stand against the world."

So he went with them all together, and it was not long before they met a man with a little hat on, and he wore it just over one ear.

"Manners! Manners!" said the leader, "with your hat like that, you look like a fool."

"I dare not put it straight," answered the other, "if I did, there would be such a terrible frost that the very

birds would be frozen and fall dead from the sky to the ground."

"Oh, come with me," said the leader, "we six together may well stand against the whole world."

So the six went on until they came to a town where the king had caused it to be made known that whoever would run a race with his daughter and win it might become her husband, but that whoever lost must lose his head into the bargain. And the leader came forward and said one of his men should run for him.

"Then," said the king, "his life too must be put in pledge, and if he fails, his head and yours too must fall."

When this was quite settled and agreed upon, the leader called the runner, and strapped his second leg on to him.

"Now, look out," said he, "and take care that we win."

It had been agreed that the one who should bring water first from a far distant brook should be accounted winner. Now the king's daughter and the runner each took a pitcher, and they started both at the same time, but in one moment, when the king's daughter had gone but a very little way, the runner was out of sight, for his running was as if the wind rushed by. In a short time he reached the brook, filled his pitcher full of water, and turned back again. About halfway home, however, he was overcome with weariness, and setting down his pitcher, he lay down on the ground to sleep. But in order to awaken soon again by not lying too soft he had taken a horse's skull that lay near and placed it under his head for a pillow.

In the meanwhile the king's daughter, who really was a good runner, good enough to beat an ordinary man, had reached the brook, and filled her pitcher, and was hastening with it back again, when she saw the runner lying asleep.

"The day is mine," said she with much joy, and she emptied his pitcher and hastened on. And now all had been lost but for the huntsman who was standing on the castle wall, and with his keen eyes saw all that happened.

"We must not be outdone by the king's daughter,"

said he, and he loaded his rifle and took so good an aim that he shot the horse's skull from under the runner's head. The runner awoke and jumped up, and saw his pitcher standing empty and the king's daughter far on her way home. But, not losing courage, he ran swiftly to the brook, filled the pitcher with water, and he got home ten minutes before the king's daughter.

The king was vexed, and his daughter yet more so, that she should be beaten by a discharged common soldier, and they took counsel together how they might rid themselves of him and of his companions.

"I have a plan," said the king, "do not fear but that we shall be quit of them forever." Then he went out to the men and bade them to feast and be merry, and he led them into a room, made of iron. In the room was a table set out with costly food.

"Now, go in there and make yourselves comfortable," said the king.

And when they had gone in, he had the door locked and bolted. Then he called the cook, and told him to make a big fire underneath the room, so that the iron floor of it should be red hot. And the cook did so, and the six men began to feel the room growing very warm. As the heat grew greater and greater, and they found the doors and windows fastened, they began to think it was an evil plan of the king's to suffocate them.

"He shall not succeed, however," said the man with the little hat, "I will bring on a frost that shall make the fire feel ashamed of itself, and creep out of the way."

So he set his hat straight on his head, and immediately there came such a frost that all the heat passed away and the food froze in the dishes. After an hour or two had passed, and the king thought they must have all perished in the heat, he caused the door

to be opened, and went himself to see how they fared. And when the door flew back, there they were all six quite safe and sound, and they said they were quite ready to come out, so that they might warm themselves, for the great cold of that room had caused the food to freeze in the dishes. Full of wrath, the king went to the cook and scolded him, and asked why he had not done as he was ordered.

"It is hot enough there – you may see for yourself," answered the cook. And the king looked and saw an immense fire burning underneath the room of iron, and he began to think that the six men were not to be got rid of in that way. And he thought of a new plan by which it might be managed, so he sent for the leader and said to him,

"If you will give up your right to my daughter, and take gold instead, you may have as much as you like."

"Certainly, my lord king," answered the man, "let me have as much gold as my servant can carry, and I give up all claim to your daughter."

And the king agreed that he should come again in a fortnight to fetch the gold. The man then called together all the tailors in the kingdom, and set them to work to make a sack, and it took them a fortnight. And when it was ready, the strong man who had been found rooting up trees took it on his shoulder, and went to the king.

"Who is this immense fellow carrying on his shoulder a bundle of stuff as big as a house?" cried the king, terrified to think how much gold he would carry off. And a tonne of gold was dragged in by sixteen strong men, but he put it all into the sack with one hand, saying, "Why don't you bring some more? This hardly covers the bottom!" So the king bade them fetch by degrees the whole of his treasure, and even then the sack was not half full.

"Bring more!" cried the man, "These few scraps go no way at all!" Then at last seven thousand waggons laden with gold collected through the whole kingdom were driven up, and he threw them in his sack, oxen and all.

"I will not look too closely," said he, "but take what I can get, so long as the sack is full." And when all was put in there was still plenty of room.

"I must make an end of this," he said, "if it is not full, it is so much the easier to tie up." And he hoisted it on his back, and went off with his comrades.

When the king saw all the wealth of his realm carried off by a single man he was full of wrath, and he bade his cavalry mount, and follow after the six men,

and take the sack away from the strong man.

Two regiments were soon up to them, and called them to consider themselves prisoners, and to deliver up the sack, or be cut in pieces.

"Prisoners, say you?" said the man who could blow, "Suppose you first have a little dance together in the air," and holding one nostril, and blowing through the other, he sent the regiments flying head over heels, over the hills and far away. But a sergeant who had nine wounds and was a brave fellow, begged not to be put to so much shame. And the blower let him down easily, so that he came to no harm, and he bade him go to the king and tell him that whatever regiments he liked to send more should be blown away just the same. And the king, when he got the message, said, "Let the fellows be, they have some right on their side." So the six comrades carried home their treasure, divided it among them, and lived contented till they died.

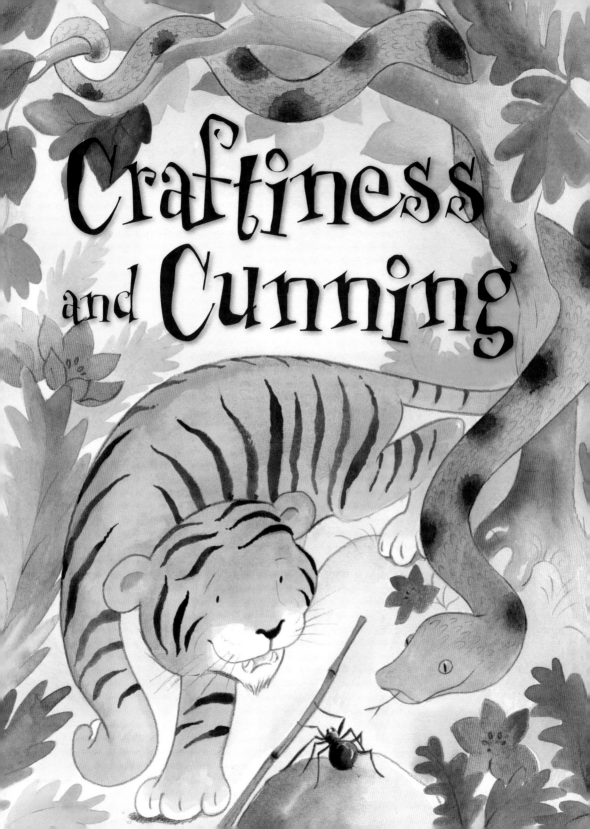

Craftiness and Cunning

The Swineherd

By Hans Christian Andersen

THERE WAS ONCE a poor prince. He possessed a kingdom which, though small, was large enough for him to marry on, and married he wished to be.

Now it was certainly a little bold of him to say to the emperor's daughter, "Will you marry me?" but he did, for his name was known far and wide. There were hundreds of princesses who would gladly have said yes, but would she say the same?

Well, we shall see.

On the grave of the prince's father grew a rose tree, a very beautiful rose tree. It only bloomed every five years, and then bore but a single rose, but oh, such a rose! Its scent was so sweet that when you smelt it you forgot all your cares and troubles. And he had also a nightingale that could sing as if all the beautiful melodies in the world were shut up in its little throat. This rose and this nightingale the princess was to have, and so they were both put into silver caskets and sent to her.

The emperor had them brought to him in the great hall, where the princess was playing 'Here comes a duke a-riding' with her ladies-in-waiting. And when she caught sight of the big caskets that contained the presents, she clapped her hands for joy.

"If only it were a little pussycat!" she said. But the rose tree with the beautiful rose came out.

"But how prettily it is made!" said all the ladies-in-waiting.

"It is more than pretty," said the emperor.

But the princess felt it, and then she almost began to cry.

"Ugh! Papa," she said, "it is not artificial, it is real!"

"Ugh!" said all the ladies-in-waiting, "It is real!"

"Let us see first what is in the other casket before we begin to be angry," said the emperor, and out came the nightingale. It sang so beautifully that one could scarcely utter a cross word against it.

"Superbe! Charmant!" said the ladies-in-waiting, for they all chattered French, each one worse than the other.

"How much the bird reminds me of the musical snuff box of the late empress!" said an old courtier. "Ah, yes, it is the same tone, the same execution!"

"Yes," said the emperor, and then he wept like a little child.

"I hope that this, at least, is not real?" asked the princess.

"Yes, it is a real bird," said those who had brought it.

"Then let the bird fly away," said the princess, and with that, she would not allow the prince to come.

But he was not put off. He painted his face brown and black, drew his cap well over his face, and knocked at the door. "Good day, emperor," he said. "Can I get a place here as servant in the castle?"

"Yes," said the emperor, "but there are so many who ask for a place that I don't know whether there will be one for you, but, still, I will think of you. Actually, it has just occurred to me that I want someone to look after the swine, for I have so very many of them."

And the prince got the job of imperial swineherd. He had a wretched little room close to the pigsties. Here he had to stay, but the whole day he sat working, and when evening came he had made a pretty little pot. All round it were little bells, and when the pot boiled they jingled most beautifully and played the tune:

"Where is Augustus dear? Alas!

He's not here, here, here!"

But the most wonderful thing was, that when one held one's finger in the steam of the pot, then at once one could smell what dinner was ready in any fireplace in the town. That was indeed something quite different from the rose.

Now the princess came walking past with all her ladies-in-waiting, and when she heard the tune she stood still and her face beamed with joy, for she also could play 'Where is Augustus dear?'

It was the only tune she knew, but that she could play with one finger.

"Why, that is what I play!" she said. "He must be a most accomplished swineherd! Listen! Go down and ask him what the instrument costs."

And one of the ladies-in-waiting had to go down,

but she put on wooden clogs because of the mud. "What will you take for the pot?" asked the lady-in-waiting.

"I will have ten kisses from the princess," said the swineherd.

"Oh my, heaven forbid!" said the lady-in-waiting.

"Yes, I will sell it for nothing less," replied the swineherd.

"What did he say?" asked the princess urgently, when the lady-in-waiting returned.

"I really hardly like to tell you," answered the lady-in-waiting.

"He is disobliging!" said the princess. But she had only gone a few steps when the bells rang out so prettily:

"Where is Augustus dear? Alas! he's not here, here,
   here."

"Listen!" said the princess. "'Ask him whether he will take ten kisses from my ladies-in-waiting."

"No, thank you," said the swineherd. "Ten kisses from the princess, or else I keep my pot."

"That is very tiresome!" said the princess. "But you must put yourselves in front of me, so no one can see."

And the ladies-in-waiting placed themselves in front of the princess and then spread out their dresses, so the swineherd got his ten kisses, and she got the pot.

What happiness that was! The whole night and the whole day the pot was made to boil. There was not a fireplace in the whole town where they did not know what was being cooked, whether it was at the chancellor's or at the shoemaker's.

The ladies-in-waiting danced and clapped their hands.

"We know who is going to have soup and pancakes – isn't it interesting?"

"Yes, very interesting!" said the first lady-in-waiting.

"But don't say anything about it, for I am the emperor's daughter."

"Oh, no, of course we won't!" said everyone.

The swineherd – that is to say, the prince (though they did not know) – let no day pass without making something, and one day he made a rattle which, when it was turned round, played all the waltzes and polkas

that had ever been known since the world began.

"But that is superbe!" said the princess as she passed by. "I have never heard a more beautiful composition. Listen! Go down and ask him what this instrument costs, but I won't kiss him again."

"He wants a hundred kisses from the princess," said the lady-in-waiting who had gone down to ask him.

"He is mad!" said the princess, and then she went on, but she had only gone a few steps when she stopped.

"One ought to encourage art," she said. "I am the emperor's daughter! Tell him he shall have, as before, ten kisses, the rest he can take from my ladies-in-waiting."

"But we don't at all like being kissed by him," said the ladies-in-waiting.

"That's nonsense," said the princess, "and if I can kiss him, you can, too."

So the ladies-in-waiting had to go down to him again.

"A hundred kisses from the princess," said he, "or each keeps his own."

"Put yourselves in front of

us," she said then, and so all the ladies-in-waiting put themselves in front, and he began to kiss the princess.

"What can that commotion be by the pigsties?" asked the emperor, who was standing on the balcony. He rubbed his eyes and put on his spectacles. "Why those are the ladies-in-waiting playing their games, I must go down to them." What a hurry he was in!

As soon as he came into the yard he walked very softly, and the ladies-in-waiting were so busy counting the kisses and seeing fair play that they never noticed the emperor. He stood on tiptoe.

"What is that?" he said, when he saw the kissing, and then he threw one of his slippers at their heads just as the swineherd was taking his eighty-sixth kiss.

"Be off with you!" said the emperor, for he was very angry. And the princess and the swineherd were driven out of the empire.

Then the princess stood still and wept, the swineherd was scolding, and the rain was streaming down.

"Alas, what an unhappy creature I am!" sobbed the princess. "If only I had taken the beautiful prince! Alas, how unfortunate I am!"

And the swineherd went behind a tree, washed the black and brown off his face, threw away his old clothes, and then stepped forward in his splendid dress, looking so beautiful that the princess was obliged to curtsey.

"I now come to this. I despise you!" he said. "You would have nothing to do with a noble prince, you did not understand the rose or the nightingale, but you would kiss the swineherd for the sake of a toy. This is what you get for it!" And he went into his kingdom and shut the door in her face, and she had to stay outside singing:

"Where's my Augustus dear?
   Alas! he's not here, here, here!"

Master and Man

By T Crofton Croker

BILLY MAC DANIEL was once as likely a young man as ever emptied a glass, or handled a club. Fearing and caring for nothing, Billy Mac Daniel fell into bad company, for surely the fairies (also known as the good people) are the worst of all company anyone could come across.

It so happened that Billy was going home one frosty night not long after Christmas. The moon was round and bright, and he felt pinched with cold.

"By my word," chattered Billy, "a drop of good liquor would be no bad thing to keep a man's soul from freezing in him, and I wish I had a full measure of the best."

"Never wish it twice, Billy," said a little man in a three-cornered hat, bound with gold lace, and with great silver buckles on his shoes, and he held out a glass as big as himself, filled with good liquor.

"Success, my little fellow," said Billy Mac Daniel, unafraid, though he knew the little man belonged to 'the good people'. "Here's to your health, anyway, and thank you kindly, no matter who pays for the drink," and he took the glass and drained it to the very bottom without ever taking a second breath.

"Success," said the little man, "and you're heartily welcome, Billy, but don't think to cheat me as you have done others – out with your purse and pay me."

"I am to pay you?" said Billy, "Could I not just take you up and put you in my pocket?"

"Billy Mac Daniel," said the little man, getting very angry, "you shall be my servant for seven years and a day, and that is the way I will be paid, so get ready to follow me."

When Billy heard this, he was sorry for having used such bold words towards the little man, and he felt that he had to follow the little man all night across the country, without any rest.

As the sun began to rise, the little man turned round to Billy and said, "You may now go home, Billy, but don't fail to meet me in the fort-field tonight, or it may be the worse for you in the long run. If I find you a good servant, you will find me a good master."

Home went Billy Mac Daniel, and though he was tired and weary, he could not get a wink of sleep for thinking about the little man. He was afraid not to do his bidding, so up he got in the evening, and went to the fort-field. He was not long there before the little man came towards him and said, "Billy, I want us to go on a long journey tonight, so saddle two horses."

"If I may be so bold, sir," said Billy, "I would ask which is the way to your stable, for not a thing do I see except the old thorn tree in the corner of the field, and the stream running at the bottom of the hill."

"Go over to that bit of a bog, and bring me two of the strongest rushes you can find," said the little man.

Billy did so, wondering what the little man would do, and he picked two of the stoutest rushes he could find, and brought them back to his master.

"Get up, Billy," said the little man, taking one of the rushes from him and striding across it.

"Where?" said Billy.

"Why, upon horseback, like me," said the little man.

"Are you after making a fool of me," said Billy, "bidding me get on horseback upon that bit of rush?"

"Up! Up! And no words," said the little man, looking very angry. So Billy, thinking all this was in joke, straddled the rush.

"Borram! Borram! Borram!" cried the little man three times (which, in English, means 'become big'), and Billy did the same after him. Suddenly the rushes swelled up into fine horses, and away they went at full speed. Billy had put the rush between his legs, without much minding how he did it, so he found himself sitting on horseback the wrong way. It was rather awkward, with his face to the horse's tail, and so quickly had his steed started off with him that he had no power to turn round. There was nothing for it but to hold on by the tail.

At last they came to their journey's end, and stopped at the gate of a fine house. "Now, Billy," said the little man, "do as you see me do, and follow me close."

The little man then said some queer kind of words, out of which Billy didn't understand, but repeated.

In they both went through the keyhole of the door, and through one keyhole after another, until they got into the wine cellar, full of all kinds of wine.

The little man fell to drinking as hard as he could, and Billy did the same. "The best of masters are you surely," said Billy to him.

"I have made no bargain with you," said the little man, "and will make none, but up and follow me." Away they went, through keyhole after keyhole. They mounted the rushes at the hall door, and scampered off, kicking the clouds before them like snowballs, as soon as the words, 'Borram, Borram, Borram', had passed their lips.

When they came back to the fort-field, the little man dismissed Billy, bidding him to be there the next night at the same hour. Thus did they go on, night after night, shaping their course one night here, and another night there, sometimes north, sometimes east, and sometimes south, until there was not a gentleman's wine cellar in all Ireland they had not visited.

One night Billy's master said to him, "Billy, I shall want an extra horse tonight, for maybe we may bring back more company than we take." So Billy brought a third rush, much wondering who it might be that would travel back in their company.

Away they went, Billy leading the third horse, and never stopped until they came to a snug farmer's house, in the county Limerick. Within the house there was a great deal of noise and the little man stopped outside. Then turning round all of a sudden, said, "Billy, I will be a thousand years old tomorrow!"

"God bless us, sir," said Billy, "will you?"

"Don't say those words again, Billy, as you will be my ruin forever. I have come all this way because I think it is time for me to get married. And in this house is young Darby Riley who is going to be married to Bridget Rooney. She is a tall and comely girl, and has come of decent people, I think of marrying her myself, and taking her off with me."

"And what will Darby Riley say to that?" said Billy.

"Silence!" said the little man, putting on a severe look. He began saying the queer words that had the power of passing him through the keyhole as free as air, and which Billy thought himself mighty clever to be able to say after him.

In they both went. For the better viewing the company, the little man perched on one of the big beams and Billy did the same.

There they were, both master and man, looking down upon the fun that was going forward, and under

them were the priest
and piper, the family of
Darby Riley, the family of Bridget
Rooney, and plenty to eat and drink on the
table for every one of them.

Now it happened, just as Mrs Rooney cut the pig's
head, that the bride gave a sneeze, which made
everyone at table start, but no one said 'God bless us'.
The bridal feast went on without the blessing.

"Ha!" exclaimed the little man, throwing one leg from under him with a joyous flourish, and his eye twinkled with a strange light. "I have half of her now, surely. Let her sneeze but twice more, and she is mine."

Again the fair Bridget sneezed, but it was so gently that few except the little man seemed to notice, and no one thought of saying 'God bless us'.

All this time, Billy could not help thinking what a terrible thing it was for a nice girl of nineteen to marry an ugly little man, who was a thousand years old.

At this moment, the bride gave a third sneeze, and Billy roared out with all his might, "God bless you!"

No sooner was it uttered than the little man, his face glowing with rage, shrieked out in the shrill voice, "I discharge you from my service, Billy Mac Daniel – take that for your wages," and gave poor Billy a most furious kick in the back, which sent his unfortunate servant sprawling upon his face and hands right in the middle of the dinner table.

If Billy was astonished, how much more so was every one of the company into which he was thrown. But when they heard his story, Father Cooney laid down his knife and fork, and married the young couple there and then!

Baba Yaga, the Bony-legged Witch

A Russian folk tale

THERE WAS ONCE a wicked woman who hated her stepdaughter so much that she pushed the little girl out of the house and told her to go and borrow a needle and thread from Baba Yaga, the bony-legged witch. The girl's father was at work, so she had no one to turn to and she was terrified. Baba Yaga, the bony-legged witch, lived in the middle of the deep, dark forest, in a hut that moved about on hens' legs. Nevertheless, the little girl dared not disobey her cruel stepmother, so off she went, alone and frightened.

The little girl was soon among tall, prickly trees that whispered all around her, and she quite forgot which way was which. Tears began to glisten in her eyes and

slowly roll
down her
flushed cheeks.

"Do not weep,
little girl," came a
cheerful voice. The little
girl looked up to see that a nightingale
was talking to her. "You are a kind-hearted girl and I
will tell you what I can to help you. Along the path,
you will come across some objects. Pick them up and
make sure you use them wisely."

So the girl set off again. As she walked along, she
saw a neatly folded handkerchief lying among the pine
needles, and she put it in her pocket. A little further
on, she spied some ribbons that were dangling from
the branches. She took those and slipped them into her
pocket, too. A few steps on, she spotted a little can of
oil, laying among some rocks. She picked up the oil can
and placed it with the other things. Next, she came
across a large bone and a maple leaf sprinkled with
some juicy morsels of meat – then her pocket was full.

It wasn't long before some big iron gates came into
view up ahead, and beyond them was the hut of
Baba Yaga running about on its hens' legs. The little
girl shivered with fear. Suddenly, a howling wind rose

up, sending the branches of the trees whipping fiercely around her head. "I'll never get near that horrible hut at this rate," the little girl sighed, ducking the boughs coming at her thick and fast. Then she remembered the things she had collected along the way. Pulling out the ribbons from her pocket, she tied them carefully onto the trees. As soon as she did, the wind dropped to a gentle breeze and the branches became still.

Then the little girl tried to push open the gates, but a dreadful creaking and groaning tore through the air. She took the oil can from her pocket and covered the hinges with oil. After that, the gate opened without a squeak, and the girl passed through.

All of a sudden, a drooling, snarling dog came running at her out of nowhere, barking ferociously. Quick as a flash, the girl threw the big, juicy bone to the dog. He forgot his attack immediately and lay down to gnaw at his unexpected treat.

Now the only obstacle left to face was the hut itself, scuttling about on its awful scaly legs. And there, standing in the shadows, was the ugliest woman the girl had ever seen – a thin, bony figure with dark, shining eyes and long, green hair. It had to be Baba Yaga, the bony-legged witch.

"Come in, my dear," grinned the witch, showing her sharp, iron teeth. "While I'm searching for that needle and thread you want, you can have a nice bath and do my spinning for me." Baba Yaga gripped the girl's arm with her clawlike fingers and pulled her into the house. "Run her a bath and be quick!" she screamed at her pale-faced maid, before whispering, "Make sure you scrub her well, all ready for eating." With a wry smile, Baba Yaga swept from the room, leaving them alone.

The pale-faced maid began to bustle about, filling the bath with water, and fetching soap and a hard, dirty scrubbing brush. The little girl saw that she was trembling with fear. "I am sorry that you have to live and work here," the little girl said. "Here, have this handkerchief as a little present to cheer you up."

"Oh, thank you," the maid sighed, gazing in delight at beautiful silky red handkerchief. "I will use a teacup instead of a jug to fill the bath, so you have more time to escape." Then the little girl noticed a skinny black cat cowering in the corner. "You don't look as if you've eaten properly for ages," she said, stroking his tatty fur. "Here, have these scraps of meat."

"Oh, thank you," the skinny black cat purred, washing his paws. "I will do the spinning for you, so you have more time to escape. Now take this magic towel and comb, and run for your life. When you hear Baba Yaga coming, throw each of them behind you, one by one. Be quick and go right away."

So the girl took the magic towel and comb, and ran as quickly as she could into the shadows of the towering trees. Back at the hut, the cat sat at the spinning wheel, tangled the wool into a ball to hide behind, and began to spin.

Several times, the witch passed the open door of the room and peered in. But when she heard the whirr of the spinning wheel and saw the pile of tangled wool, she went away, content. But by and by, the witch began to get suspicious that the pile of wool wasn't getting smaller. "Are you sure you know how to spin properly?" she screeched.

"Yes," yowled the cat, trying to sound like the girl but failing.

Baba Yaga realized she had been tricked. She screamed with fury, her face turning scarlet. Rushing into the room, she grabbed the cat by the scruff of the neck. "Why did you let the girl escape?" she howled.

"You've never given me anything but leftovers," the cat hissed. "That kind girl gave me tasty morsels of meat."

Furious, Baba Yaga stalked over to the pale-faced maid and slapped her. "Why did you let the girl escape?" she growled.

"You've never given me a single present," the pale-faced maid shouted. "That kind girl gave me a lovely hanky."

Storming outside, Baba Yaga kicked the dog who was happily chomping on his bone. "Why did you let the girl escape?"

"You've never given me a bone or a treat," the dog barked. "That kind girl gave me a big, juicy bone to chew on."

With incredible force, Baba Yaga kicked the iron gates. "Why did you let the girl escape?" she shouted.

"You let us get all stiff and rusty," they creaked. "That kind girl soothed our aching joints with lashings of lovely oil."

Finally, Baba Yaga threatened the birch trees with an axe. "Why did you let the girl escape?" she howled.

"You've never once decorated our branches," they roared, "but that kind girl dressed us with ribbons."

Gnashing her iron teeth wildly, she jumped on her broomstick and raced off through the deep, dark forest after the little girl. Hearing the swish of the air, the

little girl knew the witch was coming and so threw down the magic towel. Suddenly, a wide rushing river appeared before Baba Yaga, soaking her broomstick so badly that it could no longer fly. Spitting and cursing, Baba Yaga had to leave her broomstick and slowly wade across the river. Once she was free of the water, she began to run after the little girl.

Hearing the pounding of Baba Yaga's footsteps, the little girl knew the witch was coming, and so threw down the magic comb. All of a sudden, a rainforest sprang up in front of Baba Yaga, so thick and tangled that Baba Yaga could do nothing to find her way through it. Squawking and screaming, she stormed back to her dreary hut, shouting all the way.

With her home in sight, the little girl heaved a sigh of relief, especially when standing at the door of her house was her beloved father. She rushed to tell him all about her stepmother's evil plot. Her father was horrified. He sent the wicked woman out of the house at once and drove her into the magic rainforest. From that day to this, she has never been seen again.

Whatever became of her, the little girl and her father lived happily on their own, and pleased with her genorosity and thoughtful nature, the nightingale came to visit every day.

The Giant's Wife

An Irish legend

IN THE DAYS when giants lived in the north of Ireland, Finn McCool was the biggest, strongest, most handsome of them all – or so he thought. With his bare hands, Finn could rip a pine tree out of the ground. He could leap across a river in one bound. He could split a boulder in half with one swish of his axe. Surely he was the greatest giant who ever lived.

Now Finn had heard that there were clans of giants living in Scotland who had competitions throwing tree trunks and

carrying boulders. That sounded to him like great fun. So Finn decided to build a road right across the sea, so he could walk across to see these Scottish giants without getting his feet wet. Pulling on his big black workboots, he kissed his wife Oonagh goodbye, and promised, "I'll be back in about a week – ten days, tops." Then he strode off over the hills to the coast.

Finn began to work hard, ripping rocks from the mountains and throwing them into the sea until they piled up above the water and began to form a road. He was only three days into the job when a friend of his arrived at the seashore. "Finn, I don't mean to worry you, to be sure," his friend said, "but there's gossip about a strange giant who's on his way to your house to flatten you. Some say that he's leapt across the sea from Scotland without needing a boat or a bridge. People say that he keeps a thunderbolt in his pocket. I've heard, too, that he has a magic little finger with as much strength in it as ten men put together!"

"Pah!" cried Finn, "I don't believe a word of it!" But secretly, he began to feel a little uneasy.

"One thing's for sure," his friend continued, "the stranger knows that everyone thinks you're the biggest, strongest, most handsome giant in all of Ireland, and he doesn't like it one little bit. He's made up his mind to find you and mince you into pieces!"

"We'll see about that!" bellowed Finn. "I'm going home right now to sit and wait for this pipsqueak of a giant. If he dares to show his face at my front door, I'll stamp on him and squash him like an ant!" Although Finn sounded brave, he was really rather worried.

The minute Finn arrived home, he sat down glumly at the kitchen table and told Oonagh all about the stories of the strange giant.

"If it's true, he'll beat me into mashed potatoes!" Finn moaned.

"You men are always boasting about your muscles, but sometimes you should use your brains instead," Oonagh laughed. "Now do as I say and leave everything else to me."

Oonagh quickly found nine round, flat stones and put them on a plate with a round flat oatcake, which she cleverly marked with a thumbprint so she could see which one it was. Meanwhile, Finn built an enormous baby's cradle and put it by the fireside, just as Oonagh had told him. Just then, Finn and Oonagh felt the ground begin to shake underneath them and a dark shadow fell across the house.

"It's him! He's here!" panicked Finn, running to and fro. "What shall I do?"

"Calm down," urged Oonagh, handing her husband a bonnet and a nightdress. "Put these on and climb into the cradle!"

Finn was far too scared to argue, and soon he was dressed up like a baby and lying cuddled up in the crib. Oonagh shoved a huge bottle of milk into his mouth and went to answer the door.

"WHERE IS FINN MCCOOL?" roared the massive giant. He was the biggest giant Oonagh had ever seen – and the ugliest! "WHEN I FIND HIM, I'M GOING TO RIP HIM TO SHREDS!" the giant bellowed.

"I'm afraid you've missed my husband," Oonagh

smiled sweetly. "He's away at the coast, building a road across the sea to Scotland. He'll be finished by teatime. You can come and wait for him if you like."

The massive giant growled something under his breath that may or may not have been a thank you.

Oonagh beckoned him inside. "Well, you'd better come in and have something to eat. You'll need to get your strength up if you're going to fight Finn. I have to say, you look like a dwarf next to my husband!"

In the cradle, Finn's teeth began to chatter. What on earth was his wife annoying the giant like that for?

"Have an oatcake," Oonagh offered the stranger, putting one of the round, flat rocks on his plate.

The greedy giant crammed it into his mouth and took a huge bite. "OW!" he roared, spitting bits of broken teeth all over the table.

"Oh dear, didn't you like it?" Oonagh fussed. "They're the baby's favourite!" She gave Finn the oatcake with the thumbprint. He ate it happily.

The strange giant peered into the cradle. "That's Finn McCool's baby?" he asked, highly surprised. "He's a whopper of a lad, isn't he?"

"Yes," sighed Oonagh, tickling her husband under the chin while Finn cooed and gurgled as best he could. "He's got teeth already, you know. Here, put

your finger into his mouth and feel. Go on."

Slowly, nervously, the giant put his little finger inside Finn's mouth.

CRUNCH! Finn bit down as hard as he possibly could – right through the bone!

"AAAAAAARRRRRRGGGGGGGGHHHHHHH!" roared the giant. "If Finn McCool's baby is that strong, I'm not hanging around to find out what Finn McCool is like!" And with that, he was out of the door and away before Finn could even leap out of the cradle.

Finn McCool never finished his road across the sea. If you go to Ireland today, you can still see it poking out into the water, half-finished. He wanted to rest with his beautiful, clever wife. So that's what he did!

Anansi and Mr Snake

A Caribbean folk tale

LONG, LONG AGO, deep in the luscious rainforests, animals and birds could talk and act very much like humans do. They spent their days working and playing together, and for most of the time, they lived in absolute harmony.

At the end of every day, all the creatures liked to gather to hear a bedtime story. As the sun dipped into the ocean, they would come out of the long, lush leaves of the dark, thick rainforest, and settle on the sandy shore. Every night, a different creature would sit at the head of the group and tell them a tale.

No one knew where the stories had come from, for none of them had ever been written down, but were

passed on from generation to generation. Each creature told their story in their own style, leaving out parts that they didn't like, and adding in new ideas. And so the old stories were kept alive – made fresh and new, exciting and fun. The creatures never tired of telling or listening to the fanciful tales, night after night.

Storytelling time was known as Tiger time and all the stories were known as Tiger tales – because Tiger said so. Tiger was the strongest, most powerful animal – and so if Tiger wanted to use his name, they certainly didn't argue! Hardly anyone ever disagreed with Tiger. He made the creatures tremble and shake just by swinging his tail.

However, one particular evening, a small creature called Anansi dared to stand up to Tiger. Anansi was a spider who knew how to turn himself into a man... or maybe he was a man who knew how to turn himself into a spider. Whatever the case, he bravely stepped forwards out of the storytelling circle and spoke to Tiger.

"Mighty Mr Tiger..." Anansi began. But Tiger pretended not to notice him.

"Mighty and handsome Mr Tiger..." Anansi said, a little louder. But Tiger merely turned his head and sniffed.

"Mighty and handsome and intelligent Mr Tiger..." Anansi tried again, even louder this time. But Tiger just opened his jaws, yawned and looked away.

Now Anansi was really fed up – not just at Tiger's rudeness, but also because all the other creatures were smirking and sniggering.

"TIGER! ARE YOU DEAF?" Anansi shouted at the top of his voice.

In one bound, Tiger was nose to nose with Anansi. Anansi gulped, while all the other creatures shrank back nervously.

"Would you care to repeat that?" Tiger snarled.

"I said, excuse me, Mr Tiger, sir," Anansi squeaked.

"Hmmm," Tiger growled, settling down.

Anansi plucked up courage and continued. "Mr Tiger, sir – there are so many things named after you. I'd like something to be named after me, too."

All the creatures fell about laughing at Anansi's boldness. Even Tiger couldn't suppress a chuckle.

"What did you have in mind, little spider?" Tiger grinned.

"I'd like some tales to be called Anansi stories," Anansi announced.

Tiger was taken aback. He didn't want to share his stories with anyone. "Oh, I don't know about that," he

sniffed. "I'll have to think about it and let you know." He paused for a moment, then said, "I've thought about it – and the answer is… no."

But Anansi persisted. "Maybe I can pay you for some stories?"

Tiger chuckled again. "Whatever could you offer me, little spider, that I might want?" he said.

"I could bring you Mr Snake, all tied up, so you could make him say sorry," Anansi said.

Now, everyone knew that Tiger and Snake had fallen out. Neither could remember who had started the argument, but each was refusing to talk until the other one gave in and apologized.

Tiger thought carefully. He would love to see Snake grovel – but how on earth would the little spider manage it?

"Very well – it's a good trade," Tiger agreed. "You have set yourself such a difficult task that if you can achieve it, you deserve the stories."

With delight gleaming in his eyes, Anansi raced off to the riverbank. He waited outside Snake's hole until out of the darkness slithered Snake.

"May I have a word?" Anansi asked. "I've been telling everyone that you're the longest creature, but they've been laughing and saying that you're not."

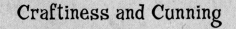

"Have they, indeed?" bristled Snake, stretching out his coils. "Who do they think is longer?"

"Crocodile," Anansi fibbed. "But I thought if you measured yourself against a length of bamboo, I could then measure crocodile, and we could settle the argument. We both know that you're the longest!"

"That'sss true," hissed Snake. "Let'sss do it."

"Shall I tie you on?" Anansi suggested. "That way, we'll be sure to measure you when you're as stretched out as possible."

"Good idea," Snake agreed.

Anansi stretched and tied Snake to the bamboo. At last the job was done and he stepped back, gleefully.

"Congratulations! You're definitely longer than Crocodile," Anansi cheered. "But you're much more stupid!" And with that, he fetched Tiger.

Astonished, yet thrilled, Tiger kept his promise. From that day onwards, many tales were told about Anansi the spider – and they're called Anansi stories.

A Midsummer Night's Dream

Retold by E Nesbit

HERMIA AND LYSANDER were in love, but Hermia's father wished her to marry another man, named Demetrius.

Now, in Athens, where they lived, there was a wicked law, by which any girl who refused to marry according to her father's wishes, might be put to death. Hermia's father was so angry with her for refusing to do as he wished, that he actually brought her before the duke of Athens to ask that she might be killed, if she still refused to obey him. The duke gave her four days to think about it, and, at the end of that time, if she still refused to marry Demetrius, she would have to die.

Lysander of course was nearly mad with grief, and it seemed to him the best thing to do was for Hermia to run away to his aunt's house at a place beyond the reach of that cruel law, and there he would come to her and marry her. But before she started, she told her friend, Helena, what she was going to do.

Helena had been Demetrius' sweetheart long before his marriage with Hermia had been thought of, and being very silly, like all jealous people, she could not see that it was not poor Hermia's fault that Demetrius wished to marry her instead of his own lady, Helena. She knew that if she told Demetrius that Hermia was going, as she was, to the wood outside Athens, he would follow her, 'and I can follow him, and at least I shall see him,' she said to herself. So she went to him, and betrayed her friend's secret.

Now this wood where Lysander was to meet Hermia, and where the other two had decided to follow them, was full of fairies, as most woods are, if one only had the eyes to see them. In this wood, on this night, were the king and queen of the fairies, Oberon and Titania. Now fairies are very wise people, but now and then they can be quite as foolish as mortal folk. Oberon and Titania, who might have been as happy as the days were long, had thrown away all their joy in a foolish quarrel. They never met without saying disagreeable things to each other, and scolded each other so dreadfully that all their little fairy followers, for fear, would creep into acorn cups and hide there.

So, instead of keeping one happy court and dancing all night through in the moonlight as is fairies' use, the king with his attendants wandered through one part of the wood, while the queen with hers kept state in another. And the cause of all this trouble was a little Indian boy whom Titania had taken to be one of her followers. Oberon wanted the child to follow him and be one of his fairy knights, but the queen would not give him up.

On this night, in a mossy moonlit glade, the king and queen of the fairies met.

"Ill met by moonlight, proud Titania," said the king.

"What! Jealous, Oberon?" answered the queen. "You spoil everything with your quarrelling. Come, fairies, let us leave him. I am not friends with him now."

"It rests with you to make up the quarrel," said the king. "Give me that little Indian boy, and I will again be your humble servant and suitor."

"Set your mind at rest," said the queen. "Your whole fairy kingdom buys not that boy from me. Come, fairies."

And she and her train rode off down the moonbeams.

"Well, go your ways," said Oberon. "But I'll be even with you before you leave this wood."

Then Oberon called his favourite fairy, Puck the spirit of mischief. He used to slip into the dairies and take the cream away, and get into the churn so that the butter would not come, and turn the beer sour, and lead people out of their way on dark nights and then laugh at them, and tumble people's stools from under them when they were going to sit down, and upset their hot ale over their chins when they were going to drink.

"Now," said Oberon to this little sprite, "fetch me the flower called Love-in-idleness. The juice of that little purple flower laid on the eyes of those who sleep will make them, when they wake, love the first thing they see. I will put some of the juice of that flower on my Titania's eyes, and when she wakes she will love the first thing she sees, were it lion, bear, or wolf, or bull, or meddling monkey, or a busy ape."

While Puck was gone, Demetrius passed through the glade followed by poor Helena, and still she told him how she loved him and reminded him of all his promises, and still he told her that he did not and could not love her, and that his promises were nothing. Oberon was sorry for poor Helena, and when Puck returned with the flower, he bade him follow Demetrius and put some of the juice on his eyes, so that he might love Helena when he woke and looked on her, as much as she loved him. So Puck set off, and wandering through the wood found, not Demetrius, but Lysander, on whose eyes he put the juice, but when

Lysander woke, he saw not his own Hermia, but Helena, who was walking through the wood looking for the cruel Demetrius. Directly he saw her, he loved her, and left his own lady, under the spell of the purple flower.

When Hermia woke she found Lysander gone, and wandered about the wood trying to find him. Puck went back and told Oberon what he had done, and Oberon soon found that he had made a mistake, and set about looking for Demetrius, and having found him, put some of the juice on his eyes. And the first thing Demetrius saw when he woke was also Helena. So now Demetrius and Lysander were both following her through the wood, and it was

Hermia's turn to follow her lover as Helena had done before. The end of it was that Helena and Hermia began to quarrel, and Demetrius and Lysander went off to fight. Oberon was very sorry to see his kind scheme to help these lovers turn out so badly. So he said to Puck:

"These two young men are going to fight. You must overhang the night with drooping fog, and lead them so astray, that one will never find the other. When they are tired out, they will fall asleep. Then drop this other herb on Lysander's eyes. That will give him his old sight and his old love. Then each man will have the lady who loves him, and they will all think that this has been only a midsummer night's dream. Then when this is done, all will be well with them."

So Puck went and did as he was told, and when the two had fallen asleep without meeting each other, Puck poured the juice on Lysander's eyes, and said:

"When thou wakest,
Thou takest
True delight
In the sight
Of thy former lady's eye:
Jack shall have Jill;
Nought shall go ill."

Meanwhile Oberon found Titania asleep on a bank where grew wild thyme, oxlips, and violets, and woodbine, musk-roses and eglantine. There Titania always slept a part of the night, wrapped in the enameled skin of a snake. Oberon stooped over her and laid the juice on her eyes, saying:

"What thou seest when thou wake,

Do it for thy true love take."

Now, it happened that when Titania woke the first thing she saw was a stupid clown, one of a party of players who had come out into the wood to rehearse their play. This clown had met with Puck, who had clapped an ass's head on his shoulders so that it looked as if it grew there. Directly Titania woke and saw this dreadful monster, she said, "What angel is this? Are you as wise as you are beautiful?"

"If I am wise enough to find my way out of this wood, that's enough for me," said the foolish clown.

"Do not desire to go out of the wood," said Titania. The spell of the love-juice was on her, and to her the clown seemed the most beautiful creature on the earth. "I love you," she went on. "Come with me, and I will give you fairies to attend on you."

So she called four fairies, whose names were Peaseblossom, Cobweb, Moth, and Mustardseed.

"You must attend this gentleman," said the queen. "Feed him with apricots and dewberries, purple grapes, green figs, and mulberries. Steal honey-bags for him from the bumble-bees, and with the wings of painted butterflies fan the moonbeams from his sleeping eyes."

"I will," said one of the fairies, and all the others said, "I will."

"Now, sit down with me," said the queen to the clown, "and let me stroke your dear cheeks, and stick musk-roses in your smooth, sleek head, and kiss your fair large ears, my gentle joy."

"Where's Peaseblossom?" asked the clown with the ass's head. He did not care much about the queen's affection, but he was very proud of having fairies to wait on him.

"Ready," said Peaseblossom.

"Scratch my head, Peaseblossom," said the clown. "Where's Cobweb?"

"Ready," said Cobweb.

"Kill me," said the clown, "the red bumble-bee on the top of the thistle yonder, and bring me the honey-bag. Where's Mustardseed?"

"Ready," said Mustardseed.

"Oh, I want nothing," said the clown. "Only just help Cobweb to scratch. I must go to the barber's, for

methinks I am marvellous hairy about the face."

"Would you like anything to eat?" said the fairy queen.

"I should like some good dry oats," said the clown – for his donkey's head made him desire donkey's food – "and some hay to follow."

"Shall some of my fairies fetch you new nuts from the squirrel's house?" asked the queen.

"I'd rather have a handful or two of good dried peas," said the clown. "But please don't let any of your people disturb me – I am going to sleep."

Then said the queen, "And I will wind thee in my arms."

And so when Oberon came along he found his beautiful queen lavishing kisses and endearments on a clown with a donkey's head.

And before he released her from the enchantment, he persuaded her to give him the little Indian boy he so much desired to have. Then he took pity on her, and threw some juice of the disenchanting flower on her pretty eyes, and then in a moment she saw plainly the donkey-headed clown she had been loving, and knew how foolish she had been.

Oberon took off the ass's head from the clown, and left him to finish his sleep with his own silly head lying

on the thyme and violets.

Thus all was made plain and straight again. Oberon and Titania loved each other more than ever. Demetrius thought of no one but Helena, and Helena had never had any thought of anyone but Demetrius.

As for Hermia and Lysander, they were as loving a couple as you could meet in a day's march, even through a fairy wood.

So the four mortal lovers went back to Athens and were married; and the fairy king and queen live happily together in that very wood at this very day.

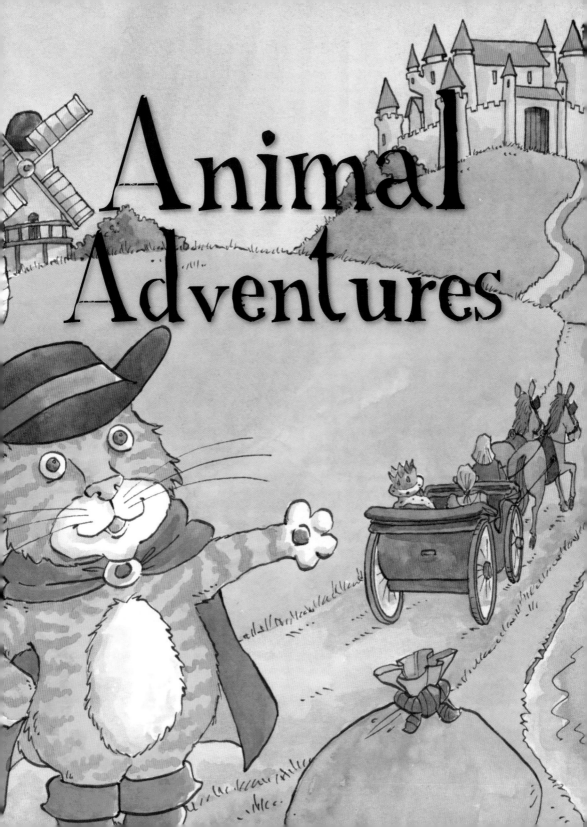

Animal Adventures

The Spider and the Toad

From *Wood Magic* by Richard Jeffries

ONE MORNING AS LITTLE 'SIR' BEVIS (such was his pet name) was digging in the farmhouse garden, he saw a daisy, and throwing aside his spade, he sat down on the grass to pick the flower to pieces.

A flutter of wings sounded among the blossom on an apple tree close by, and instantly Bevis sat up, knowing it must be a goldfinch thinking of building a nest in the branches. If the trunk of the tree had not been so big, he would have tried to climb it at once, but he knew he could not do it, nor could he see the bird for the leaves and bloom. A puff of wind came and showered the petals down upon him; they fell like snowflakes on his face and dotted the grass.

Buzz! A great humble-bee, with a band of gold across his back, flew up, and hovered near, wavering to and fro in the air as he stayed to look at a flower.

Buzz! Bevis listened, and knew very well what he was saying. It was, 'This is a sweet little garden, my darling; a very pleasant garden; all grass and daisies, and apple trees, and narrow patches with flowers and fruit trees one side, and a wall and currant bushes another side, and a low box-hedge and a haha, where you can see the high mowing grass quite underneath you; and a round summerhouse in the corner, painted as blue inside as a hedge-sparrow's egg is outside; and then another haha with iron railings, which you are always climbing up, Bevis, on the fourth side, with stone steps leading down to a meadow, where the cows are feeding, and where they have left all the buttercups standing as tall as your waist, sir. The gate in the iron railings is not fastened, and besides, there is a gap in the box-hedge, and it is easy to drop down the haha wall, but that is mowing grass there. You know very well you could not

come to any harm in the meadow; they said you were not to go outside the garden, but that's all nonsense, and very stupid. I am going outside the garden, Bevis. Good morning, dear. Buzz!' And the great humble-bee flew slowly between the iron railings, out among the buttercups, and away up the field.

Bevis went to the railings, and stood on the lowest bar; then he opened the gate a little way, but it squeaked so loud upon its rusty hinges that he let it shut again. He walked round the garden along beside the box-hedge to the patch by the lilac trees; they were single lilacs, which are much more beautiful than the double, and all bowed down with a mass of bloom. Some rhubarb grew there, and to bring it up the faster, they had put a round wooden box on it, hollowed out from the sawn butt of an elm.

One of these round wooden boxes had been split and spoilt, and half of it was left lying on the ground. Under this shelter a toad had his house. Bevis peered in at him, and touched him with a twig to make him move an inch or two, for he was so lazy, and sat there all day long, except when it rained. Sometimes the Toad told him a story, but not very often, for he was a silent old philosopher, and not very fond of anybody. He had a nephew, quite a lively young fellow, in the cucumber frame on the other side of the lilac bushes, at whom Bevis also peered nearly every day after they had lifted the frame and propped it up with wedges.

The gooseberries were no bigger than beads, but he tasted two, and then a thrush began to sing on an ash tree in the hedge of the meadow. 'Bevis! Bevis!' said the thrush, and he turned round to listen: 'Have you forgotten the meadow, and the buttercups, and the sorrel? You know the sorrel, don't you, that tastes so pleasant if you nibble the leaf? And I have a nest in the bushes, not very far up the hedge, and you may take just one egg; there are only two yet. But don't tell any more boys about it, or we shall not have one left. That is a very sweet garden, but it is small. I like all these fields to fly about in, and the swallows fly ever so much farther than I can; so far away and so high, that I cannot tell you how they find their way home to the chimney. But they will tell you, if you ask them. Good morning! I am going over the brook.'

Bevis went to the iron railings and got up two bars, and looked over; but he could not yet make up his mind, so he went inside the summerhouse, which had one small round window. All the lower part of the blue walls was scribbled and marked with pencil, where he had written and drawn, and put down his ideas and notes. The lines were somewhat intermingled, and crossed each other, and some stretched out long distances, and came back in sharp angles. But Bevis knew very well what he meant when he wrote it all. Taking a stump of cedar pencil from his pocket, he added a few scrawls to the inscriptions, and then stood on the seat to look out of the round window, which was darkened by an old cobweb.

Once upon a time there was a very cunning spider, a very cunning spider indeed. The old Toad by the rhubarb told Bevis there had not been such a cunning spider for many summers; he knew almost as much about flies as the old Toad, and caught such a great number that the Toad began to think there would be none left for him. Now the Toad was extremely fond of flies, and he watched the Spider with envy, and grew more angry about it every day.

As he sat blinking and winking by the rhubarb in his house all day long, the Toad never left off thinking,

thinking, thinking about the Spider. And as he kept thinking, thinking, thinking, so he told Bevis, he recollected that he knew a great deal about a good many other things besides flies. So one day, after several weeks of thinking, he crawled out of his house in the sunshine, which he did not like at all, and went across the grass to the iron railings, where the Spider had then got his web. The Spider saw him coming, and being very proud of his cleverness, began to taunt and tease him.

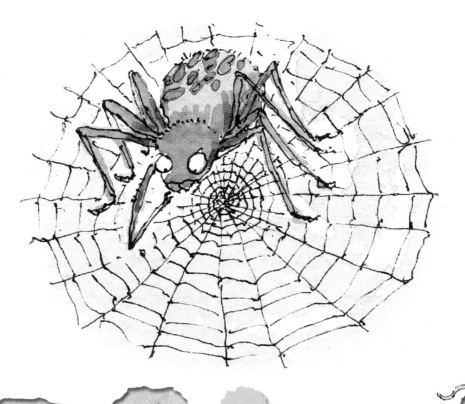

"Your back is all over warts, and you are an old toad," he said. "You are so old, that I heard the swallows saying their great, great, great grandmothers, when they built in the chimney, did not know when you were born. And you have got foolish, and past doing anything, and so stupid that you hardly know when it is going to rain. Why, the sun is shining bright, you stupid old Toad, and there isn't a chance of a single drop falling. You look very ugly down there in the grass. Now, don't you wish that you were me, and could catch more flies than you could eat? Why, I can catch wasps and bees, and tie them up so tight with my threads that they cannot sting nor even move their wings, nor so much as wriggle their bodies. I am the very cleverest and most cunning spider that ever lived."

"Indeed, you are!" replied the Toad. "I have been thinking so all the summer; and so much do I admire you, that I have come all this way, across in the hot sun, to tell you something."

"Tell me something!" said the Spider, much offended. "I know everything."

"Oh, yes, honoured sir," said the Toad; "you have such wonderful eyes, and such a sharp mind, it is true that you know everything about the sun, and the moon, and the earth, and flies. But, as you have studied all these great and important things, you could hardly see all the very little trifles like a poor old toad."

"Oh yes, I can. I know everything – everything!"

"But, sir," went on the Toad so humbly, "this is such a very little thing, and a spider like you in such a high position of life, could not mind me telling you such a mere nothing."

"Well, I don't mind," said the Spider, "you may go on, and tell me, if you like."

"The fact is," said the Toad, "while I have been sitting in my hole, I have noticed that such a lot of the flies that come into this garden presently go into the summerhouse there, and when they are in the summerhouse, they always go to that little round window, which is sometimes quite black with them; for it is the nature of flies to buzz over glass."

"I do not know so much about that," said the Spider; "for I have never lived in houses, being an independent insect; but it is possible you may be right. At any rate, it is not of much consequence. You had better go up into the window, old Toad." Now this was a sneer on the part of the Spider.

"But I can't climb up into the window," said the Toad; "all I can do is to crawl about the ground, but you can run up a wall quickly. How I do wish I was a

spider, like you. Oh, dear!" And then the Toad turned round, after bowing to the clever Spider, and went back to his hole.

Now the Spider was secretly very much mortified and angry with himself, because he had not noticed this about the flies going to the window in the summerhouse. At first he said to himself that it was not true; but he could not help looking that way now and then, and every time he looked, there was the window crowded with flies. They had all the garden to buzz about in, and all the fields, but instead of wandering under the trees, and over the flowers, they preferred to go into the summerhouse and crawl over the glass of the little window, though it was very dirty from so many feet. For a long time, the Spider was too proud to go there too; but one day such a splendid bluebottle fly got in the window and made such a tremendous buzzing, that he could not resist it any more.

So he left his web by the railings, and climbed up the blue-painted wall, over Bevis' writings and marks, and spun such a web in the window as had never before been seen. It was the largest and the finest, and the most beautiful web that had ever been made, and it caught such a number of flies that the Spider grew fatter every day. In a week's time he was so big that he could no longer hide in the crack he had chosen, he was quite a giant, and the Toad came across the grass one night and looked at him, but the Spider was now so bloated he would not recognize the Toad.

But one morning a robin came to the iron railings, and perched on the top, and put his head a little on one side, to show his black eye the better. Then he flew inside the summerhouse, alighted in the window, and gobbled up the Spider in an instant. The old Toad shut his eye and opened it again, and went on thinking, for that was just what he knew would happen. Ever so many times in his very long life he had seen spiders go up there, but no sooner had they got fat than a robin or a wren came in and ate them. Some of the clever spider's web was there still when Bevis looked out of the window, all dusty and draggled, with the skins and wings of some gnats and a dead leaf entangled in it.

Pinocchio is Swallowed by the Dogfish

From *Pinocchio* by Carlo Collodi

WHILST PINOCCHIO was swimming, he saw in the midst of the sea a rock that seemed to be made of white marble, and on it there stood a beautiful little goat who bleated lovingly and made signs to him to approach.

I leave you to imagine how rapidly poor Pinocchio's heart began to beat. He swam with redoubled strength and energy towards the white rock; and he was already half-way there when he saw, rising up out of the water and coming to meet him, the horrible head of a sea-monster. His wide-open, cavernous mouth and his three rows of enormous teeth would have been terrifying to look at even in a picture.

This sea-monster was the gigantic Dogfish. Only to think of poor Pinocchio's terror at the sight of the monster. He tried to escape, but that immense, wide-open mouth came towards him with the speed of an arrow.

"Be quick, Pinocchio, for pity's sake!" cried the beautiful little goat, bleating.

And Pinocchio swam desperately with his arms, his chest, his legs, and his feet.

"Quick, Pinocchio, the monster is close upon you!"

And Pinocchio swam quicker than ever. He had nearly reached the rock, and the little goat, leaning over towards the sea, had stretched out her forelegs to

help him out of the water!

But it was too late! The monster had overtaken him and, drawing in his breath, he swallowed Pinocchio.

When he came to himself again, he could not in the least imagine in what world he was. All around him it was quite dark, and the darkness was so black that it seemed to him that he had fallen head downwards into an inkstand full of ink. He listened, but he could hear no noise; only from time to time great gusts of wind blew in his face.

At first he could not understand where the wind came from, but at last he discovered that it came out of the monster's lungs, for the Dogfish suffered very much from asthma.

Pinocchio began to cry and scream, and to sob out: "Help! help! Will nobody come to save me?"

"Who do you think could save you?" said a voice in the dark that sounded like a guitar out of tune.

"Who is speaking?" asked Pinocchio, frozen with terror.

"It is I! I am a poor Tunny who was swallowed by the Dogfish at the same time that you were."

"I want to get away from here. I want to escape. Is this Dogfish very big?" asked the puppet.

"Big! Why, only imagine, his body is two miles long

without counting his tail."

Whilst they were talking, Pinocchio thought that he saw a light a long way off.

"What is that little light I see in the distance?" he asked.

"It is most likely some companion in misfortune who is waiting, like us, to be digested."

"I will go and find him. Perhaps the fish could show us how to escape?"

"I hope it may be so, with all my heart, dear puppet."

Pinocchio, having left Tunny, began to grope his way in the dark through the body of the Dogfish, taking a step at a time in the direction of the light.

The farther he advanced, the brighter became the light; and he walked and walked until at last he reached it. There he found a little table spread out and on it a lighted candle stuck into a green glass bottle, and, seated at the table, was a little old man.

At this sight, Pinocchio was filled with such great and unexpected joy. At last he uttered a cry of joy, and, opening his arms, he threw them around the little old man's neck, and began to shout:

"Oh, my dear papa! I have found you at last! I will never leave you more, never more, never more!"

"Then my eyes tell me true?" said the little old man,

rubbing his eyes; "then you are really my dear Pinocchio?"

"Yes, yes, I am Pinocchio, really Pinocchio! Oh, if you only knew what misfortunes have been poured on my head when I couldn't find my way back to you! Then one day, the Pigeon, seeing that I was crying, said to me, 'I have seen your father who was building a little boat to go in search of you.' So we flew all night, and then in the morning the fishermen said, 'There is a poor man in a boat who is on the point of being drowned,' and I recognized you at once and I made signs to you to return to land."

"I also recognized you," said Geppetto, "and I would willingly have returned to the shore, but what was I to do! A great wave upset my boat. Then a horrible Dogfish swallowed me as if I had been a little apple tart."

"And how long have you been shut up here?" asked Pinocchio.

"Since that day – it must be nearly two years ago; two years, my dear Pinocchio!"

"And how have you managed to live? And where did you get the candle? And the matches to light it?"

"Stop, and I will tell you everything. In the same storm in which my boat was upset a merchant vessel sunk. The sailors were all saved, but the vessel went to the bottom, and the Dogfish swallowed it. Fortunately for me, the vessel was laden with preserved meat in tins, biscuit, bottles of wine, dried raisins, cheese, coffee, sugar, candles, and boxes of wax matches. With this, I have been able to live for two years. But now there is nothing left in the larder, and this candle that you see burning is the last that remains."

"Then, dear little papa," said Pinocchio, "there is no time to lose. We must think of escaping through the mouth of the Dogfish. I am a good swimmer, and I will carry you safely to shore."

Geppetto shook his head. "Do you suppose a puppet like you could have the strength to swim with me on his shoulders!"

"Try it and you will see!"

Without another word Pinocchio took the candle in his hand, and, going in front to light the way, he said to his father: "Follow me, and don't be afraid."

And they walked for some time and when they had arrived at the point where the monster's big throat began, they thought it better to stop to look around and to choose the best moment for escaping. The Dogfish, being old and suffering from asthma, slept with his mouth open. Pinocchio looked up and could see a large piece of starry sky and beautiful moonlight.

"This is the moment to escape," he whispered, turning to his father; "the Dogfish is sleeping, the sea is calm, and it is as light as day. Follow me, dear papa, and in a short time we shall be in safety."

They immediately climbed up the throat of the sea-monster, and, having reached his immense mouth, they began to walk on tiptoe down his tongue.

Before taking the final leap the puppet said to his father: "Get on my shoulders and put your arms tightly around my neck. I will take care of the rest."

Then Pinocchio began to swim, out of the Dogfish and into the sea, where they were surrounded by fish. After a while, his strength began to fail. He was gasping and panting for breath. He could do no more, and the shore was still far off.

He swam until he had no breath left; then he turned his head to Geppetto and said in broken words: "Papa, help me, I am dying!"

"I know that voice! You are Pinocchio!"

"Yes, and you?"

"I am the Tunny, your prison companion in the body of the Dogfish."

"And how did you manage to escape?"

"I followed your example and escaped after you."

"Tunny, you have arrived at the right moment! Please help us or we are lost."

"You must both take hold of my tail and leave it to me to guide you. I will take you to the shore."

Geppetto and Pinocchio accepted the offer at once; but, instead of holding on by his tail, they

thought it would be more comfortable to get on the Tunny's back.

Having reached the shore, Pinocchio sprang first on land that he might help his father to do the same. He then turned to the Tunny and said to him: "My friend, you have saved my papa's life. I can find no words with which to thank you properly. Permit me at least to give you a kiss as a sign of my eternal gratitude!"

The Tunny put his head out of the water and Pinocchio, kneeling on the ground, kissed him. The poor Tunny felt extremely touched, and, ashamed to let himself be seen crying like a child, he plunged under the water and disappeared.

The Horse and the Olive

By James Baldwin

ON A STEEP STONY hill in Greece there lived in early times a few very poor people who had not yet learned to build houses. They made their homes in little caves, which they dug in the earth or hollowed out among the rocks; and their food was the flesh of wild animals, which they hunted in the woods, with now and then a few berries or nuts. They did not even know how to make bows and arrows, but used slings and clubs and sharp sticks for weapons; and the little clothing they had was made of skins.

They lived on the top of the hill, because they were safe there from the savage beasts of the great forest around them, and safe also from the wild men who

sometimes roamed through the land. The hill was so steep on every side that there was no way of climbing it save by a single narrow footpath which was always guarded by someone at the top.

One day when the men were hunting in the woods, they found a strange youth whose face was so fair and who was dressed so beautifully that they could hardly believe him to be a man like themselves. His body was so slender and lithe, and he moved so nimbly among the trees, that they fancied him to be a serpent in the guise of a human being; and they stood still in wonder and alarm. The young man spoke to them, but they could not understand a word that he said; then he made signs to them that he was hungry, and they gave him something to eat and were no longer afraid. Had they been like the wild men of the woods, they might have killed him at once.

But they wanted their women and children to see the serpent man, as they called him, and hear him talk; and so they took him home with them to the top of the hill. They thought that after they had made a show of him for a few days, they would kill him and offer his body as a sacrifice to the unknown being whom they dimly fancied to have some sort of control over their lives.

But the young man was so fair and gentle that, after they had all taken a look at him, they began to think it would be a great pity to harm him. So they gave him food and treated him kindly; and he sang songs to them and played with their children, and made them happier than they had been for many a day. In a short time he learned to talk in their language; and he told them that his name was Cecrops, and that he had been shipwrecked on the seacoast not far away; and then he told them many strange things about the land from which he had come and to which he would never be able to return. The poor people listened and wondered; and it was not long until they began to love him and to look up to him as one wiser than themselves. Then they came to ask him about everything that was to be done, and there was not one of them who refused to do his bidding.

So Cecrops – the serpent man, as they still called him – became the king of the poor people on the hill. He taught them how to make bows and arrows, and how to set nets for birds, and how to take fish with hooks. He led them against the savage wild men of the woods, and helped them kill the fierce beasts that had been so great a terror to them. He showed them how to build houses of wood and to thatch them with the

reeds which grew in the marshes. He taught them how to live in families instead of herding together like senseless beasts as they had always done before. And he told them about great Jupiter and the Mighty Folk who lived amid the clouds on the mountain top.

By and by, instead of the wretched caves among the rocks, there was a little town on the top of the hill, with neat houses and a market place; and around it was a strong wall with a single narrow gate just where the footpath began to descend to the plain. But as yet the place had no name.

One morning while the king and his wise men were sitting together in the market place and planning how to make the town become a rich, strong city, two strangers were seen in the street. Nobody could tell how they came there. The guard at the gate had not seen them; and no man had ever dared to climb the narrow footway without his leave. But there the two strangers stood. One was a man, the other a woman; and they were so tall, and their faces were so grand and noble, that those who saw them stood still and wondered and said not a word.

The man had a robe of purple and green wrapped round his body, and he bore in one hand a strong staff with three sharp spear points at one end. The woman

was not beautiful, but she had wonderful gray eyes; and she carried a spear and a shield.

"What is the name of this town?" asked the man.

The people stared at him in wonder. Then an old man answered and said, "It has no name. We who live on this hill used to be called Cranæ; but since King Cecrops came, we have been so busy that we have had no time to think of names."

"Where is this King Cecrops?" asked the woman.

"He is in the market place with the wise men," was the answer.

"Lead us to him at once," said the man.

When Cecrops saw the two strangers coming into the market place, he stood up and waited for them to speak. The man spoke first: "I am Neptune," said he, "and I rule the sea."

"And I am Athena," said the woman, "and I give wisdom to men."

"I hear that you are planning to make your town become a great city," said Neptune, "and I have come to help you. Give my name to the place, and let me be your protector and patron, and the wealth of the whole world shall be yours. Ships from every land shall bring you merchandise and gold and silver; and you shall be the masters of the sea."

"My uncle makes you fair promises," said Athena; "but listen to me. Give my name to your city, and let me be your patron, and I will give you that which gold cannot buy: I will teach you how to do a thousand things of which you now know nothing. I will make your city my favorite home, and I will give you wisdom that shall sway the minds and hearts of all men until the end of time."

The king bowed, and turned to the people, who had all crowded into the market place.

"Which of these mighty ones shall we elect to be the protector and patron of our city?" he asked. "Neptune offers us wealth; Athena promises us wisdom. Which shall we choose?"

"Neptune and wealth!" cried many.

"Athena and wisdom!" cried as many others.

At last when it was plain that the people could not agree, an old man whose advice was always heeded stood up and said: "These mighty ones have only given us promises, and they have promised things of which we are ignorant. For who among us knows what wealth is or what wisdom is? Now, if they would only give us some real gift, right now and right here, which we can see and handle, we should know better how to choose."

"That is true! That is true!" cried the people.

"Very well, then," said the strangers, "we will each give you a gift, right now and right here, and then you may choose between us."

Neptune gave the first gift. He stood on the highest point of the hill where the rock was bare, and bade the people see his power. He raised his three-pointed spear high in the air, and then brought it down with great force. Lightning flashed, the earth shook, and the rock was split halfway down to the bottom of the hill. Then out of the yawning crevice there sprang a wonderful creature, white as milk, with long slender legs, an arching neck, and a mane and tail of silk.

The people had never seen anything like it before, and they thought it a new kind of bear or wolf or wild boar that had come out of the rock to devour them.

Some of them ran and hid in their houses, while others climbed upon the wall, and still others grasped their weapons in alarm. But when they saw the

creature stand quietly by the side of Neptune, they lost their fear and came closer to see and admire its beauty.

"This is my gift," said Neptune. "This animal will carry your burdens for you; he will draw your chariots; he will pull your wagons; he will let you sit on his back and will run with you faster than the wind."

"What is his name?" asked the king.

"His name is Horse," answered Neptune.

Then Athena came forward. She stood a moment on a green grassy plot where the children of the town liked to play in the evening. Then she drove the point of her spear deep down in the soil. At once the air was filled with

music, and out of the earth
there sprang a tree with
slender branches and
dark green leaves and
white flowers.

"This is my gift," said
Athena. "This tree will
give you food when you are
hungry; it will shelter
you from the sun when
you are faint; it will
beautify your city; and the oil from its fruit will be
sought by the world."

"What is it called?" asked the king.

"It is called Olive," answered Athena.

Then the king and his wise men began to talk about
the two gifts.

"I do not see that Horse will be of much use to us,"
said the old man who had spoken before. "For, as to the
chariots and wagons, we have none of them, and
indeed do not know what they are; and who among us
will ever want to sit on this creature's back and be
borne faster than the wind? But Olive will be a thing of
beauty and a joy for us and our children forever."

"Which shall we choose?" asked the king, turning to

the people.

"Athena has given us the best gift," they all cried, "and we choose Athena and wisdom!"

"Be it so," said the king, "and the name of our city shall be Athens."

From that day the town grew and spread, and soon there was not room on the hilltop for all the people. Then houses were built in the plain around the foot of the hill, and a great road was built to the sea, three miles away; and in all the world there was no city more fair than Athens.

In the old market place on the top of the hill the people built a temple to Athena, the ruins of which may still be seen. The olive tree grew and flourished; and, when you visit Athens, people will show you the very spot where it stood. Many other trees sprang from it, and in time became a blessing both to Greece and to all the other countries round the great sea. As for the horse, he wandered away across the plains towards the north and found a home at last in distant Thessaly beyond the River Peneus. And I have heard it said that all the horses in the world have descended from that one which Neptune brought out of the rock; but of the truth of this story there may be some doubts.

Puss in Boots

Retold from the original tale
by Charles Perrault

A CERTAIN MILLER was so poor that when he died, all he left his three sons were his mill, his mule and a cat.

"Bagsy me the mill," said the eldest son.

"Bagsy me the mule," said the middle son.

"Oh, great!" said the youngest son. "I suppose I'm left with the cat then." (As you can tell, he wasn't very happy about it. But youngest children often start off with a bad deal in fairytales, so he should really have seen it coming.)

"Stop your moaning!" scolded the cat. "If you stick with me, I can guarantee that you'll be thanking your dear old dad later. Now fetch me a large bag and leave

me to get on with things. Oh – and get me a smart pair of boots made from the finest red leather, just like I've always wanted..."

The youngest son didn't argue. Firstly, the cat had never talked before, so he was speechless with shock. And secondly, he didn't have a better plan to suggest anyway. So he took what little money he had saved under the mattress and did exactly what the cat had told him...

As soon as Puss had finished purring with delight at how fine he looked in his smart boots of the finest red leather, he hurried along to a field and lay down quite still with his bag wide open beside him. After a while – hop! hop! hop! – along came a plump bunny. Pop! the silly rabbit jumped straight into the bag. Zip! Puss shut the bag. Whistling merrily, he took his catch to the palace and presented it to the king. "My master, the Marquis of Carabas, sends you this gift," Puss announced, bowing low.

"Give him my warmest thanks," the king announced, smiling graciously.

As soon as Puss was gone, the king turned to his chamberlain and whispered: "Whoever this Marquis is, he must be very rich and important to send his messengers in such smart boots!"

The next day the cat was back again – with a present of two partridges. And the day after that – with three pheasants. Every day for three months, Puss arrived at court with a gift for the king from his master, the Marquis of Carabas. "What a thoughtful, kind-hearted man this Marquis of Carabas is!" the king exclaimed as his royal pantry filled up with delicious game.

One day, Puss learned that the king was going to take a drive along the river with his beautiful daughter. "Right, you're going for a swim!" the cat commanded the miller's youngest son.

"But – but – I don't have any swimming trunks!" the Marquis of Carabas protested, but Puss was already dragging him along to a certain spot on the riverbank. Before he knew it, the cat had taken away all his clothes and he was swimming around obediently among the waterweed.

Just then, the royal carriage came trundling by. "Help! Help!'" shouted Puss, running out onto the road and flagging it down. "The Marquis of Carabas is drowning!"

The princess squealed with fright as she peered out of the carriage and saw a man splashing about in the water. At once, the king ordered his guards into the river to pull him out.

"Your majesty," purred the cat, as the soldiers began trying to give the startled miller's son the kiss of life. "As if it wasn't bad enough that the Marquis of Carabas has nearly drowned, while he was in the water, robbers have stolen all his clothes!"

The king tut-tutted and sent his chamberlain galloping back to the palace to bring a selection of his very own robes for the Marquis to wear. Soon the miller's son was looking exceedingly handsome in the king's best suit, and the princess was blushing a deep pink. "It's the very least I can do in return for all the kind gifts you have been sending me!" the king said earnestly. The miller's son had no idea what the king was talking about, but he thought it best just to nod and smile all the same. "You will come and ride with us a while, won't you?" insisted the king, and the miller's son was ushered up into the royal carriage to sit next to the princess.

Puss was highly excited that his scheme was working, and he ran ahead down the road. By and by, he came to a hayfield of mowers, and he said, "Good people, if you don't tell the king that this field belongs to the Marquis of Carabas, I'll make you all into cat food."

It wasn't long before the royal carriage passed by and, sure enough, the king leaned out of the window and asked, "Who does this land belong to?"

"It b-b-b-belongs to the M-m-m-arquis of C-c-c-arabas," the terrified mowers stuttered.

"You have a fine estate," the king beamed at the miller's youngest son, and the so-called Marquis nodded and smiled.

Soon the royal carriage came to a cornfield of harvesters. The miller's youngest son was just as surprised as the king to learn from the harvesters that the cornfield belonged to him, too! A little further

down the road, and a group of dairymaids insisted that their cows belonged to the Marquis of Carabas.

"My!" the king grinned. "What splendid lands you have!" And the princess's cheeks turned rosy with pleasure.

While the royal carriage rolled along, Puss was a long way down the road at a fearful ogre's castle. It was the ogre who owned all the land that Puss had been giving to the Marquis of Carabas (though luckily, the ogre didn't know about that!). "Mr Ogre," began Puss politely. "I have come to pay my respects to you because I have heard that you have remarkable powers. Is it true that you can turn yourself from a big, hulking ogre into a tiny, sneaky mouse?"

"Easy-peasy!" growled the ogre. He disappeared before Puss's very eyes and suddenly there was a mouse scurrying about on the floor. It took Puss only a few seconds to pounce and gobble him up, and that was the end of the ogre.

By the time the royal carriage pulled up outside the castle, Puss was waiting outside to greet it. "Welcome to the home of the Marquis of Carabas," Puss announced proudly. The 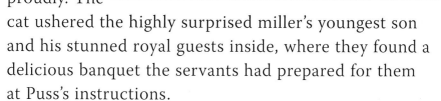 cat ushered the highly surprised miller's youngest son and his stunned royal guests inside, where they found a delicious banquet the servants had prepared for them at Puss's instructions.

"My dear Marquis," beamed the king. "I am most impressed with your riches – er, I mean generosity. If there's anything I can do for you, just say the word."

The miller's son glanced at the princess, who hissed under her breath, "Go on! Ask him!"

So the Marquis of Carabas cleared his throat and said, "Actually, I'd quite like to marry your daughter!" and the king roared with happy laughter.

The couple were married that very day, and the miller's youngest son lived as the rich and prosperous

Marquis of Carabas for the rest of his life. So his story has a happy ending after all. (And that's what happens in fairytales, so he should really have seen it coming.) As for Puss – well, he lived happily at the castle too. There were plenty of mice to catch, and that's all he needed to be content – as well as his smart boots of the finest red leather, of course!

Tom Sawyer in Church

From *The Adventures of Tom Sawyer*
by Mark Twain

ABOUT HALF-PAST TEN the cracked bell of the small church began to ring, and presently the people began to gather for the morning sermon. The Sunday school children distributed themselves about the house and occupied pews with their parents, so as to be under supervision. Aunt Polly came, and Tom and Sid and Mary sat with her – Tom being placed next to the aisle, in order that he might be as far away from the open window and the seductive outside summer scenes as possible.

The crowd filed up the aisles: the aged and needy postmaster, who had seen better days; the mayor and his wife – for they had a mayor there, among other

unnecessaries; the justice of the peace; the widow
Douglass, fair, smart, and forty, a generous, good-
hearted soul and well-to-do, her hill mansion the only
palace in the town, and the most hospitable and much
the most lavish in the matter of festivities that
St Petersburg could boast; the bent and venerable
Major and Mrs Ward; lawyer Riverson, the new
notable from a distance; next the belle of the village,
followed by a troop of lawn-clad and ribbon-decked
young heart-breakers; then all the young clerks in town
in a body – for they had stood in the vestibule sucking
their cane-heads, a circling wall of oiled and simpering
admirers, till the last girl had run their gauntlet; and
last of all came the Model Boy, Willie Mufferson,
taking as heedful care of his mother as if she were cut
glass. He always brought his mother to church, and
was the pride of all the matrons. The boys all hated
him, he was so good. And besides, he had been
'thrown up to them' so much. His white handkerchief
was hanging out of his pocket behind, as usual on
Sundays – accidentally. Tom had no handkerchief, and
he looked upon boys who had as snobs.

The congregation being fully assembled, the bell
rang once more, to warn laggards and stragglers, and
then a solemn hush fell upon the church which was

only broken by the tittering and whispering of the
choir in the gallery. The choir always tittered and
whispered all through the service. There was once a
church choir that was not ill-bred, but I have forgotten
where it was, now. It was a great many years ago, and I
can scarcely remember anything about it, but I think it
was in some foreign country.

The minister gave out the hymn, and read it through
with a relish, in a peculiar style which was much
admired in that part of the country. His voice began on
a medium key and climbed steadily up till it reached a
certain point, where it bore with strong emphasis upon
the topmost word and then plunged down as if from a
spring-board:

"Shall I be car-ri-ed to the skies,
On flow'ry beds of ease,
Whilst others fight to win the prize,
And sail thro' bloody seas?"

He was regarded as a wonderful reader. At church
'sociables' he was always called upon to read poetry;
and when he was through, the ladies would lift up their
hands and let them fall helplessly in their laps, and
'wall' their eyes, and shake their heads, as much as to
say, 'Words cannot express it; it is too beautiful, too
beautiful for this mortal earth.'

After the hymn had been sung, the Rev. Mr. Sprague turned himself into a bulletin-board, and read off 'notices' of meetings and societies and things till it seemed that the list would stretch out to the crack of doom – a queer custom which is still kept up in America, even in cities, away here in this age of abundant newspapers. Often, the less there is to justify a traditional custom, the harder it is to get rid of it.

And now the minister prayed. A good, generous prayer it was, and went into details: it pleaded for the church, and the little children of the church; for the other churches of the village; for the village itself; for the county; for the State; for the State officers; for the United States; for the churches of the United States; for Congress; for the President; for the officers of the Government; for poor sailors, tossed by stormy seas; for the oppressed millions groaning under the heel of European monarchies and Oriental despotisms; for such as have the light and the good tidings, and yet have not eyes to see nor ears to hear withal; for the heathen in the far islands of the sea; and closed with a supplication that the words he was about to speak might find grace and favor, and be as seed sown in fertile ground, yielding in time a grateful harvest of good. Amen.

There was a rustling of dresses, and the standing congregation sat down. The boy whose history this book relates did not enjoy the prayer, he only endured it – if he even did that much. He was restive all through it; he kept tally of the details of the prayer, unconsciously – for he was not listening, but he knew the ground of old, and the clergyman's regular route over it – and when a little trifle of new matter was interlarded, his ear detected it and his whole nature resented it; he considered additions unfair, and scoundrelly. In the midst of the prayer a fly had lit on the back of the pew in front of him and tortured his spirit by calmly rubbing its hands together, embracing its head with its arms, and polishing it so vigorously that it seemed to almost part company with the body, and the slender thread of a neck was exposed to view; scraping its wings with its hind legs and smoothing them to its body as if they had been coat-tails; going through its whole toilet as tranquilly as if it knew it was perfectly safe. As indeed it was; for as sorely as Tom's hands itched to grab for it they did not dare – he believed his soul would be instantly destroyed if he did such a thing while the prayer was going on. But with the closing sentence his hand began to curve and steal forward; and the instant the 'Amen' was out the

fly was a prisoner of war. His aunt detected the act and made him let it go.

The minister gave out his text and droned along monotonously through an argument that was so prosy that many a head by and by began to nod – and yet it was an argument that dealt in limitless fire and brimstone and thinned the predestined elect down to a company so small as to be hardly worth the saving. Tom counted the pages of the sermon; after church he always knew how many pages there had been, but he seldom knew anything else about the discourse. However, this time he was really interested for a little while. The minister made a grand and moving picture of the assembling together of the world's hosts at the millennium when the lion and the lamb should lie down together and a little child should lead them. But the pathos, the lesson, the moral of the great spectacle were lost upon the boy; he only thought of the conspicuousness of the principal character before the on-looking nations; his face lit with the thought, and he said to himself that he wished he could be that child, if it was a tame lion.

Now he lapsed into suffering again, as the dry argument was resumed. Presently he bethought him of a treasure he had and got it out. It was a large black beetle with formidable jaws – a 'pinchbug,' he called it. It was in a percussion-cap box. The first thing the beetle did was to take him by the finger. A natural fillip followed, the beetle went floundering into the aisle and lit on its back, and the hurt finger went into the boy's mouth. The beetle lay there working its helpless legs, unable to turn over. Tom eyed it, and longed for it; but it was safe out of his reach. Other people uninterested in the sermon found relief in the beetle, and they eyed it too. Presently a vagrant poodle dog came idling along, sad at heart, lazy with the summer softness and the quiet, weary of captivity, sighing for change. He spied the beetle; the drooping tail lifted and wagged. He surveyed the prize; walked around it; smelt at it from a safe distance; walked around it again; grew bolder, and took a closer smell; then lifted his lip and made a gingerly snatch at it, just missing it; made another, and another; began to enjoy the diversion; subsided to his stomach with the beetle between his paws, and continued his experiments;

grew weary at last, and then indifferent and absent-minded. His head nodded, and little by little his chin descended and touched the enemy, who seized it. There was a sharp yelp, a flirt of the poodle's head, and the beetle fell a couple of yards away, and lit on its back once more. The neighboring spectators shook with a gentle inward joy, several faces went behind fans and handkerchiefs, and Tom was entirely happy. The dog looked foolish, and probably felt so; but there was resentment in his heart, too, and a craving for revenge. So he went to the beetle and began a wary attack on it again; jumping at it from every point of a circle, lighting with his fore-paws within an inch of the creature, making even closer snatches at it with his teeth, and jerking his head till his ears flapped again.

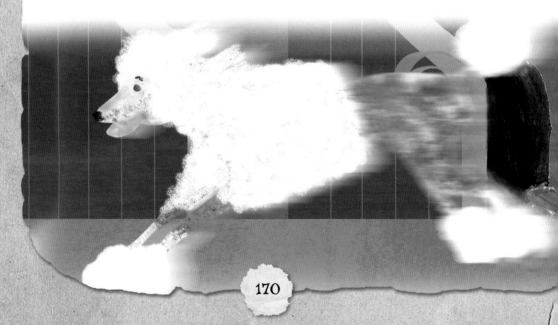

But he grew tired once more, after a while; tried to amuse himself with a fly but found no relief; followed an ant around, with his nose close to the floor, and quickly wearied of that; yawned, sighed, forgot the beetle entirely, and sat down on it. Then there was a wild yelp of agony and the poodle went sailing up the aisle; the yelps continued, and so did the dog; he crossed the house in front of the altar; he flew down the other aisle; he crossed before the doors; he clamored up the home stretch; his anguish grew with his progress, till presently he was but a woolly comet moving in its orbit with the gleam and the speed of light. At last the frantic sufferer sheered from its course, and sprang into its master's lap; he flung it out of the window, and the voice of distress quickly

thinned away and died in the distance.

By this time the whole church was red-faced and suffocating with suppressed laughter, and the sermon had come to a dead standstill. The discourse was resumed presently, but it went lame and halting, all possibility of impressiveness being at an end; for even the gravest sentiments were constantly being received with a smothered burst of unholy mirth, under cover of some remote pew-back, as if the poor parson had said a rarely facetious thing. It was a genuine relief to the whole congregation when the ordeal was over and the benediction pronounced.

Tom Sawyer went home quite cheerful, thinking to himself that there was some satisfaction about divine service when there was a bit of variety in it. He had but one marring thought; he was willing that the dog should play with his pinchbug, but he did not think it was upright in him to carry it off.

The Story of Arachne

By James Baldwin

THERE WAS A YOUNG GIRL in Greece whose name was Arachne. Her face was pale but fair, and her eyes were big and blue, and her hair was long and like gold. All that she cared to do from morn till noon was to sit in the sun and spin; and all that she cared to do from noon till night was to sit in the shade and weave.

And oh, how fine and fair were the things which she wove in her loom! Flax, wool, silk – she worked with them all; and when they came from her hands, the cloth which she had made of them was so thin and soft and bright that men came from all parts of the world to see it. And they said that cloth so rare could not be made of flax, or wool, or silk, but that the warp was of

rays of sunlight and the woof was of threads of gold.

Then as, day by day, the girl sat in the sun and span, or sat in the shade and wove, she said: "In all the world there is no yarn so fine as mine, and in all the world there is no cloth so soft and smooth, nor silk so bright and rare."

"Who taught you to spin and weave so well?" someone asked.

"No one taught me," she said. "I learned how to do it as I sat in the sun and the shade; but no one showed me."

"But it may be that Athena, the queen of the air, taught you, and you did not know it."

"Athena, the queen of the air? Bah!" said Arachne. "How could she teach me? Can she spin such skeins of yarn as these? Can she weave goods like mine? I should like to see her try. I can teach her a thing or two."

She looked up and saw in the doorway a tall woman wrapped in a long cloak. Her face was fair to see, but stern, oh, so stern! And her grey eyes were so sharp and bright that Arachne could not meet her gaze.

"Arachne," said the woman, "I am Athena, the queen of the air, and I have heard your boast. Do you still mean to say that I have not taught you how to spin and weave?"

"No one has taught me," said Arachne; "and I thank no one for what I know;" and she stood up, straight and proud, by the side of her loom.

"And do you still think that you can spin and weave as well as I?" said Athena.

Arachne's cheeks grew pale, but she said: "Yes. I can weave as well as you."

"Then let me tell you what we will do," said Athena. "Three days from now we will both weave; you on your loom, and I on mine. We will ask all the world to come and see us; and great Jupiter, who sits in the clouds, shall be the judge. And if your work is best, then I will weave no more so long as the world shall last; but if my work is best, then you shall never use loom or spindle or distaff again. Do you agree to this?"

"I agree," said Arachne.

"It is well," said Athena. And she was gone.

When the time came for the contest in weaving, all the world

was there to see it, and great Jupiter sat among the clouds and looked on.

Arachne had set up her loom in the shade of a mulberry tree, where butterflies were flitting and grasshoppers chirping all through the livelong day. But Athena had set up her loom in the sky, where the breezes were blowing and the summer sun was shining; for she was the queen of the air.

Then Arachne took her skeins of finest silk and began to weave. And she wove a web of marvelous beauty, so thin and light that it would float in the air, and yet so strong that it could hold a lion in its meshes; and the threads of warp and woof were of many colours, so beautifully arranged and mingled one with another that all who saw were filled with delight.

"No wonder that the maiden boasted of her skill," said the people.

And Jupiter himself nodded.

Then Athena began to weave. And she took of the sunbeams that gilded the mountain top, and of the snowy fleece of the summer clouds, and of the blue ether of the summer sky, and of the bright green of the summer fields, and of the royal purple of the autumn woods – and what do you suppose she wove?

The web which she wove in the sky was full of

enchanting pictures of flowers and gardens, and of castles and towers, and of mountain heights, and of men and beasts, and of giants and dwarfs, and of the mighty beings who dwell in the clouds with Jupiter. And those who looked upon it were so filled with wonder and delight, that they forgot all about the beautiful web which Arachne had woven. And Arachne herself was ashamed and afraid when she saw it; and she hid her face in her hands and wept.

"Oh, how can I live," she cried, "now that I must never again use loom or spindle or distaff?"

And she kept on, weeping and weeping and weeping, and saying, "How can I live?"

Then, when Athena saw that the poor maiden would never have any joy unless she were allowed to spin and weave, she took pity on her and said:

"I would free you from your bargain if I could, but that is a thing which no one can do. You must hold to your agreement never to touch loom or spindle again. And yet, since you will never be happy unless you can spin and weave, I will give you a new form so that you can carry on your work with neither spindle nor loom."

Then she touched Arachne with the tip of the spear which she sometimes carried; and the maiden was changed at once into a nimble spider,

which ran into a shady place in the grass and began
merrily to spin and weave a beautiful web.

I have heard it said that all the spiders which have
been in the world since then are the children of
Arachne; but I doubt whether this be true. Yet, for
aught I know, Arachne still lives and spins and weaves;
and the very next spider that you see may be
she herself.

Lads and Lasses

The Saviours of the Train

From *The Railway Children* by E Nesbit

*T*HE RUSSIAN gentleman was so delighted with the strawberries that the three racked their brains to find some other surprise for him. But all the racking did not bring out any idea more novel than wild cherries.

The cherry trees were some way from Three Chimneys, so Mother let them take their lunch with them in a basket. And the basket would do to bring the cherries back in if they found any. She also lent them her silver watch so that they should not be late for tea.

Near the tunnel was a flight of steps leading down to the line – just wooden bars roughly fixed into the earth – a very steep and narrow way.

"We'd better get down," said Peter; "I'm sure the cherries would be quite easy to get at from the side of the steps. You remember it was there we picked the cherry blossoms that we put on the rabbit's grave."

So they went along the fence towards the little swing gate that is at the top of these steps. And they were almost at the gate when Bobbie said: –

"Hush. Stop! What's that?"

"That" was a very odd noise – it was a sort of

rustling, whispering sound. As they listened it stopped, and then it began again. And this time it did not stop, but it grew louder and more rustling and rumbling.

"Look," cried Peter "the tree over there!"

And, as Peter pointed, the tree was moving – not just the way trees ought to move when the wind blows, but all in one piece, as though it were a live creature and were walking down the side of the cutting.

"It's moving!" cried Bobbie.

"It's magic," said Phyllis, breathlessly. "I always knew this railway was enchanted. What is it? It's much too magic for me. I don't like it. Let's go home."

But Bobbie and Peter clung fast to the rail and watched breathlessly. And Phyllis made no movement towards going home by herself.

The trees moved on and on. Some stones and loose earth fell and rattled on the railway metals below.

"It's ALL coming down," Peter tried to say, but he found there was hardly any voice to say it with. And, indeed, just as he spoke, the great rock, on the top of which the walking trees were, leaned slowly forward. The trees, ceasing to walk, stood still and shivered. Leaning with the rock, they seemed to hesitate a moment, and then rock and trees and grass and bushes, with a rushing sound, slipped right away from the face of the cutting and fell on the line with a blundering crash that could have been heard half a mile off. A cloud of dust rose up.

"Oh," said Peter, in awestruck tones, "isn't it exactly like when coals come in? – if there wasn't any roof to the cellar and you could see down."

"Look what a great mound it's made!" said Bobbie.

"Yes," said Peter, slowly. He was still leaning on the fence. Then he stood upright.

"The 11.29 down hasn't gone by yet. We must let them know at the station, or there'll be a most frightful accident."

"Let's run," said Bobbie, and began.

But Peter cried, "Come back!" and looked at Mother's watch. He was very prompt and businesslike, and his face looked whiter than they had ever seen it.

"No time," he said; "it's two miles away, and it's past eleven."

"Couldn't we climb up a telegraph post and do something to the wires?" suggested Phyllis.

"We don't know how," said Peter.

"They do it in war," said Phyllis; "I've heard of it."

"They only CUT them, silly," said Peter, "and that doesn't do any good. And we couldn't cut them even if we got up, and we couldn't get up. If we had some cloth, we could get down on the line and wave it."

"But the train wouldn't see us till it got round the corner, and then it could see the mound just as well as us," said Phyllis.

"If we only had some cloth," Peter repeated, "we could go round the corner and wave to the train."

"We might wave, anyway."

"They'd only think it was just US, as usual. We've waved so often before. Anyway, let's get down."

They got down the steep stairs. Bobbie was pale and shivering. Peter's face looked thinner than usual. Phyllis was red-faced and damp with anxiety.

"Oh, how hot I am!" she said; "and I thought it was going to be cold; I wish we hadn't put on our – " she stopped short, and then ended in quite a different tone – "our flannel petticoats."

Bobbie turned at the bottom of the stairs.

"Oh, yes," she cried; "Let's take them off."

They did, and with the petticoats rolled up under their arms, ran along the railway. They reached the corner that hid the mound from the straight line of railway that ran half a mile without curve or corner.

"Now," said Peter, taking hold of the largest petticoat.

"You're not" – Phyllis faltered – "you're not going to TEAR them?"

"Shut up," said Peter, with brief sternness.

"Oh, yes," said Bobbie, "tear them into little bits if you like. Don't you see, Phil, if we can't stop the train, there'll be a real live accident, with people KILLED. Oh, horrible! Here, Peter, you'll never tear it through the band!"

She took the flannel petticoat from him and tore it off an inch from the band. Then she tore the other in the same way.

"There!" said Peter, tearing in his turn. He divided each petticoat into three pieces. "Now, we've got six flags." He looked at the watch again. "And we've got seven minutes. We must have flagstaffs."

The knives given to boys are, for some odd reason, seldom of the kind of steel that keeps sharp. The young saplings had to be broken off. Two came up by the roots. The leaves were stripped from them.

"We must cut holes in the flags, and run the sticks through the holes," said Peter. And the holes were cut. The knife was sharp enough to cut flannel with. Two of the flags were set up in heaps of loose stones between the sleepers of the down line. Then Phyllis and Roberta took each a flag, and stood ready to wave it as soon as the train came in sight.

"I shall have the other two myself," said Peter, "because it was my idea to wave something."

"They're our petticoats, though," Phyllis was beginning, but Bobbie interrupted –

"Oh, what does it matter who waves what, if we can only save the train?"

Perhaps Peter had not rightly calculated the number of minutes it would take the 11.29 to get from the station to the place where they were, or perhaps the train was late. Anyway, it seemed a very long time that they waited.

It seemed to her that they had been standing there for hours and hours, holding those silly little flannel flags that no one would ever notice. The train wouldn't care. It would go rushing by them and tear round the corner and go crashing into that awful mound. And everyone would be killed. And then came the distant rumble and hum of the metals, and a puff of white steam showed far away along the stretch of line.

"Stand firm," said Peter, "and wave like mad! When it gets to that big furze bush step back, but go on waving! Don't stand ON the line, Bobbie!"

The train came rattling along very, very fast.

"They don't see us! They won't see us! It's all no good!" cried Bobbie.

The two little flags on the line swayed as the nearing train shook and loosened the heaps of loose stones that held them up. One of them slowly leaned over and fell on the line. Bobbie jumped forward and caught it up, and waved it; her hands did not tremble now.

It seemed that the train came on as fast as ever. It was very near now.

"Keep off the line, you silly cuckoo!" said Peter.

"It's no good," Bobbie said again.

"Stand back!" cried Peter, suddenly, and he dragged Phyllis back by the arm.

But Bobbie cried, "Not yet, not yet!" and waved her two flags right over the line. The front of the engine looked black and enormous.

"Oh, stop, stop, stop!" cried Bobbie. No one heard her. At least Peter and Phyllis didn't, for the oncoming rush of the train covered the sound of her voice with a mountain of sound. But afterwards she used to wonder whether the engine itself had not heard her, for it slackened swiftly, slackened and stopped, not twenty yards from the place where Bobbie's two flags waved over the line. She saw the great black engine stop dead, but somehow she could not stop waving the flags. And when the driver and the fireman had got off the engine and Peter and Phyllis had gone to meet them and pour out their excited tale of the awful mound just round the corner, Bobbie still waved the flags.

When the others turned towards her she was lying across the line with her hands flung forward and still gripping the sticks of the little flannel flags.

The engine-driver picked her up, carried her to the train, and laid her on the cushions.

"Gone right off in a faint," he said, "poor little woman. And no wonder. I'll just 'ave a look at this 'ere mound of yours, and then we'll run you back to the station and get her seen to."

It was horrible to see Bobbie lying so white and quiet, with her lips blue, and parted.

They sat by Bobbie on the blue cushions, and the train ran back. Before it reached their station Bobbie had sighed and opened her eyes, and rolled herself over and begun to cry. This cheered the others wonderfully. They had seen her cry before, but they had never seen her faint. They had not known what to do when she was fainting, but now she was only crying they could thump her on the back and tell her not to, just as they always did. And presently, when she stopped crying, they were able to laugh at her for being such a coward as to faint.

When the station was reached, the three were the heroes of an agitated meeting on the platform.

The praises they got for their "prompt action," their

"common sense," their "ingenuity," were enough to have turned anybody's head. Phyllis enjoyed herself thoroughly. She had never been a real heroine before, and the feeling was delicious. Peter's ears got very red. Yet he, too, enjoyed himself. Only Bobbie wished they all wouldn't. She wanted to get away.

"You'll hear from the Company about this, I expect," said the Station Master.

Bobbie wished she might never hear of it again. She pulled at Peter's jacket.

"Oh, come away! I want to go home," she said.

So they went. And as they went, everyone sent up a cheer.

"Oh, listen," cried Phyllis; "that's for US!"

"Yes," said Peter. "I say, I am glad I thought about waving something."

"How lucky WE put on our flannel petticoats!" said Phyllis.

Bobbie said nothing. She was thinking of the horrible mound, and the train rushing towards it.

"And it was US that saved them," said Peter.

"How dreadful if they had all been killed!" said Phyllis; "wouldn't it, Bobbie?"

"We never got any cherries, after all," said Bobbie.

The others thought her rather heartless.

The White Cat

By E Nesbit

THE WHITE CAT lived at the back of a shelf at the darkest end of the inside attic, which was nearly dark all over. It had lived there for years, because one of its white china ears was chipped, so that it was no longer a possible ornament for the spare bedroom.

Tavy found it at the end of a wicked and glorious afternoon. He had been left alone. The servants were the only other people in the house. He had promised to be good. He had meant to be good. And he had not been. The last thing he had done was to explore the attic, where he was never allowed to go, and to knock down the white cat from its shelf.

The sound of its fall brought the servants. The cat was not broken – only its other ear was chipped. Tavy was put to bed. But he got out as soon as the servants had gone downstairs, crept up to the attic, secured the cat, and washed it in the bath. So that when mother came back from London, Tavy, dancing impatiently at the head of the stairs, in a very wet nightgown, flung himself upon her and cried, "I've been awfully naughty, and I'm frightfully sorry, and please may I have the white cat for my very own?"

He was much sorrier than he had expected to be when he saw that mother was too tired even to want to know, as she generally did, exactly how naughty he had been. She only kissed him, and said, "I am sorry you've been naughty, my darling. Go back to bed now."

Tavy was ashamed to say anything more about the china cat, so he went back to bed. But he took the cat with him, and talked to it and kissed it, and went to sleep with its smooth shiny shoulder against his cheek.

In the days that followed, he was extravagantly good. Being good seemed as easy as being bad usually was. This may have been because mother seemed so tired and ill, and gentlemen in black coats and high hats came to see mother, and after they had gone she used to cry. These things going on in a house sometimes make people good, sometimes they act just the other way. Or it may have been because he had the china cat to talk to. Anyhow, whichever way it was, at the end of the week mother said, "Tavy, you've been a great comfort to me. You have tried very hard to be good."

It was difficult to say, "No, I haven't, at least not since the first day," but Tavy got it said, and was hugged for his pains.

"You wanted," said mother, "the china cat. Well, you may have it. But you must be very careful not to break it. And you mustn't give it away. It goes with the house. Your Aunt Jane made me promise to keep it in the family. It's very, very old. Don't take it out of doors for fear of accidents."

"I love the white cat, mother," said Tavy. "I love it better than all my toys."

Then mother told Tavy several things, and that night when he went to bed Tavy repeated them all faithfully to the china cat, who was about six inches high and looked very intelligent.

"So you see," he ended, "the wicked lawyer's taken nearly all mother's money, and we've got to leave our own lovely big white house, and go and live in a horrid little house. And mother does hate it so."

"I don't wonder," said the china cat very distinctly.

"What!" said Tavy, halfway into his nightshirt.

"I said, I don't wonder, Octavius," said the china cat, and rose from her sitting position, stretched her china legs and waved her white china tail.

"You can speak?" said Tavy.

"Can't you see I can? Hear I mean?" said the cat. "I belong to you now, so I can speak to you. I couldn't before. It wouldn't have been good manners."

Tavy, his nightshirt round his neck, sat down on the edge of the bed with his mouth open.

"Come, don't look so silly," said the cat, taking a walk along the high wooden mantelpiece, "anyone would think you didn't like me to talk to you."

"I'd love you to," said Tavy recovering himself a little.

"Well then," said the cat.

"May I touch you?" Tavy asked timidly.

"Of course! I belong to you. Look out!" The china cat gathered herself together and jumped. Tavy caught her.

It was quite a shock to find when one stroked her that the china cat, though alive, was still china, hard, cold, and smooth to the touch, and yet perfectly brisk and absolutely bendable as any flesh-and-blood cat.

"I wish you were a real cat," said Tavy.

"I am," said the cat. "Now how shall we amuse ourselves? I suppose you don't care for mousing?"

"I never tried," said Tavy, "and I think I rather wouldn't."

"Very well then, Octavius," said the cat. "I'll take you to the white cat's castle. Get into bed. Bed makes a good travelling carriage, especially when you haven't any other. Shut your eyes."

Tavy did as he was told. He shut his eyes, but could not keep them shut. He opened them a tiny, tiny chink, and sprang up. He was not in bed. He was on a couch of soft cloth, and the couch stood in a splendid hall, whose walls were of gold and ivory. By him stood the white cat, no longer china, but a real life cat with fur.

"Here we are," she said. "The journey didn't take

long, did it? Now we'll have that splendid supper, out of the fairytale, with the invisible hands waiting on us."

She clapped her paws – paws now as soft as white velvet – and a tablecloth floated into the room, then knives and forks and spoons and glasses, the table was laid, the dishes drifted in and they began to eat. There happened to be every single thing Tavy liked best to eat. After supper there was music and singing, and Tavy, having kissed a white, soft, furry forehead, went to bed in a gold four-poster with a counterpane of butterflies' wings. He awoke at home. On the mantelpiece sat the white cat, looking as though butter would not melt in her mouth. And all her furriness had gone with her voice. She was silent and china.

Tavy spoke to her. But she would not answer. Nor did she speak all day. Only at night when he was getting into bed she suddenly mewed and said, "Make haste, there's a play acted tonight at my castle."

Tavy made haste, and was rewarded by another glorious evening in the castle of the white cat.

And so the weeks went on. Days full of an ordinary little boy's joys and sorrows; nights spent by a little prince in the magic castle of the white cat.

Then came the day when Tavy's mother spoke to him, and he told the china cat what she had said.

"I knew this would happen," said the cat. "It always does. So you're to leave your house next week. Well, there's only one way out of the difficulty. Draw your sword, Tavy, and cut off my head and tail."

"And then will you turn into a princess, and shall I have to marry you?" Tavy asked with horror.

"No, dear – no," said the cat reassuringly. "I shan't turn into anything. But you and mother will turn into happy people. I shall just not be any more – for you."

"Then I won't do it," said Tavy.

"But you must. Come, draw your sword, like a brave fairy prince, and cut off my head."

The sword hung above his bed, with the helmet and breastplate Uncle James had given him last Christmas.

"I'm not a fairy prince," said the child. "I'm Tavy – and I love you."

"You love your mother better," said the cat. "Come cut my head off. The story always ends like that. You love mother best. It's for her sake."

"Yes." Tavy was trying to think it out. "Yes, I love mother best. But I won't cut off your head."

"Then," said the cat, "I must do what I can!"

She stood up, waving her white china tail, and before Tavy could stop her she had leapt, not, as before, into his arms, but onto the wide hearthstone.

It was all over – the china cat lay broken. The sound of the smash brought mother running.

"What is it?" she cried. "Oh, Tavy – the china cat!"

"She did it," sobbed Tavy. "She wanted me to cut off her head and I wouldn't."

"Don't talk nonsense, dear," said mother sadly. "That only makes it worse. Pick up the pieces."

"There's only two pieces," said Tavy. "Couldn't you stick her together again?"

"Why," said mother, holding the pieces close to the candle. "She's been broken before. And mended."

"I knew that," said Tavy, still sobbing. "Oh, my dear white cat!"

"Come, crying won't mend her," said mother. "Look, there's another piece, close to the shovel."

"That's not a piece of cat," he said, and picked it up.

It was a pale parchment label, tied to a key. Mother held it to the candle and read, "Key of the lock behind the knot in the mantelpiece panel in the white parlour."

"Tavy! I wonder! But where did it come from?"

"Out of my white cat, I suppose," said Tavy, his tears stopping. "Are you going to see what's in the mantelpiece panel,

Mother? Are you?"

They went downstairs to the white parlour. But they could not see any knot in the mantelpiece panel, because it was all painted white. But mother's fingers felt softly all over it, and found a round raised spot. It was a knot, sure enough. Then she scraped round it with her scissors, till she loosened the knot, and poked it out with the scissors point.

"I don't suppose there's any keyhole there really," she said. But there was. And what is more, the key fitted. The panel swung open, and inside was a little cupboard with two shelves. What was on the shelves? There were

199

old laces and old embroideries, old jewellery and old silver, there was money, and there were dusty old papers that Tavy thought most uninteresting. But mother did not think them uninteresting. She laughed, and cried, or nearly cried, and said:

"Oh, Tavy, this was why the china cat was to be taken such care of!"

Then she told him how, one-hundred-and-fifty years before, the head of the house had gone out to fight for the pretender, and had told his daughter to take the greatest care of the china cat. "I will send you word of the reason by a sure hand," he said, for they parted on the open square, where any spy might have overheard anything. And he had been killed by an ambush not ten miles from home – and his daughter had never known. But she had kept the cat.

"And now it has saved us," said mother. "We can stay in the dear old house, and there are two other houses that will belong to us too, I think. And, oh, Tavy, would you like some pound cake and ginger wine, dear?"

Tavy did like. And had it.

The china cat was mended, but it was put in the glass-fronted corner cupboard in the drawing-room, because it had saved the house.

Now I dare say you'll think this is all nonsense, and a

made-up story. Not at all. If it
were, how would you account
for Tavy's finding,
the very next
night, fast asleep on
his pillow, his
own white cat –
the furry friend that the china cat used to turn into
every evening – the dear hostess who had amused him
so well in the white cat's fairy palace?

It was she, beyond a doubt, and that was why Tavy
didn't mind a bit about the china cat being taken from
him and kept under glass. You may think that it was
just any old stray white cat that had come in by
accident. Tavy knows better. It has the very same
tender tone in its purr that the magic white cat had. It
will not talk to Tavy, it is true, but Tavy can and does
talk to it. But the thing that makes it perfectly certain
that it is the white cat is that the tips of its two ears are
missing just as the china cat's ears were. If you say that
it might have lost its ear-tips in battle you are the kind
of person who always makes difficulties, and you may
be quite sure that the kind of splendid magics that
happened to Tavy will never happen to you.

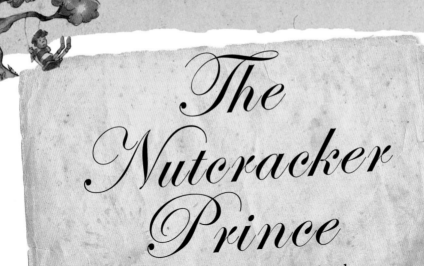

The Nutcracker Prince

Retold from the original tale
by Ernst Hoffmann

*D*R DROSSELMEIER was an old man with a secret. In his youth, he had been the most nimble-fingered craftsman in the royal court.

Dr Drosselmeier had made clocks that were mechanical wonders. Some chimed with a hundred tinkling bells. Others were decorated with tiny musicians that danced and played their instruments as they struck the hour. Some even had secret doors, out of which little birds fluttered and flew around the room, chirruping the passing minutes. Yes, Dr Drosselmeier's clocks had been the talk of the palace. But the most amazing thing he had ever made was a mouse-trap.

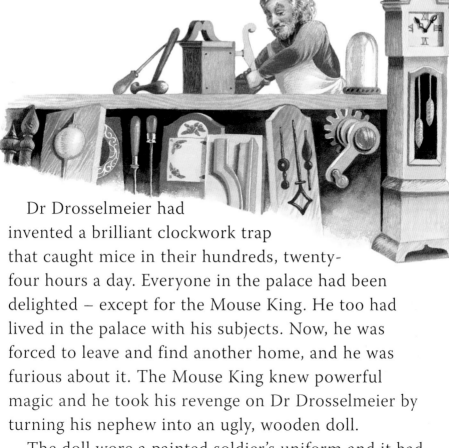

Dr Drosselmeier had
invented a brilliant clockwork trap
that caught mice in their hundreds, twenty-
four hours a day. Everyone in the palace had been
delighted – except for the Mouse King. He too had
lived in the palace with his subjects. Now, he was
forced to leave and find another home, and he was
furious about it. The Mouse King knew powerful
magic and he took his revenge on Dr Drosselmeier by
turning his nephew into an ugly, wooden doll.

The doll wore a painted soldier's uniform and it had
a prince's crown painted mockingly onto its head, and
its jaws moved so it could crack nuts between its teeth.
The Mouse King's spell was so strong that there was
only one way to undo it. Firstly, the nutcracker prince
had somehow to kill the evil Mouse King. And
secondly, a little girl had to love him, in spite of his

ugliness. Well, Dr Drosselmeier had no idea where the Mouse King had gone, and he certainly didn't know a little girl kind enough to take pity on the poor, ugly wooden doll. And so his nephew had stayed a nutcracker.

From that moment on, Dr Drosselmeier had never made another clock. He lost all heart for mechanical things and so he lost his job at the palace, too. Dr Drosselmeier blamed himself entirely for his nephew's dreadful disappearance and he had never breathed a word of what had happened to anyone. But ever since, he had been trying to find a way to break the Mouse King's spell… and at last, he thought he had.

Dr Drosselmeier's goddaughter, Clara, had grown into the kindest little girl anyone could wish to meet. If any little girl was going to take pity on the stiff, glaring nutcracker prince, it would be Clara.

Now it was Christmas Eve, and Dr Drosselmeier had arrived at Clara's house trembling with excitement. He wasn't excited because there was a party going on with games and music and dancing. No, Dr Drosselmeier was excited because tonight was the night he hoped the evil magic would be undone and his nephew would return to life.

While the party guests talked and joked and laughed

together, Dr Drosselmeier set about emptying the huge bag he had brought with him. It was filled with gingerbread and shortcake, candy walking sticks and sugar pigs, nuts and bon bons, nougat and humbugs... High and low, in every corner of the room, Dr Drosselmeier heaped piles of all the Mouse King's favourite things to eat. That should tempt him out from wherever he's hiding, thought Dr Drosselmeier, determinedly.

Then it was time to give Clara her Christmas present. The little girl's eyes opened wide with excitement as she stripped off the sparkly paper. But her face suddenly fell as she saw the ugly nutcracker prince. Then, gently, Clara stroked the doll's face. He wasn't cute, he wasn't cuddly – he wasn't even new! But that was exactly why Clara decided she loved him. She couldn't bear to think of leaving him all alone, laughed at and unloved – especially at Christmas time. Clara clutched the nutcracker prince close to her and hugged him tight. And Dr Drosselmeier slipped away from the party, his heart light with hope...

When the party was over and it was bedtime at last, Clara tucked the wooden doll up next to her. "I love you," she whispered, just before she fell asleep. "I'll look after you always." And that night, Clara had a very strange dream. She dreamt that the nutcracker prince woke up beside her. He smiled at Clara and held her hand, and led her downstairs. There was scuffling and squeaking coming from the drawing room, and when Clara peeped around the door she saw a terrible sight. There were mice everywhere! They were climbing all over Dr Drosselmeier's goodies, fighting and biting to get at the sweets. And worst of all, a horrible seven-headed mouse was standing in the middle of the carpet, cackling with glee at all the arguing and the mess. The seven-headed mouse wore seven gold crowns and Clara could tell he must be the king of the evil creatures.

Very bravely, the nutcracker prince charged at the gruesome Mouse King with a sword glinting in his hand and began to fight furiously. But he was completely outnumbered. The mice swarmed to their king's defence. They dragged the nutcracker prince to the ground and he disappeared under a thousand biting, clawing bodies. Just as the Mouse King threw back his head and began to laugh, Clara tore her slipper off her foot and threw it at him with all her might. WHAM! It hit the Mouse King on four of his seven horrible heads. He staggered to and fro for a second, and then collapsed dead to the floor.

As soon as the mice saw that their leader was no more, their courage deserted them. They hurried to scoop up his body and then they were gone, streaming off through cracks in the wall, holes in the skirting and gaps in the floorboards.

The nutcracker prince ran to Clara and kissed her. "Thank you for all you have done for me," he whispered, and there were tears sparkling in his painted eyes. "Let me repay you by taking you on a wonderful journey to my kingdom, the realm of sweets..."

It was the most wonderful dream Clara had ever had. She travelled through forests made of barley sugar, crossed rivers that ran with lemonade, picked flowers of sherbert, walked on paths of chocolate, and visited the nutcracker prince's gingerbread castle. In fact, Clara was very sorry to be woken up – even though it was Christmas Day itself! She hugged the wooden doll and told him, "You're the best present I've ever had," and she could have sworn that his smile was even broader than usual.

Meanwhile, across the city, Dr Drosselmeier had also woken up to find the best present he'd ever had. There sprawled underneath his Christmas tree, sleeping an exhausted but peaceful sleep, was his brave, handsome nephew…

Sleeping Beauty

Retold from the original tale by Charles Perrault

LONG, *LONG* ago, when fairies were still able to grant wishes, there lived a king and queen who wanted, more than anything in the whole world, to have a baby daughter. When their wish was finally granted and a beautiful tiny princess lay in her cradle, the king and queen decided to have a great candlelit party to celebrate.

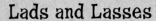

They invited the twelve most important fairies in the
land and a great many other people besides.

As well as the thousands of glittering candles,
there were golden tables piled high with all kinds
of delicious food, and the royal orchestra played
their most cheerful tunes. The twelve fairies all
lined up to present their christening gifts to the
tiny princess. Their gifts were those that only a
fairy can give: beauty, kindness, grace, honesty
and the like. The princess smiled happily in her
cradle as one by one the fairies tiptoed up.

The eleventh fairy had just promised the
princess a sweet singing voice, when
there was a great roll of thunder and
all the candles flickered out.
There stood quite the most
wicked fairy anyone
had ever seen. She
was dressed all in
black, her

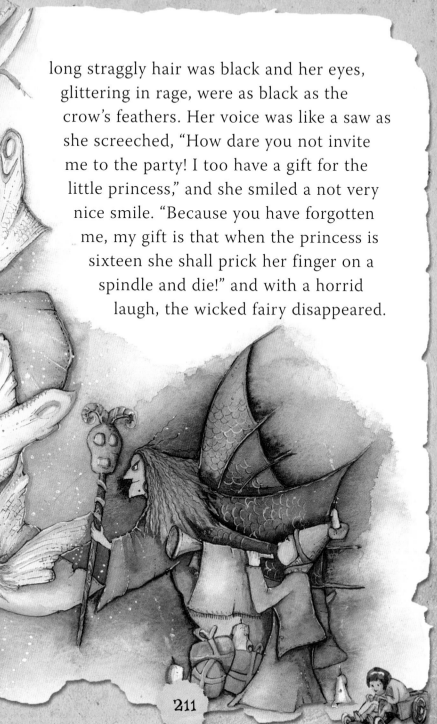

long straggly hair was black and her eyes, glittering in rage, were as black as the crow's feathers. Her voice was like a saw as she screeched, "How dare you not invite me to the party! I too have a gift for the little princess," and she smiled a not very nice smile. "Because you have forgotten me, my gift is that when the princess is sixteen she shall prick her finger on a spindle and die!" and with a horrid laugh, the wicked fairy disappeared.

211

As the candles were hastily relit, everyone started talking at once. Then a quiet voice was heard over all hubbub. It was the twelfth fairy.

"I cannot undo this wicked spell," she whispered, "but I can decree that the princess will not die. She will instead fall into a deep sleep for a hundred years," and all the fairies slipped away leaving the court in despair.

The king, of course, immediately ordered that all the spinning wheels in the land were to be burned. After a while, everyone grew less frightened, and as the princess grew up into the most lovely girl, the wicked fairy's prediction slipped from most people's memories.

On her sixteenth birthday the princess went exploring. At the top of a tower she did not remember seeing before, she found an old woman, sitting at a spinning wheel.It was, of course, the wicked fairy in disguise. The princess was fascinated and, as she bent forward to look at the cloth, her hand caught the sharp spindle and she immediately fell to the ground as though dead. With a swirl of smoke and a nasty laugh, the wicked fairy disappeared.

Everyone else in the palace fell asleep at the same moment. The king fell asleep with his ministers, the queen and her maids fell asleep in her dressing room. The cook fell asleep in the kitchen in the middle of baking a cake, the groom fell asleep as he fed the horses in the stables and even the little linnet the princess had in a golden cage by her bedside fell asleep on its perch. A great high thorn hedge grew up and soon the palace was completely hidden. Time stood still and all was silent.

Many, many years passed. The tale of the sleeping princess spread far and wide, and many came to try to find her. But no one could get through the thorn hedge. And so after even more years, people forgot what lay behindthe hedge.

Then one day a handsome prince came riding through the woods. As he reached the thorn hedge, thousands of pink roses burst into bloom and a path appeared, leading through the hedge towards the palace. It was a hundred years to the day since the princess had pricked her finger. The prince was astonished by the sight that met his eyes. Everywhere people lay asleep, frozen in the midst of whatever they had been doing when the spell caught them.

214

The prince climbed the tower, and there he found the princess, looking as lovely as ever. He bent over and kissed her, and immediately the spell was broken. The king and his ministers carried on just where they had left off. The queen chose which dress she wanted to wear and the maids brushed her hair. The cook put her cake in the oven and the groom led the horses out into the courtyard. And even the little linnet in her golden cage sang a joyful song.

As for the princess... Well, she and the prince had fallen in love with each other on the spot, and were married the very next day. They all lived happily ever after, and the wicked fairy was never ever seen again.

The Counterpane Fairy

By Katharine Pyle

*T*EDDY WAS ALL alone, for his mother had been up with him so much the night before that at four o'clock in the afternoon she said that she was going to lie down.

He lay staring out of the window at the grey clouds sweeping across the April sky. He grew lonelier and lonelier and a lump rose in his throat. A big tear trickled down his cheek and dripped off his chin.

"Oh dear, oh dear!" said a little voice just back of the hill his knees made as he lay with them drawn up in bed, "What a hill to climb!"

Teddy stopped crying and gazed wonderingly at where the voice came from, and over the top of his knees appeared a brown peaked hood, a tiny withered face, a brown cloak, and last of all two small feet in buckled shoes. It was a little old woman, so weazened and brown that she looked more like a dried leaf.

She seated herself on Teddy's knees and gazed at him solemnly, and she was so light that he felt her weight no more than if she had been a feather.

Teddy lay staring at her for a while, and then he asked, "Who are you?"

"I'm the Counterpane Fairy," said the little figure, in a thin little voice. "I came to you, because you were lonely and sick, and I thought maybe you would like me to show you a story."

"Do you mean tell me a story?" asked Teddy.

"No," said the fairy, "I mean show you a story. It's a game I invented after I joined the Counterpane Fairies.

Choose any one of the squares of the counterpane and I will show you how to play it. That's all you have to do – choose a square."

Teddy looked the counterpane over carefully. "I think I'll choose that yellow square," he said, "because it looks so nice and bright."

"Very well," said the Counterpane Fairy. "Look straight at it and don't turn your eyes away until I count seven times seven and then you shall see the story of it."

Teddy fixed his eyes on the square and the fairy began to count. "One – two – three – four," she counted, Teddy heard her voice, thin and clear as the hissing of the logs on the hearth. "Don't look away from the square," she cried. "Five – six – seven," it seemed to Teddy that the yellow silk square was turning to a mist before his eyes and wrapping everything about him in a golden glow. "Thirteen – fourteen," the fairy counted on and on. "Forty-six – forty-seven – forty-eight – forty-nine!"

At the words 'forty-nine', the Counterpane Fairy clapped her hands and Teddy looked about him. He was no longer in a golden mist. He was standing in a wonderful enchanted garden. The sky was like the golden sky at sunset, and the grass was so thickly set with tiny yellow flowers that it looked like a golden carpet. From this garden stretched a long flight of glass steps. They reached up and up and up to a great golden castle with shining domes and turrets.

"Listen!" said the Counterpane Fairy. "In that golden castle there lies an enchanted princess. For more than a hundred years she has been lying there waiting for the hero who is to come and rescue her, and you are the hero who can do it if you will."

With that the fairy led him to a little pool close by, and bade him look in the water. When Teddy looked, he saw himself standing there in the golden garden, and he did not appear as he ever had before. He was tall and strong and beautiful, like a hero.

"Yes," said Teddy, "I will do it."

Without pausing longer, he ran to the glass steps and began to mount them.

Up and up and up he went. Once he turned and waved his hand to the Counterpane Fairy in the golden garden below. She waved her hand, and he heard her voice faint and clear, "Goodbye! Goodbye! Be brave and strong, and beware of that that is little and grey."

Then Teddy turned his face toward the castle, and in a moment he was standing before the great gates.

He raised his hand and struck the door. There was

no answer, so he opened the door and
went in. The hall was five-sided,
and all of pure gold, as clear and
shining as glass. Upon three sides
of it were three arched doors – one
was of emerald, one was of ruby, and
one was of diamond. They were arched, and tall, and
wide – fit for a hero to go through. The question was,
behind which one lay the enchanted princess?

While Teddy stood there looking at them and
wondering, he heard a little thin voice, that seemed to
be singing to itself, and this is what it sang:

"In and out and out and in, quick as a flash I weave
and spin. Some may mistake and some forget, but
I'll have my spider web finished yet."

On the fourth side of the wall there hung a curtain
of silvery-grey spider web, and the voice seemed to
come from it. The hero went toward it, but he saw
nothing, for the spider that was spinning it moved so
fast that no eyes could follow it. Presently it paused up
in the corner of the web, and then Teddy saw it. It
looked very little to have spun a curtain of silvery web.

"Mistress Spinner! Mistress Spinner!" cried Teddy.
"Can you tell me where to find the enchanted princess
who lies asleep waiting for me to rescue her?"

The spider sat quite still for a while, and then it said in a voice as thin as a hair:

"You must go through the emerald door, you must go through the emerald door. What so fit as the emerald door for the hero who would do great deeds?"

Teddy did not so much as stay to thank the little grey spinner, he was in such a hurry to find the princess, but turning he sprang to the emerald door, flung it open, and stepped outside.

He found himself standing on the glass steps, and as his foot touched the topmost one the whole flight closed up like an umbrella, and in a moment Teddy was sliding down the smooth glass pane, faster and faster and faster until he could hardly catch his breath.

The next thing he knew he was standing in the golden garden, and there was the Counterpane Fairy beside him looking at him sadly. "You should have known better than to try the emerald door," she said, "and now shall we break the story?"

"Oh, no, no!" cried Teddy, and he was still the hero. "Let me try once more."

Then the Counterpane Fairy smiled. "Very well," she said, "you shall try again. But remember what I told you: beware of that that is little and grey, and take this with you, for it may be of use." Stooping, she picked up a blade of grass from the ground and handed it to him.

The hero took it wondering, and in his hands it was changed to a sword that shone so brightly that it dazzled his eyes. Then he turned, and there was the long flight of glass steps leading up to the golden castle just as before, so thrusting the magic sword into his belt, he ran nimbly up and up and up, and not until he reached the very topmost step did he turn to wave farewell to the Counterpane Fairy below. She waved her hand to him. "Remember," she called, "beware of what is little and grey."

He opened the door and went into the five-sided golden hall, and there were the three doors just as before, and the spider spinning and singing:

"Now the brave hero is wiser indeed, he may have failed once, but he still may succeed. Dull are the emeralds, diamonds are bright, so is his wisdom that shines as the light."

"The diamond door!" cried Teddy. "Yes, that is the door that I should have tried. How could I have thought the emerald door was it?" and opening the diamond door he stepped through it.

He hardly had time to see that he was standing at the top of the glass steps, before they had become a smooth glass hill, and there he was spinning down

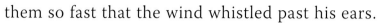

them so fast that the wind whistled past his ears.

In less time than it takes to tell, he was back again for the third time in the golden garden, with the Counterpane Fairy standing before him.

"So!" said the Counterpane Fairy. "Did you know no better than to open the diamond door?"

"No," said Teddy, "I knew no better."

"Then," said the fairy, "if you can pay no better heed to my warnings than that, the princess must wait for another hero, for you are not the one."

"Let me try but once more," cried Teddy.

"Then you may try once more and for the last time," said the fairy, "but beware of what is little and grey." Stooping she picked from the grass beside her a fallen acorn cup and handed it to him. "Take this with you," she said, "for it may serve you well."

As he took it from her, it was changed in his hand to a goblet of gold set round with precious stones. Turning he ran for the third time up the flight of glass steps. As soon as he reached the great golden hall he walked over to the curtain of spider web. The spider was spinning so fast that it was little more than a grey streak, but presently it stopped up in the corner of the web. As the hero looked at it he saw that it was little and grey. Then it began to sing to him:

"Great hero, wiser than ever before, try the red door, try the red door. Open the door that is ruby, and then, you never need search for the princess again."

"No, I will not open the ruby door," cried Teddy. "Twice have you sent me back to the golden garden, and now you shall fool me no more."

As he said this he saw that a corner of the web was unfinished, and underneath was something that looked like a little yellow door. Suddenly he knew that this was the door he must go through. He pulled at the curtain of web but it was as strong as steel. Quickly he snatched from his belt the magic sword, and with one blow the curtain was cut in two, and fell at his feet.

He heard the spider calling but paid no heed, for he had opened the door and entered.

Beyond was a great gold courtyard with a fountain splashing into a golden basin in the middle. But what he saw first was the princess, who lay stretched out as if asleep upon a couch all covered with cloth of gold.

He knew she was a princess, because she was so beautiful and because she wore a golden crown.

He stood looking at her without stirring, and at last he whispered, "Princess! I have come to save you."

Still she did not stir. He bent and touched her, but she lay there in her enchanted sleep. Then, seeing the fountain he filled the magic cup and sprinkled the hands and face of the princess with the water.

Then her eyes opened and she rose to her feet and caught the hero by the hand. "You have broken the enchantment," she cried, "and now you shall be the king of the golden castle and—"

"So that is the story of the yellow square," said the Counterpane Fairy.

Teddy looked about him. He was lying in bed with the silk coverlet over his little knees.

"Did you like it?" asked the fairy.

Teddy heaved a deep sigh. "Oh! Wasn't it beautiful?" he said. Then he lay for a while thinking and smiling. "Wasn't the princess lovely?"

The Counterpane Fairy got up. "Well, I must be journeying on," she said.

Then the door opened and his mother came in. She smiled at him lovingly, and the little brown Counterpane Fairy was gone.

Heroic Deeds

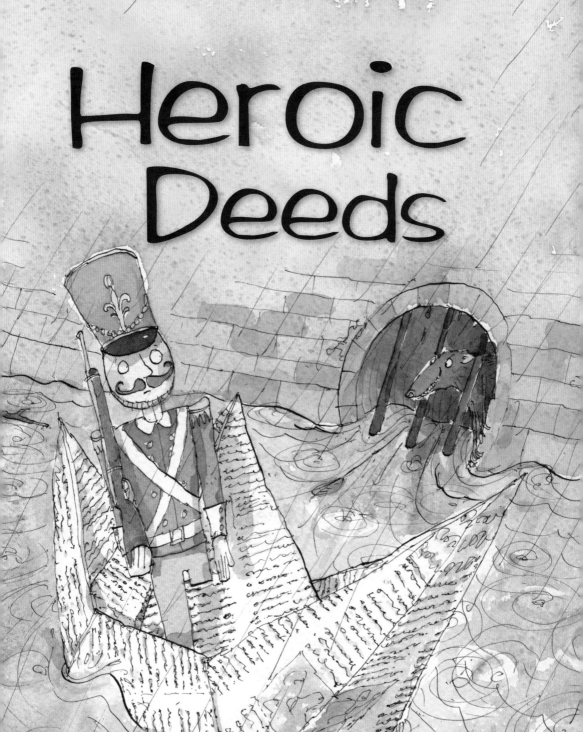

The Rebellious Titans and Gods

A Greek myth

BEFORE THE BEGINNING of time, there was nothing but an emptiness called Chaos. Out of the darkness emerged three beings who became known as Gaea, Tartarus and Eros.

Gaea, the earth goddess wished for some company, so she gave birth to Uranus, the god of the sky, and he surrounded her on all sides. Next, the mountains and the sea sprang from Gaea, shaping the landscape of the world.

Soon, Gaea and Uranus created three children together – giants, each with fifty heads and one hundred arms! Shortly after, three more children were born to them – again giants. But this time, they each had just one eye in the middle of their forehead. They came to be known as the Cyclopes.

With such immense strength and power, Uranus became fearful that the children would eventually try to overthrow him and take control of the universe themselves. So one by one, Uranus seized them, throwing them down into the depths of Tartarus, the underworld, from where they could not possibly threaten him.

Furious and devastated, Gaea began to hate Uranus for his cold-hearted, ruthless actions. With time, she gave birth to thirteen more children – the immortal Titans. Among them were the god of the sun Helios, the goddess of the moon Selene, the god of the waters Oceanus, the goddess of prophecy Themis, the strongest Titan Atlas, and finally Prometheus – the most intelligent Titan, who created the human race out of soft clay.

Yet Gaea's bitterness towards Uranus only increased with time. The day came when she put a mighty, curved sickle into the hands of her youngest Titan son,

Cronus. "I want to punish your cruel father and free your brothers and sisters from their underground banishment," she explained. "If you kill your father, you can rule in his place."

His eyes gleaming greedily, Cronus did what he was told. Across the universe echoed his father's cries of agony. Rivers of blood flowed from his wounds, and from this stream of wickedness sprang forth three evil creatures, the Furies, and a race of terrifying warrior giants.

Being immortal, Uranus couldn't die, so Cronus threw his father's body into the ocean. "Now I reign over all things!" Cronus roared.

To Gaea's despair, Cronus proved to be just as much of a tyrant as her husband. Relishing his control over the universe, he refused to free the hundred-handed giants and the Cyclopes from Tartarus.

Outraged, Gaea warned, "Your cruelty will come full circle! The day will come when your children will destroy you, just as you have destroyed your own father."

Cronus simply sneered. In his arrogance, he thought that he could cheat the prophecy. He would make sure that he had no children. If he had none, then how could they vanquish him?

Cronus was married to his sister, Rhea. In due course, a baby daughter Hestia was born. Cronus didn't hesitate in swallowing her whole. To Rhea's horror and misery, Cronus did exactly the same with their next four babies – Demeter, Hera, Hades and Poseidon. By the time Rhea was due to give birth to their fifth child, her heart was breaking with grief. She went to Gaea and begged for help. "Mother," she sobbed, "how can I fool Cronus, so I can keep my baby? I can't stand to lose another!"

Gaea eagerly came up with a plan. She hid Rhea away in a mountainside cave on the island of Crete. There, unseen, Rhea gave birth to a baby boy called Zeus. Rhea left Zeus in Gaea's care, and hurried home. Then she wrapped a rock in a blue blanket and presented it to Cronus. "Here is your newborn son!" she proclaimed. Cronus didn't spare a second to look at the infant. He simply opened his jaws and gulped

the bundle down. Smirking with satisfaction, he thought of how he had defeated his destiny once again...

And so, unknown to his father, Zeus grew up safely into a strong, courageous god. When he came of age, he disguised himself as one of Cronus' servants and waited. Then, when one day Cronus called for a drink to be brought to him, the disguised Zeus carefully took him a chalice of sweet-tasting poison instead.

In one gulp, Cronus drained the drink – and immediately realized that something was wrong. Clutching and clawing at his stomach, cramps and spasms stabbed inside him. Suddenly, up came the rock he had swallowed, followed by Poseidon, Hades, Hera, Demeter and Hestia – who were all fully grown ... and furious!

"Behold your son, Zeus, and all your other children!" Rhea said proudly. "They are ready to rule in your place, with justice and wisdom, instead of cruelty and tyranny. Your fate has come!"

"You will regret this because this means war!" bellowed Cronus, striding away to prepare for battle.

While Cronus was rousing all the other Titans to fight at his side, Zeus sped down to Tartarus with his brothers and sisters to release the hundred-handed

giants and the Cyclopes. Of course, the monsters were
so grateful that they pledged their allegiance to the
gods and goddesses and vowed to fight with them.
Then the Cyclopes presented Zeus and his brothers
with special gifts to help them in their mighty task. To
Zeus, they gave the weapons of thunder and lightning.
To Poseidon, they gave a magic trident for stirring up
sea-storms and creating earthquakes. To Hades, they
gave a helmet of invisibility.

It was now time for the gods and goddesses to
return to the upper world and begin the battle.

Enraged, the Titans were ready and waiting, forming
a formidable flank behind Cronus. With blood-
curdling war cries, they flung themselves forwards
across the heavens into the attack.

As the Titans advanced, the hundred-handed giants
tore great chunks of rock off the mountains and hurled
them at the enemy. The two sides clashed together, in
an embroiled mass of arrows, spears and swords. The
blows of the mighty warriors made the earth tremble
and shake until the awful rumblings were heard down
in the depths of Tartarus itself. The cries and groans of
the injured echoed around the mountains and across
the heavens. And still the Titans and the gods fought,
inflicting terrible wounds on each other. As immortals,

none of them could die.

When Zeus unleashed his ear-splitting thunderclaps and blinding lightning bolts, the stench of smouldering flesh filled the air as the Titans were set alight. While the Titans threw themselves into the sea, trying to quench the burning flames, the hundred-handed giants saw their chance. Seizing the howling Titans one by one, the giants dragged them below the earth down to the underworld. There, they bound them in the strongest of chains and left them for all eternity.

How the victorious gods and goddesses rejoiced! At last, tyranny had been overthrown and they would rule together, spreading fairness and heroism throughout the universe. The gods decided upon their kingdoms – Hades won the underworld and became the king of the dead. Poseidon won the sea and became lord of the oceans. And Zeus won the sky, and became ruler of the world. All three leaders determined not only to keep peace and harmony among immortal beings, but also to teach humans how to live prosperous lives – to respect their fellow people, all other living creatures, and above all, the gods themselves.

Contented, the gods and goddesses made their own home on Mount Olympus. And there they have ruled ever since.

The Treasure Stone of the Fairies

By William Elliot Griffis

LONG AGO, when London was a village and Cardiff only a hamlet, there was a boy who tended sheep on the hillsides. His father was a hardworking farmer, who every year tried to grow out of the stony ground some oats, barley, leeks and cabbage. In summer, he worked hard, from the first croak of the raven to the last hoot of the owl, to provide food for his wife and baby daughter. When his boy was born, he took him to the church to be christened Gruffyd, but everybody called him 'Gruff'.

In time, several little sisters came to keep the boy company. His mother always kept her cottage, which was painted pink, very neat and pretty, with vines covering the outside, while flowers bloomed indoors. These were set in pots and on shelves near the latticed windows. They seemed to grow finely, because so good a woman loved them. The copper doorframe was kept bright, and the broad borders on the clay floor, along the walls, were always fresh with whitewash. The pewter dishes on the sideboard shone as if they were moons, and the china cats on the mantelpiece, in silvery lustre, reflected both sun and candle light. Daddy often declared he could use these polished metal plates for a mirror when he shaved his face. Puss, the cat, was always happy purring away on the hearth, as the kettle boiled to make the sour oat jelly, which daddy loved so well.

Mother Gruffyd was always neat, with her striped apron, her high peaked hat, with its scalloped lace and quilled fastening around her chin, her little short shawl, with its pointed, long tips, tied in a bow, and her bright red petticoat folded back from her frock. Her white collar and neck cloth knotted at the top, and fringed at the ends, added fine touches to her picturesque costume.

In fact, young Gruffyd was proud of his mother and he loved her dearly. He thought no woman could be quite as sweet as she was.

Once, at the end of the day, on coming back home, from the hills, the boy met some lovely children. They were dressed in very fine clothes, and had elegant manners. They came up, smiled, and invited him to play with them. He joined in their sports, and was too much interested to take note of time. He kept on playing with them until it was pitch dark.

Among other games, which he enjoyed, had been that of 'The king in his counting house, counting out his money,' and 'The queen in her kitchen, eating bread and honey,' and 'The girl hanging out the clothes,' and 'The saucy blackbird that snipped off her nose.' In playing these, the children had aprons full of what seemed to be real coins, the size of crowns, or five-shilling pieces, each worth a dollar. These had 'head and tail,' beside letters on them and the boy

supposed they were real.

But when he showed these to his mother, she saw at once from their lightness, and because they were so easily bent, that they were only paper, and not silver.

She asked her boy where he had got them. He told her what a nice time he had enjoyed. Then she knew that these, his playmates, were fairy children. Fearing that some evil might come of this, she charged him, her only son, never to go out again alone, on the mountain. She mistrusted that no good would come of making such strange children his companions.

But the lad was so fond of play, that one day, tired of seeing nothing but byre and garden, while his sisters liked to play girls' games more than those which boys cared most for, and the hills seeming to beckon him to come to them, he disobeyed, and slipped out and off to the mountains. He was soon missed and a search was made for him.

Yet nobody had seen or heard of him. Though inquiries were made on every road, in every village, and at all the fairs and markets in the neighbourhood, two whole years passed by, without a trace of the boy.

But early one morning of the twenty-fifth month, before breakfast, his mother, on opening the door, found him sitting on the steps, with a bundle under his

arm, but dressed in the same clothes, and not looking a day older or in any way different, from the very hour he disappeared.

"Why my dear boy, where have you been, all these months, which have now run into the third year?"

"Why, mother dear, how strange you talk. I left here yesterday, to go out and to play with the children, on the hills, and we have had a lovely time. See what pretty clothes they have given me for a present."

When she tore open the package, the mother was all the more sure that she was right, and that her fears had been justified. In it she found only a dress of white paper. Examining it carefully, she could see neither seam nor stitches. She threw it in the fire, and again warned her son against fairy children.

But soon, after a great calamity, both father and mother changed their minds about fairies.

They had put all their savings into the venture of a ship, which had for a long time made trading voyages from Cardiff. Every year, it came back bringing great profit to the owners and shareholders. In this way, his father was able to eke out his income, and keep his family comfortably clothed, while all the time the table was well supplied with good food. Nor did they ever turn from their door anyone who asked for food.

But in the same month of the boy's return, bad news came that the good ship had gone down in a storm. All on board had perished, and the cargo was totally lost in the deep sea, far from land. In fact, no word except that of dire disaster had come to hand.

Now it was a tradition, as old as the days of King Arthur, that on a certain hill a great boulder could be seen, which was quite different from any other kind of rock to be found within miles. It was partly imbedded in the earth, and beneath it, lay a great, yes, an untold treasure. The grass grew luxuriantly around this stone, and the sheep loved to rest at noon in its shadow. Many men had tried to lift, or pry it up, but in vain. The tradition, unaltered and unbroken for centuries, was to the effect, that none but a good man could ever budge this stone. Any and all unworthy men might dig, or pull, or pry, until doomsday, but in vain. Till the right one came, the treasure was as safe as if in heaven.

But the boy's father and mother were now very poor and his sisters now grown up wanted pretty clothes so badly, that the lad hoped that he or his father might be the deserving one. He would help him to win the treasure for he felt sure that his parent would share his gains with all his friends.

Though his neighbours were not told of the

generous intentions credited to the boy's father, by his loving son, they all came with horses, ropes, crowbars, and tackle, to help. Yet after many a long days' toil, between the sun's rising and setting, their end was failure. Everyday, when darkness came on, the stone lay there, as hard and fast as ever. So they gave up.

On the final night, the lad saw that his father and mother were holding hands, while their tears flowed together, and they were praying for patience.

Seeing this, before he fell asleep, the boy resolved that on the morrow, he would go up to the mountains, and talk to his fairy friends about the matter.

So early in the morning, he hurried to the hill tops, and going into one of the caves, met the fairies and told them his troubles. Then he asked them to give him again some of their money.

"Not this time, but something better. Under the great rock there are treasures waiting for you."

"Oh, don't send me there! For all the men and horses of our parish have been unable to budge the stone."

"We know that," answered the principal fairy, "but you should try to move it. Then you will see what is certain to happen."

Going home, to tell what he had heard, his parents had a hearty laugh at the idea of a boy succeeding where men, with the united strength of many horses and oxen, had failed.

Yet, after brooding for a while, they were so dejected, that anything seemed reasonable. So they said, "Go ahead and try it."

Returning to the mountain, the fairies, in a band, went with him to the great rock.

One touch of his hand, and the mighty boulder trembled, like an aspen leaf in the breeze. A shove, and the rock rolled down from the hill and crashed in the valley below.

There, underneath, were little heaps of gold and silver, which the boy carried home to his parents, who became the richest people in the country round about.

Bucephalus

By James Baldwin

OLD PHILONICUS of Thessaly was the most famous horse-raiser of his time. His stables were talked about from the Adriatic Sea to the Persian Gulf, and many of the best war steeds in Greece and Asia Minor had been bred and partially trained by him. He prided himself particularly on his 'ox-headed' horses – broad-browed fellows, with large polls and small, sharp ears, set far apart. Proud creatures these were, and strong, and knowing, and high-spirited – just the kind for war steeds; and that was about all that horses were valued for in those days.

Among these 'ox-heads' there was one which excelled all others in courage, beauty, and size, but which, nevertheless, was a source of great concern to his master. He seemed to be altogether untamable, and, although he was now fourteen years old, there was not a horseman in Greece who had ever been able to mount him. He was a handsome creature – coal-black, with a white star in his forehead. One eye was grey and the other brown. Everybody admired him, and people came great distances to see him. Had Philonicus been less shrewd, he would have sold him for half the price of a common steed, and been glad that he was rid of him. But, like most men who spend their lives among horses, he knew a thing or two. He kept the horse's untamableness a secret, and was careful that only his good points should be exhibited. Everybody who had any use for such an animal wanted to buy him.

"What is the price?"

"Thirteen thousand dollars."

That answer usually put an end to the talk. For, as an ordinary horse might be bought at that time for about seventy dollars, and a thoroughbred war steed for two hundred, who was going to pay such a fabulous price? Half a dozen fine houses could be built for that money. There were rich men who made Philonicus some very handsome offers – a thousand dollars, five thousand, eight thousand – but he held steadily to his first price,

and the longer he held to it the more anxious everybody became to buy.

At last, however, after the horse had reached middle age, shrewd Philonicus got his price. King Philip of Macedon, who was ambitious to become the first man of Greece, was the purchaser; and Philonicus, after hearing the gold pieces jingle in his strong-box, led the great Bucephalus up to the Macedonian capital and left him safely housed in the king's stalls. He was careful, no doubt, to get back into his own country before Philip had had time to give the steed any kind of examination.

You may imagine what followed. When the horse was brought out upon the parade ground for trial the skilfullest riders in Macedon could not mount him. He reared and plunged, and beat madly around with his sharp hoofs, until everybody was glad to get safely out of his reach. The greatest horse-tamers of the country were called, but they could do nothing.

"Take him away!" cried the king, at last, in great rage. "That man Philonicus has sold me an utterly wild and unbroken beast, under pretense of his being the finest horse in the world; but he shall rue it."

But now Bucephalus would not be led away. The horse-tamers tried to throw ropes over his feet; they beat him with long poles; they pelted him with stones.

"What a shame to spoil so fine a horse! The awkward cowards know nothing about handling him!" cried the king's son, Alexander, who was standing by.

"Are you finding fault with men who are wiser than yourself?" asked the king, growing still more angry. "Do you, a boy twelve years old, pretend to know more about handling horses than these men, whose business it is?"

"I can certainly handle this horse better," said the prince.

"Suppose you try it!"

"I wish that I might."

"How much will you forfeit if you try, and fail?"

"I will forfeit the price which you paid for the horse," answered Alexander.

Everybody laughed, but the king said, "Stand away, and let the lad try his skill."

Alexander ran quickly to the horse and turned his head toward the sun, for he had noticed that the animal was afraid of his own shadow. Then he spoke softly and gently to him, and kindly stroked his neck. The horse seemed to know that he had found a friend, and little by little his uneasiness left him. Soon with a light spring the lad leaped nimbly upon his back, and

without pulling the reins too hard, allowed him to start off at his own gait; and then, when he saw that the horse was no longer afraid, but only proud of his speed, he urged him with voice and spur to do his utmost. The king and his attendants were alarmed, and expected every moment to see the boy unseated and dashed to the ground. But when he turned and rode back, proud of his daring feat, everybody cheered and shouted – everybody but his father, who wept for joy and, kissing him, said: "You must look for a kingdom which is worthy of you, my son, for Macedonia is too small for you."

After that, Bucephalus would allow his groom to mount him barebacked; but when he was saddled nobody but Alexander dared touch him. He would even kneel to his young master, in order that he might mount more easily; and for sixteen years thereafter he served him as faithfully as horse ever served man. Of course, he was with Alexander when he conquered Persia, and he carried him into more than one hard-fought battle. At one time (I think it was in Hyrcania) he was stolen; but his master made proclamation that unless he were forthcoming within a certain time, every man, woman and child in the province should be put to death, and it was not long before he was brought back.

In the great battle that was fought with King Porus, of India, Alexander recklessly rode too far into the enemy's ranks. The horse and his rider became the target for every spear, and for a time it seemed as if neither could escape. But the gallant Bucephalus, pierced by many weapons, and with streams of blood flowing from his neck and sides, turned about and, overriding the foes which beset them, rushed back to a place of safety. When he saw that his master was out of danger and among friends, the horse sank down upon the grass and died.

Historians say that this happened in the

year 327 BC, and that Bucephalus had reached the good old age – for a horse – of thirty years. Alexander mourned for him as for his dearest friend, and the next city which he founded he named Bucephalia, in honor of the steed that had served him so well.

Gilgamesh and Humbaba

From the epic poem *Gilgamesh*

GILGAMESH WAS A MIGHTY king, ruler of the great city of Uruk. His father, Lugalbanda, had been a noble king before him and his mother was the wise goddess Ninsun. Gilgamesh was especially favoured by the gods. The great mother goddess Nintu had helped to create him. The sun god Shamash had bestowed beauty upon him. The storm god Adad had filled him with courage. The god of learning and intelligence Ea had given him wisdom. Indeed, Gilgamesh had been granted many divine gifts, but he had not been given the gift he prized most of all – immortality. Gilgamesh was human, and like all humans, he would eventually die.

One day, Gilgamesh was sitting with his dearest friend, the warrior Enkidu, when he declared, "Before I die, I want to win a place among the greatest heroes who have ever lived. Then, people will tell tales of my glorious deeds for thousands of years to come, and my name shall live on through the ages."

"O great Gilgamesh," Enkidu replied, "you are already a renowned ruler of a powerful people and a magnificent city, admired throughout the land. How do you intend to achieve even greater fame? Surely you are as famous as you can be!"

Gilgamesh paused. There was an excited gleam in his eyes. He announced, "I am going to slay the giant, Humbaba!"

Enkidu gasped. "Tell me you are not serious! Everyone who has heard of Humbaba quakes in fear at his name! Humbaba has a ferocious face like a great dragon, a terrifying roar like a rampaging river, gnashing teeth like a bloodthirsty lion, and fiery breath that scorches everything in his path. The divine ruler

Enlil appointed Humbaba to scare travellers away from the mountain home of the gods, which lies in the deep, dark Cedar Forest of Lebanon – so wild and treacherous that you can enter it and never find your way out again."

"All that is true," smiled Gilgamesh. "Nevertheless, I am determined to track this monster down and slay him! The whole world will talk of my adventure. Say you will come with me, Enkidu."

Enkidu shook his head. "My lord, I am not yet ready to die," he exclaimed.

"Come, Enkidu," coaxed Gilgamesh, "would you rather wait for death to find you, or go out and greet it face to face. I am going to slay Humbaba. Poets will sing forever more of Gilgamesh, King of Uruk!"

Enkidu sighed. "My king, if your mind is made up, then I shall remain at your side until the very end."

Gilgamesh hurried off to prepare. First, he made a sacrifice at the temple of Shamash. "O radiant one," he begged, "take pity on my mortality. Help me to conquer Humbaba and win everlasting fame."

Then Gilgamesh called the elders of Uruk to a meeting and informed them of his plan. They were horrified and protested angrily, but Gilgamesh was defiant and could not be persuaded otherwise.

Finally, he told his mother of his plans. She wept and wailed, and prayed to the gods to change his mind. But finally, she kissed Gilgamesh and Enkidu goodbye. "Go forth with my blessing, but return safely home to me."

Gilgamesh took the bravest warriors of Uruk, along with supplies and weapons, including a mighty axe especially forged by his smiths for felling Humbaba. Then Enkidu led the way out of the high gates of Uruk and down the road that led towards Humbaba's lair. To reach the gateway to the Cedar Forest of Lebanon, it should have taken six weeks of marching night and day. However, with motivated hearts, Gilgamesh, Enkidu and the warriors covered the distance in only three days. Before they entered the eerie gloom of the woods, Gilgamesh gave a stirring speech. "No one who follows me should be afraid. If we die, we die making lasting names for ourselves. We will not disappear into the well of time and be forgotten, like cowards. So be of good courage and let us go forward together!"

"Gilgamesh's dreams prophesy victory!" announced Enkidu. "Our mighty god Shamash will help us, and we will triumph over the greatest of giants, Humbaba!"

Then Gilgamesh, Enkidu and their brave army plunged determinedly into the forest, their hearts pounding. They marched all day into its depths, before Gilgamesh gave the order to stop. He took out his axe and began cutting down one of the massive cedars – a bold ploy to attract Humbaba's attention.

In the silence of the forest, the thudding chops resounded like the beat of a battle drum. As the tree finally toppled and fell, the warriors saw bursts of flame in the distance and heard huge footsteps striding towards them. Humbaba's thunderous voice struck terror into their hearts. "Who dares enter my forest and cut down the trees of the heavenly mountain of the gods? Answer me and prepare to die!"

"I, Gilgamesh, King of Uruk, have felled your tree," Gilgamesh bellowed back, "and now I will fell you with my mighty axe!"

Gilgamesh brandished his axe overhead and charged forwards to meet the oncoming monster. Enkidu roared a mighty battle cry, and he and the warriors

followed suit. As they did so, Shamash rewarded their courage by sending mighty winds from heaven against Humbaba. The blasts beat upon him from all directions and hurled him backwards, until he was held trapped against the wall of his own house.

The huge giant thrashed and struggled, but remained pinned to the wall by the force of the wind. Quivering and quaking with fear, he cried, "Have mercy, great Gilgamesh. I swear that if you let me live, I shall become your faithful servant."

But Enkidu shook his head sternly. "Do not listen to the cunning creature," he advised. "If you set him free, you will surely never see Uruk again."

Gilgamesh listened to his friend's wise words. Raising his axe high above his head, he struck Humbaba with all his might. The giant's body hit the ground with an almighty thud, which echoed throughout the great forest for many miles.

Gilgamesh, Enkidu and the warriors returned triumphant to Uruk – not only with the head of Humbaba, but with many felled cedars to make the mighty city of Uruk even stronger.

Gilgamesh's faith in himself paid off. He got his wish and tales are still told of his courageous deed to this very day.

The Brave Tin Soldier

Retold from the original tale
by Hans Christian Andersen

A LITTLE BOY WAS once given a box of twenty-five tin soldiers as a gift. They wore smart uniforms and proudly shouldered their guns, and the little boy was very pleased with them. Only one of the tin soldiers wasn't quite perfect, for he had just one leg. He and his brothers had all been made from the same tin spoon, and there hadn't been quite enough metal to finish him off. Still, it was because he stood out as being special that the little boy put him to stand guard at the gates of the toy castle, instead of keeping him in the box with the others.

The tin soldier was very honoured to have been given an important duty, and he stood to attention,

staring straight ahead. His gaze landed on a beautiful tiny doll whom the boy had placed in the open castle doorway. She was made of the very best plastic and wore a ballet dress of thin muslin, tied at the waist with a shiny blue ribbon. She held both her arms gracefully over her head and she balanced beautifully on one leg, for just like the tin soldier, she had one leg missing. (Well, in actual fact that wasn't the truth. The girl's other leg was extended out behind her because she was a dancer. But the tin soldier wasn't in a position to see it.) That would be just the wife for me, the tin soldier thought at least ten times every day. But the tin soldier dared not go and tell the girl of his love for her, for he was on duty.

One morning, the tin soldier was unexpectedly relieved of his post. A sudden breeze blew through the open window causing the curtains to flutter and knocking the soldier right off his feet and over the windowsill. Down he tumbled through the air, until he landed headfirst on the pavement.

The tin soldier didn't cry out for he was brave-

hearted in the face of danger – not even when big drops of rain began to bombard him from above. So this is what it feels like to be out on the battlefield, the brave tin soldier thought.

Eventually the rain stopped falling and two keen-eyed boys came along and spotted the tin soldier among the puddles. The boys quickly folded some newspaper into a boat, popped the tin soldier in the middle, and set him afloat in the rainwater that rushed down the gutter at the side of the street. They ran alongside the boat as it swirled along, cheering it on its way delightedly. The tin soldier was shaking with fear inside, but he didn't flinch or move a muscle – even when the rushing water carried his newspaper boat down a drain and into the darkness under the pavement.

Suddenly a huge water-rat appeared. "Who goes there?" it demanded, twitching its whiskers and baring its long teeth.

At last, I face the enemy! thought the brave tin soldier. But before he could lower his gun and aim it, his newspaper boat was carried past the rat on the tide.

A glimmer of light appeared in the distance and the rushing of the water grew louder and louder. The tin

soldier realised with horror that he was being swept towards a sudden drop where the drain water cascaded in a waterfall into a canal below. Even worse, the churning waters were splashing over the sides of the newspaper boat and the bottom was growing soggy beneath the tin soldier's feet. "Steady! Steady! Hold the line!" the brave tin soldier told himself. Suddenly the bottom of the boat ripped and gave way. The tin soldier plunged into the deeps and the icy waters closed over his head.

Surely now I am done for! thought the tin soldier, as he sank downwards through the murky wetness. Then all at once, everything went black as a fish swallowed him. The tin soldier choked and spluttered as he was gulped down into the fish's gullet, then the waters drained away and he was left lying on his back, holding tightly onto his gun. Even though the tin soldier couldn't see in the darkness, he could just about breathe in the stinking, rotten air. So this is what it's like to be a prisoner of war in a dungeon, the brave tin soldier thought to himself. To keep up his spirits, he concentrated on the beautiful dancing girl he had left at the castle.

The tin soldier lost track of time inside the fish, but eventually he was flung to and fro as the creature was

caught on a hook
and struggled to
escape. Then everything
went quiet and still for
quite a while, until suddenly
the fish was cut open. "I
don't believe it!" came a voice
"Here's the missing tin soldier," and
a woman with a kind face reached in and pulled him
out. She gave the brave tin soldier a shower under a
running tap, carried him into the drawing room and
set him back in his old position outside his very own
castle.

The tin soldier puffed out his chest with pride. The
war is over. I am back where I belong, he thought to
himself. He stared straight ahead, and there was his
love, his sweetheart, the beautiful little dancing girl.
Tomorrow, as soon as I am off duty, I will definitely ask
her to marry me, the tin soldier decided. But then he
felt an icy wind around his ankles, and a breeze coming
through the window once more swept him off his feet
and into the air. This time he landed in the blazing
flames of the open fire – but the brave tin soldier
didn't mind, for the dancing girl was blown in too and
landed at his side. "Be brave, my love!" cried the tin

soldier, holding his gun on his shoulder, and the dancing girl burst into flames and was gone. Then the tin soldier himself began to melt... and the next day, when the woman with the kind face was raking over the ashes, she found a tiny tin heart that the fire had been unable to burn away.

My Lord Bag of Rice

By Yei Theodora Ozaka

LONG, LONG AGO there lived in Japan a brave warrior known to all as Tawara Toda, or 'My Lord Bag of Rice'. His true name was Fujiwara Hidesato, and there is a very interesting story of how he came to change his name.

One day he went out in search of adventures, for he had the nature of a warrior and could not bear to be idle. So he buckled on his two swords, took his huge bow in his hand, and slinging his quiver on his back started out. He had not gone far when he came to the bridge of Seta-no-Karashi spanning one end of the beautiful Lake Biwa. No sooner had he set foot on the bridge than he saw lying right across his path a huge

serpent-dragon. Its body was so big that it looked like the trunk of a large pine tree and it took up the whole width of the bridge. One of its huge claws rested on the parapet of one side of the bridge, while its tail lay right against the other. The monster seemed to be asleep, and as it breathed, fire and smoke came out of its nostrils.

At first Hidesato could not help feeling alarmed at the sight of this horrible reptile lying in his path, for he must either turn back or walk right over its body. He was a brave man, however, and putting aside all fear went forward dauntlessly. Crunch, crunch! He stepped now on the dragon's body, now between its coils, and without even one glance backward he went on his way.

He had only gone a few steps when he heard someone calling him from behind. On turning back he was much surprised to see that the monster dragon had entirely disappeared and in its place was a strange looking man, who was bowing most ceremoniously to the ground. His red hair streamed over his shoulders and was surmounted by a crown in the shape of a dragon's head, and his sea-green dress was patterned with shells. Hidesato knew at once that this was no ordinary mortal and he wondered much at the strange occurrence. Where had the dragon gone in such a short space of time? Or had it transformed itself into this man, and what did the whole thing mean? While these thoughts passed through his mind he had come up to the man on the bridge and now addressed him:

"Was it you that called me just now?"

"Yes, it was I," said the man, "I have an earnest request to make to you. Do you think you can grant it to me?"

"If it is in my power to do so I will," answered Hidesato, "but first tell me who you are?"

"I am the dragon king of the lake, and my home is in these waters just under this bridge."

"What is it you have to ask of me?" said Hidesato.

"I want you to kill my mortal enemy the centipede, who lives on the mountain beyond," and the

dragon king pointed to a high peak on the opposite
shore of the lake.

"I have lived for many years in this lake and I have a
large family of children and grandchildren. For some
time past we have lived in terror, for a monster
centipede has discovered our home, and night after
night it comes and carries off one of my family. I am
powerless to save them. If it goes on much longer like
this, not only shall I lose all my children, but I myself
must fall a victim to the monster. I am, therefore, very
unhappy, and in my extremity I determined to ask the
help of a human being. For many days with this
intention I have waited on the bridge in the shape of
the horrible serpent-dragon that you saw, in the hope
that some strong brave man would come along. But all
who came this way, as soon as they saw me were
terrified and ran away as fast as they could. You are the
first man I have found able to look at me without fear,
so I knew at once that you were a man of great
courage. I beg you to have pity upon me. Will you not
help me and kill my enemy the centipede?"

Hidesato felt very sorry for the dragon king on
hearing his story, and readily promised to do what he
could to help him. The warrior asked where the
centipede lived, so that he might attack the creature at

once. The dragon king replied that its home was on the mountain Mikami, but as it came every night at a certain hour to the palace of the lake, it would be better to wait till then.

So Hidesato was conducted to the palace of the dragon king, under the bridge. Strangely, as he followed his host downwards the waters parted to let them pass, and his clothes did not even feel damp as he passed through the flood. Never had Hidesato seen anything so beautiful as this palace built of white marble beneath the lake. He had often heard of the sea king's palace at the bottom of the sea, where all the servants were saltwater fish, but here was a magnificent building in the heart of Lake Biwa. The dainty goldfish, red carp, and silvery trout, waited upon the dragon king and his guest.

Hidesato was astonished at the feast that was spread for him. The dishes were crystallized lotus leaves and flowers, and the chopsticks were of the rarest ebony. As soon as they sat down, the sliding doors opened and ten lovely goldfish dancers came out, and behind them followed ten red carp musicians. Thus the hours flew by till midnight, and the beautiful music and dancing had banished all thoughts of the centipede. The dragon king was about to pass the warrior a fresh cup of wine when the palace was suddenly shaken by a tramp, tramp, tramp! It was as if a mighty army had begun to march not far away.

Hidesato and his host both rose to their feet and rushed to the balcony, and the warrior saw on the opposite mountain two great balls of glowing fire coming nearer. The dragon king stood by the warrior's side trembling with fear.

"The centipede! The centipede! Those two balls of fire are its eyes. It is coming for its prey! Now is the time to kill it."

Hidesato looked where his host pointed, and, in the dim light of the starlit evening, behind the two balls of fire he saw the long body of an enormous centipede winding round the mountains, and the light in its terrifying eyes glowed like many distant lanterns moving slowly towards the shore.

Hidesato showed no fear. He tried to calm the dragon king.

"Don't be afraid. I shall surely kill the centipede. Just bring me my bow and arrows."

The dragon king did as he was bid, and the warrior noticed that he had only three arrows left in his quiver. He took the bow, and fitting an arrow to the notch, took careful aim and let fly.

The arrow hit the centipede right in the middle of its head, but instead of penetrating, it glanced off harmless and fell to the ground.

Not daunted, Hidesato took another arrow, fitted it to the notch of the bow and let fly. Again the arrow hit the mark, it struck the centipede right in the middle of its head, only to glance off and fall to the ground. The centipede was invulnerable to weapons! When the dragon king saw that even this brave warrior's arrows were powerless to kill the centipede, he lost heart and began to tremble with fear.

The warrior saw that he had now only one arrow left in his quiver,

and if this one failed he could not kill the centipede. He looked across the waters. The huge reptile had wound its horrid body seven times round the mountain and would soon come down to the lake.

Then suddenly the warrior remembered that human saliva was deadly to centipedes. But this was no ordinary centipede. This was so monstrous that even to think of such a creature made him creep with horror. Hidesato determined to try one more time. So taking his last arrow and first putting the end of it in his mouth, he fitted the notch to his bow, took careful aim once more and let fly.

The arrow again hit the centipede in the middle of its head, but instead of glancing off harmlessly as before, it struck home to the creature's brain. Then with a convulsive shudder the serpentine body stopped moving, and the fiery light of its great eyes and hundred feet darkened to a dull glare like the sunset of a stormy day, and then went out in blackness. A great darkness now overspread the heavens, thunder rolled and lightning flashed, and the wind roared in fury, and it seemed as if the world were coming to an end. Hidesato called to the dragon king to come out with him on the balcony, for the centipede was dead and he had nothing more to fear. All the inhabitants of the palace came out shouting with joy, and Hidesato pointed to the lake. There lay the body of the dead centipede floating on the water.

The gratitude of the dragon king knew no bounds. Another feast was prepared, more sumptuous than the first. All kinds of fish, prepared in every imaginable way, raw, stewed, boiled and roasted, served on coral trays and crystal dishes, were put before him, and the wine was the best that Hidesato had ever tasted in his life. They begged him to accept a few small presents in token of their gratitude to him for delivering them forever from their terrible enemy the centipede.

The presents that they carried were as follows:

First, a large bronze bell.
Second, a bag of rice.
Third, a roll of silk.
Fourth, a cooking pot.
Fifth, another bell.

Hidesato did not want to accept all these presents, but as the dragon king insisted, he could not well refuse.

The dragon king himself accompanied the warrior as far as the bridge, and then took leave of him with many bows and good wishes, leaving the servants to

accompany Hidesato to his house with the presents.

The warrior's household and servants had been very much concerned when they found that he did not return the night before. When the servants on the watch for his return caught sight of him they called to everyone that he was approaching.

As soon as the dragon king's retainers had put down the presents, they vanished, and Hidesato told all that had happened to him.

The presents were found to be of magic power. Only the bell was ordinary, so Hidesato presented it to the temple nearby, where it was hung up, to boom out the hour of day over the neighbourhood.

However much was taken from from the single bag of rice, the supply in the bag never grew less. The roll of silk never grew shorter, though long pieces were cut off to make the warrior a new suit of clothes. No matter what was put into the cooking pot, it cooked deliciously whatever was wanted without any heating.

The fame of Hidesato's fortune spread far and wide, and as there was no need for him to spend money on rice, silk or heating, he became very rich and prosperous, and was henceforth known as 'My Lord Bag of Rice'.

Amazing Adventures

The Elephant's Child

From *Just So Stories* by Rudyard Kipling

IN THE HIGH and far-off times, the Elephant, oh best beloved, had no trunk. He had only a blackish, bulgy nose, as big as a boot, that he could wriggle about from side to side; but he couldn't pick up things with it. But there was one Elephant – a new Elephant – an Elephant's Child – who was full of 'satiable curtiosity, and that means he asked ever so many questions. And he lived in Africa, and he filled all Africa with his 'satiable curtiosities. He asked his tall aunt, the Ostrich, why her tail feathers grew just so, and his tall aunt the Ostrich spanked him with her hard, hard claw.

He asked his broad aunt, the Hippopotamus, why her eyes were red, and his broad aunt, the

Hippopotamus, spanked him with her broad, broad hoof; and he asked his hairy uncle, the Baboon, why melons tasted just so, and his hairy uncle, the Baboon, spanked him with his hairy, hairy paw. And still he was full of 'satiable curtiosity! He asked questions about everything that he saw, or heard, or felt, or smelt, or touched, and all his uncles and his aunts spanked him. And still he was full of 'satiable curtiosity!

One fine morning in the middle of the Precession of the Equinoxes this 'satiable Elephant's Child asked a new fine question that he had never asked before. He asked, "What does the Crocodile have for dinner?"

Then everybody said, "Hush!" in a loud and dreadful tone, and they spanked him immediately and directly, without stopping, for a long time.

By and by, when that was finished, he came upon Kolokolo Bird sitting in the middle of a wait-a-bit thorn-bush, and he said, "My father has spanked me, and my mother has spanked me; all my aunts and uncles have spanked me for my 'satiable curtiosity; and still I want to know what the Crocodile has for dinner!"

Then Kolokolo Bird said, with a mournful cry, "Go to the banks of the great grey-green, greasy Limpopo River, all set about with fever-trees, and find out."

That very next morning, when there was nothing

left of the Equinoxes, because the Precession had preceded according to precedent, this 'satiable Elephant's Child took a hundred pounds of bananas (the little short red kind), and a hundred pounds of sugar-cane (the long purple kind), and seventeen melons (the greeny-crackly kind), and said to all his dear families, "Goodbye. I am going to the great grey-green, greasy Limpopo River, all set about with fever-trees, to find out what the Crocodile has for dinner." And they all spanked him once more for luck, though he asked them most politely to stop.

Then he went away, a little warm, but not at all astonished, eating melons, and throwing the rind about, because he could not pick it up.

He went from Graham's Town to Kimberley, and from Kimberley to Khama's Country, and from Khama's Country he went east by north, eating melons all the time, till at last he came to the banks of the great grey-green, greasy Limpopo River, all set about with fever-trees, precisely as Kolokolo Bird had said.

Now you must know and understand, Oh Best Beloved, that till that very week, and day, and hour, and minute, this 'satiable Elephant's Child had never seen a Crocodile, and did not know what one was like. It was all his 'satiable curtiosity.

The first thing that he found was a Bi-Coloured-Python-Rock-Snake curled round a rock.

"'Scuse me," said the Elephant's Child most politely, "but have you seen such a thing as a Crocodile in these promiscuous parts?"

"Have I seen a Crocodile?" said the Bi-Coloured-Python-Rock-Snake, in a voice of dreadful scorn. "What will you ask me next?"

"'Scuse me," said the Elephant's Child, "but could you kindly tell me what he has for dinner?"

Then the Bi-Coloured-Python-Rock-Snake uncoiled himself very quickly from the rock, and spanked the Elephant's Child with his scalesome, flailsome tail.

"That is odd," said the Elephant's Child, "because my father and my mother, and my uncle and my aunt, not to mention my other aunt, the Hippopotamus, and my other uncle, the Baboon, have all spanked me for my 'satiable curtiosity – and I suppose this is the same.

So he said goodbye very politely to the Bi-Coloured-Python-Rock-Snake, and helped to coil him up on the rock again, and went on, a little warm, but not at all astonished, eating melons, and throwing the rind about, because he could not pick it up, till he trod on what he thought was a log of wood at the very edge of the great grey-green, greasy Limpopo River, all set about with fever-trees.

But it was really the Crocodile, Oh Best Beloved, and the Crocodile winked one eye – like this!

"'Scuse me," said the Elephant's Child most politely, "but do you happen to have seen a Crocodile in these promiscuous parts?"

Then the Crocodile winked the other eye, and lifted half his tail out of the mud; and the Elephant's Child stepped back most politely, because he did not wish to be spanked again.

"Come hither, Little One," said the Crocodile. "Why do you ask such things?"

"'Scuse me," said the Elephant's Child most politely, "but my father has spanked me, my mother has spanked me, not to mention my tall aunt, the Ostrich, and my tall uncle, the Giraffe, who can kick ever so hard, as well as my broad aunt, the Hippopotamus, and my hairy uncle, the Baboon, and including the

Bi-Coloured-Python-Rock-Snake, with the scalesome, flailsome tail, just up the bank, who spanks harder than any of them; and so, if it's quite all the same to you, I don't want to be spanked any more."

"Come hither, Little One," said the Crocodile, "for I am the Crocodile," and he wept crocodile-tears to show it was quite true.

Then the Elephant's Child grew all breathless, and panted, and kneeled down on the bank and said, "You are the very person I have been looking for all these long days. Will you please tell me what you have for dinner?"

"Come hither, Little One," said the Crocodile, "and I'll whisper."

Then the Elephant's Child put his head down close to the Crocodile's musky, tusky mouth, and the Crocodile caught him by his little nose, which up to that very week, day, hour, and minute, had been no bigger than a boot, though much more useful.

"I think," said the Crocodile – and he said it between his teeth, like this – "I think today I will begin with Elephant's Child!"

At this, Oh Best Beloved, the Elephant's Child was much annoyed, and he said, speaking through his nose, like this, "Led go! You are hurtig be!"

Then the Bi-Coloured-Python-Rock-Snake scuffled down from the bank and said, "My young friend, if you do not now, immediately and instantly, pull as hard as ever you can, it is my opinion that your acquaintance in the large-pattern leather ulster" (and by this he meant the Crocodile) "will jerk you into yonder limpid stream before you can say Jack Robinson."

283

Then the Elephant's Child sat back on his little haunches, and pulled, and pulled, and pulled, and his nose began to stretch. And the Crocodile floundered into the water, making it all creamy with great sweeps of his tail, and he pulled, and pulled, and pulled.

And the Elephant's Child's nose kept on stretching; and the Elephant's Child spread all his little four legs and pulled, and pulled, and pulled, and his nose kept on stretching; and the Crocodile threshed his tail like an oar, and he pulled, and pulled, and pulled, and at each pull the Elephant's Child's nose grew longer and longer – and it hurt him terribly!

Then the Elephant's Child felt his legs slipping, and he said through his nose, which was now nearly five feet long, "This is too butch for be!"

Then the Bi-Coloured-Python-Rock-Snake came down from the bank, and knotted himself in a double-clove-hitch round the Elephant's Child's hind legs. And he pulled, and the Elephant's Child pulled, and the Crocodile pulled; but the Elephant's Child and the Bi-Coloured-Python-Rock-Snake pulled hardest; and at last the Crocodile let go of the Elephant's Child's nose with a plop that you could hear all up and down the Limpopo.

Then the Elephant's Child sat down most hard and

sudden; but first he was careful to say "Thank you" to the Bi-Coloured-Python-Rock-Snake; and next he was kind to his poor pulled nose, and wrapped it all up in cool banana leaves, and hung it in the great grey-green, greasy Limpopo to cool.

"What are you doing that for?" said the Bi-Coloured-Python-Rock-Snake.

"'Scuse me," said the Elephant's Child, "but my nose is badly out of shape, and I am waiting for it to shrink.

"Then you will have to wait a long time, said the Bi-Coloured-Python-Rock-Snake. "Some people do not know what is good for them."

The Elephant's Child sat there for three days waiting for his nose to shrink. But it never grew any shorter, and, besides, it made him squint. For, Oh Best Beloved, you will see and understand that the Crocodile had pulled it out into a really truly trunk, same as all Elephants have today.

At the end of the third day a fly came and stung him on the shoulder, and before he knew what he was doing he lifted up his trunk and hit that fly dead with the end of it.

"'Vantage number one!" said the Bi-Coloured-Python-Rock-Snake. "You couldn't have done that with a mere-smear nose. Try and eat a little now."

Before he thought what he was doing the Elephant's Child put out his trunk and plucked a large bundle of grass, dusted it clean against his fore-legs, and stuffed it into his own mouth.

"Vantage number two!" said the Bi-Coloured-Python-Rock-Snake. "You couldn't have done that with a mear-smear nose. Don't you think the sun is hot?"

"It is," said the Elephant's Child, and before he thought what he was doing he schlooped up a schloop of mud from the banks of the great Limpopo, and slapped it on his head, where it made a cool schloopy-sloshy mud-cap all trickly behind his ears.

"Vantage number three!" said the Bi-Coloured-Python-Rock-Snake. "You couldn't have done that with a mere-smear nose. Now how do you feel about being spanked again?"

"'Scuse me," said the Elephant's Child, "but I should not like it at all."

"How would you like to spank somebody?" said the Bi- Coloured-Python-Rock-Snake.

"I should like it very much indeed," said the Elephant's Child.

"Well," said the Bi-Coloured-Python-Rock-Snake, "you will find that new nose of yours very useful to spank people with."

"Thank you," said the Elephant's Child, "I'll remember that; and now I think I'll go home to all my dear families and try."

So the Elephant's Child went home across Africa frisking and whisking his trunk. When he wanted fruit to eat he pulled fruit down from a tree, instead of waiting for it to fall as he used to do. When he wanted grass he plucked grass up from the ground, instead of going on his knees as he used to do. When the flies bit him he broke off the branch of a tree and used it as fly-whisk; and he made himself a new, cool, slushy-squishy mud-cap whenever the sun was hot. When he felt lonely walking through Africa he sang to himself down his trunk, and the noise was louder than several brass bands. He went especially out of his way to find a broad Hippopotamus (she was no relation of his), and he spanked her very hard, to make sure that the Bi-Coloured-Python-Rock-Snake had spoken the truth about his new trunk. The rest of the time he picked up the melon rinds that he had dropped on his way to the Limpopo – for he was a Tidy Pachyderm.

One evening he came back to all his dear families, and he coiled up his trunk and said, "How do you do?" They were glad to see him, and said, "Come here and be spanked for your 'satiable curtiosity."

"Pooh," said the Elephant's Child. "I don't think you peoples know anything about spanking; but I do, and I'll show you." Then he uncurled his trunk and knocked two of his dear brothers head over heels.

"Oh Bananas!" said they, "where did you learn that trick, and what have you done to your nose?"

"I got a new one from the Crocodile on the banks of the great grey-green, greasy Limpopo River," said the Elephant's Child.

"It looks very ugly," said his hairy uncle, the Baboon.

"It does," said the Elephant's Child. "But it's very useful," and he picked up his hairy uncle, the Baboon, by one hairy leg, and hove him into a hornet's nest.

Then that bad Elephant's Child spanked all his dear families for a long time. He pulled out his tall Ostrich aunt's tail feathers; and he caught his tall uncle, the Giraffe, and dragged him through a thorn-bush; and he shouted at his aunt, the Hippopotamus, and blew bubbles in her ear when she was sleeping in the water.

At last, his dear families went off one by one to the banks of the great Limpopo River to borrow new noses from the Crocodile. When they came back nobody spanked anybody any more; and ever since that day, all the Elephants have trunks precisely like the trunk of the 'satiable Elephant's Child.

Eva's Visit to Fairyland

By Louisa M Alcott

DOWN AMONG THE grass and fragrant clover lay little Eva by the brook-side, watching the bright waves, as they went singing by under the drooping flowers that grew on its banks. As she was wondering where the waters went, she heard a faint sound. She thought it was the wind, but not a leaf was stirring, and soon through the rippling water came a strange little boat.

It was a lily of the valley, whose tall stem formed the mast, while the broad leaves that rose from the roots, and drooped again till they reached the water, were filled with fairies, who danced to the music of the silver lily-bells above that rang a merry peal, and filled the air with their fragrant breath.

On came the fairy boat till it reached a rock, and here it stopped, while the fairies rested beneath the violet leaves, and sang with the dancing waves.

Eva looked with wonder and threw crimson fruit for the little folks to feast upon.

They looked kindly on the child, and, after whispering long among themselves, two elves flew over the shining water, and, lighting on the clover blossoms, said gently, "Little maiden, many thanks for your kindness, our queen bids us ask if you will go with us to Fairyland, and learn what we can teach you."

"I would go with you, dear fairies," said Eva, "but I cannot sail in your little boat. See! I can hold you in my hand, and could not live among you without harming your tiny kingdom, I am so large."

Then the elves laughed, saying, "You are a good child to fear doing harm to those weaker than yourself. Look in the water and see what we have done."

Eva looked into the brook, and saw a tiny child standing between the elves. "Now I can go with you," said she, "but I can no longer step from the bank to yonder stone, for the brook seems now like a great river, and you have not given me wings like yours."

But the fairies took each a hand, and flew lightly over the stream. The queen and her subjects came to meet her. "Now must we go home," said the queen, "and you shall go with us, little one."

Then there was a great bustle, as they flew about on shining wings, some laying cushions of violet leaves in the boat, others folding the queen's veil and mantle more closely round her.

The cool waves' gentle splashing against the boat, and the sweet chime of the lily-bells, lulled little Eva to sleep, and when she woke it was in Fairyland. A faint, rosy light, as of the setting sun, shone on the white pillars of the queen's palace as they passed in. They led

Eva to a bed of pure white leaves, above which drooped the fragrant petals of a crimson rose.

With the sun rose the fairies, and, with Eva, hastened away to the gardens, and soon, high up among the tree-tops, or under the broad leaves, sat the elves in little groups, taking their breakfast of fruit and pure fresh dew.

"Now, Eva," said they, "you will see that Fairies are not idle spirits. Come, we will show you what we do."

They led her to a lovely room, through whose walls of deep green leaves the light stole softly in. Here lay many wounded insects, and creatures, and pale, drooping flowers grew beside urns of healing herbs, from whose fresh leaves came a faint, sweet perfume.

Eva wondered, but silently followed her guide, little Rose-Leaf, who went to the insects – first to a little fly who lay in a flower-leaf cradle.

"Do you suffer much, dear Gauzy-Wing?" asked the Fairy. "I will bind up your poor little leg." So she folded the cool leaves tenderly about the poor fly, bathed his wings, and brought him refreshing drink, while he hummed his thanks, and forgot his pain.

They passed on, and Eva saw beside each bed a fairy, who with gentle hands and loving words soothed the suffering insects.

Then Rose-Leaf led Eva away, saying, "Come now to the Flower Palace, and see the Fairy Court."

Beneath green arches, bright with birds and flowers, went Eva into a lofty hall. Suddenly the music grew louder and sweeter, and the fairies knelt, and bowed their heads, as on through the crowd of loving subjects came the queen, while the air was filled with gay voices singing to welcome her.

She placed the child beside her, saying, "Little Eva, you shall see now how the flowers on your great earth bloom so brightly. A band of loving little gardeners go daily forth from Fairyland, to tend and watch them Now, Eglantine, what have you to tell us of your rosy namesakes on the earth?"

From a group of elves, whose rose-wreathed wands showed the flower they loved, came one bearing a tiny urn, and, answering the queen, she said:

"Over hill and valley they are blooming fresh and fair as summer sun and dew, and this have I brought to place among the fairy flowers that never pass away." Eglantine laid the urn before the queen, and placed the fragrant rose on the dewy moss beside the throne, while a murmur of approval went through the hall, as each wand waved to the little fairy who could bring so fair a gift to their good queen.

Said little Rose-Leaf to Eva, "Come now and see where we are taught to read the tales written on flower-leaves, and the sweet language of the birds, and all that can make a fairy heart wiser and better."

Then into a cheerful place they went, where were many groups of flowers, among whose leaves sat the child elves, and learned from their flower-books all that fairy hands had written there. Some studied how to watch the tender buds – when to spread them to the sunlight, and when to shelter them from rain, how to guard the ripening seeds, and when to lay them in the warm earth or send them on the summer wind to far off hills and valleys, where other fairy hands would tend and cherish them. Others learned to heal the wounded insects, who, were it not for fairy hands, would die before half their happy summer life had gone. Eva nodded to the little ones, as they peeped from among the leaves at the stranger, and then she listened to the fairy lessons. Several tiny elves sat on leaves while the teacher sat among the petals of a flower beside them, and asked questions that none but fairies would care to know.

At last, Eva said farewell to the child elves, and hastened with little Rose-Leaf to the gates. Here she saw many bands of fairies, folded in dark mantles that mortals might not know them, who, with the child among them, flew away over hill and valley. Some went to the cottages amid the hills, some to the seaside to watch above the humble fisher folks, but little Rose-Leaf and many others went into the noisy city.

Eva soon learned that the fairy band went among the poor and friendless, bringing pleasant dreams to the sick and old, sweet, tender thoughts of love and gentleness to the young, strength to the weak, and patient cheerfulness to the poor and lonely.

After their work was done, they turned towards

Fairyland, which was dressed in flowers, and the soft wind went singing by, laden with their fragrant breath. Sweet music sounded through the air, and troops of elves in their gayest robes hastened to the palace where the feast was spread.

Soon the hall was filled with smiling faces and fair forms, and little Eva, as she stood beside the queen, thought she had never seen a sight so lovely.

Long they feasted, gaily they sang, and Eva, dancing merrily among them, longed to be an elf that she might dwell forever in so fair a home.

At length the music ceased, and the queen said, as she laid her hand on little Eva's shining hair: "Dear child, tomorrow we must bear you home, therefore we will guide you to the brook-side, and there say farewell till you come again to visit us."

On a rosy morning cloud, went Eva through the sunny sky. The fresh wind bore them gently on, and soon they stood again beside the brook, whose waves danced brightly as if to welcome them.

"Now, we say farewell," said the queen, as they gathered nearer to the child.

They clung about her tenderly, and little Rose-Leaf placed a flower crown on her head, whispering softly, "When you would come to us again, stand by the brook-side and wave this in the air, and we will gladly take you to our home again. Farewell, dear Eva. Think of your little Rose-Leaf when among the flowers."

For a long time Eva watched their shining wings, and listened to the music of their voices as they flew singing home. When at last little form had vanished among the clouds, she saw that all around her, the fairest flowers had sprung up.

The Firebird

A Russian folk tale

LONG AGO IN RUSSIA, there lived a lord called Tsar Andronovich who owned a magnificent garden. At the centre of the garden lay a beautiful orchard, and in the middle of the orchard grew Tsar Andronovich's favourite tree – a tree that grew golden apples. No one was allowed to touch the golden apple tree except for Tsar Andronovich himself. But one night, an amazing firebird with wings of flame and eyes of crystal came blazing into the orchard and stole some of the fruit.

"A fortune to whoever brings me this amazing firebird alive." Tsar Andronovich declared the very next day. "This creature is even more splendid than the golden apples she has been stealing!"

Half an hour later, the Tsar's three sons galloped out of the gates in search of the firebird. The eldest and middle son, Dimitri and Vassili, thundered off together. The youngest son, Ivan, went off sadly on his own.

Ivan rode for three days. His food began to run low, and his horse was exhausted. Just as Ivan thought things couldn't get much worse, he heard a howl and out of a dark forest ran a grey wolf. Ivan's horse shot away, throwing him into the dirt. But it didn't escape far. The wolf sprang onto it and gobbled it up.

"Eat me quickly!" Ivan cried at the panting beast.

"I am not going to eat you," grinned the wolf. "I have to repay you for eating your horse. Ride on me and I will take you where you want to go."

Ivan was too tired and lonely to argue. He climbed onto the grey wolf's back and explained all about his quest to find the firebird. He had hardly finished

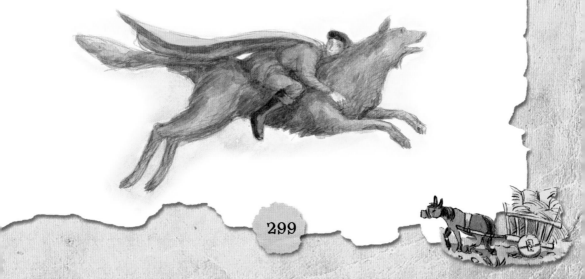

speaking when the grey wolf leapt away like an arrow. It seemed only a few seconds before they halted at a stone wall.

"Ivan, climb this wall and you will see the firebird in a golden cage," the wolf explained. "Take the firebird, but whatever you do, do not steal the golden cage."

Trembling, Ivan clambered over the wall and found himself in a courtyard below. Hanging from a tree was a golden cage with the firebird inside, just as the wolf had said. Ivan crept over to it, opened the jewelled door, and drew out the beautiful firebird. 'I really need the cage as well,' thought Ivan. He reached up and unhooked the cage. At that moment, ear-splitting alarm bells rang and guards rushed in from all sides. They dragged Ivan to their master, Tsar Dolmat.

"You must pay dearly for trying to steal my precious firebird," boomed Tsar Dolmat, his face dark with anger. Then he rubbed his beard and thought for a second. "UNLESS," he added, "you go to the ends of the earth and bring me the horse with the golden mane. If you do this, I will give you the firebird with pleasure."

Ivan crept back to the grey wolf in shame. But his friend simply said, "Ride on me and I will take you where you want to go."

The grey wolf sprang away faster than the wind. It seemed only a couple of minutes before they stopped outside some stables.

"Ivan, go into these stables and take the horse with the golden mane," the wolf told him. "But whatever you do, do not steal its golden bridle."

Cautiously, Ivan edged into the stables, crept up to the horse with the golden mane, and began to lead it out of its stall. 'I really need the bridle as well,' thought Ivan. He lifted down the bridle and a clanging peal of bells broke the silence. Soldiers dashed into the stable and hauled Ivan away to see their master, Tsar Afron.

"You must pay dearly for trying to steal my wonderful horse with the golden mane," raged Tsar Afron, shaking with fury. "UNLESS," he added, "you go to the other side of the world and bring me Tasha the Beautiful to be my bride. If you do this, I will gladly give you the horse with the golden mane."

When Ivan returned empty-handed, the wolf did not scold. He simply said, "Ride on me and I will take you where you want to go."

Ivan jumped onto the grey wolf and he sped away to the other side of the world as quick as lightning. It seemed only an hour before they drew up outside a glorious palace.

"Ivan, this time I am going to be the one who goes inside and you are going to be the one who waits," said the wolf and he sprang over the palace wall with one mighty bound. Ivan hardly had time to draw breath before the wolf came springing over again – this time with Tasha the Beautiful tossed onto his back. Ivan leapt onto the wolf and they were off through the air like a shooting star.

By the time the three arrived back at Tsar Afron's home, the grey wolf was highly surprised to find Ivan weeping bitterly.

"Why are you crying?" the grey wolf asked.

"I have fallen in love with Tasha," Ivan protested, "and she has fallen in love with me. I cannot let her go."

The grey wolf looked at Tasha the Beautiful and she nodded sadly.

"Oh very well," sighed the grey wolf. "I will turn myself into the form of Tasha the Beautiful. You can present me to Tsar Afron in her place and he will give you the horse with the golden mane. When you are two mountains away, think of me and I will be back at your side."

And so, Tsar Afron was tricked and soon Ivan was once again mounted on the grey wolf while his sweetheart, Tasha the Beautiful, rode on the horse with the golden mane.

As they drew near the villa of Tsar Dolmat, Ivan sighed a deep sigh. "Oh grey wolf," he began, "I would so like to keep this horse with the golden mane. Would you turn into the form of the horse, as you disguised yourself as Tasha before? Then I could take you to Tsar Dolmat and win the firebird. When I am two forests away, I will think of you and you will return back to my side."

The grey wolf looked at Ivan and bowed slightly.

"For you, I will do this." And so it came to pass and Tsar Dolmat was tricked. Ivan once again mounted the grey wolf while his sweetheart, Tasha the Beautiful, rode on the horse with the golden mane and carried the firebird.

By and by, the companions came to the very spot where the grey wolf had set upon Ivan's horse and eaten it. Then it was the grey wolf's turn to sigh a deep sigh. "Well, Ivan, here I took a horse from you and here I now return you with another horse, a beautiful bride and a firebird, too! You no longer need me and I must go." And with that, the grey wolf disappeared into the woods.

Ivan and Tasha went on their way in sadness, weeping for their lost friend. As they stopped to rest, the two figures of Dimitri and Vassily crept out of the shadows. They had returned from their travels empty-handed and were enraged to find their little brother not only with the firebird, but also with Tasha the Beautiful. In their bitterness, the brothers drew their swords and stabbed Ivan where he lay, dreaming. Then they swept up Tasha the Beautiful and the firebird, and were off to their father's mansion to pretend that the treasures were theirs. "Breathe a word of this and we'll kill you, too," they hissed into Tasha's

ear, making her shake with sorrow and fear.

Ivan's body lay lifeless and cold. Snow began to cover him like a thick blanket. Birds and woodland creatures slowly crept closer to find out what was lying so silent and still in the freezing weather – and among them came a grey wolf with yellow eyes and drooling jaws. He stalked right up to Ivan's body and sniffed all around. Throwing his head back, he gave a spine-chilling howl. Slowly and gently, the wolf began to lick the wound in Ivan's chest. And suddenly, Ivan sat up and began to shiver.

"Why am I asleep in this snowstorm?" he asked the grey wolf.

"Ride on me," came the gruff voice, "and I will take you where you want to go."

"Home," whispered Ivan into his friend's ear, "I want to go home." And no sooner had he finished saying the words than they were there.

Of course, when Tsar Andronovich learnt the truth, he threw the wicked Dimitri and Vassily in a dungeon.

Ivan and Tasha the Beautiful were married – Ivan rode his faithful grey wolf to the wedding and Tasha arrived on the horse with the golden mane. As for Tsar Andronovich, well, he got his precious firebird after all – and he loved her so much, he even let her eat the golden apples from his favourite tree whenever she wanted.

Thumbelina

Retold from the original tale
by Hans Christian Andersen

ONCE UPON A TIME there was a woman who wanted more than anything in the world to have a child – but she didn't know where to get one. She went to see a witch about it and the witch gave her a special seed. The woman planted the seed in a flowerpot and it grew into a bud that looked very much like the bud of a tulip. "What a beautiful flower!" the woman murmured one day, and she leant over and kissed the closed petals. POP! the bud exploded into an open flower, and sitting in the middle of it was a tiny little girl, no bigger than the woman's thumb.

The woman was overjoyed with her beautiful daughter and named her Thumbelina. The woman thought that her tiny daughter was utterly delightful and looked after her tenderly. But one night, a big, fat toad came hopping through a broken pane of glass in the woman's window. Hmmm, thought the toad, as her bulging eyes caught sight of Thumbelina sleeping in half a walnut shell. She would make a perfect wife for my son. The toad picked up the dreaming little girl, and hopped away to the marshy river where she lived. The toad placed Thumbelina on a broad, flat lily pad. Now you can't run away, the toad thought, and she swam off to break the good news to her son...

When Thumbelina woke up and saw that she was not only lost, but trapped too, she began to cry bitterly. The fish wiggled up to see what was causing all the tiny splashes and ripples, and they took pity on the sad, tiny girl. Quickly and silently, they nibbled through the lily pad's green stem and Thumbelina went floating down the river. Soon, she was far out of the toads' reach...

and still the lily pad raft floated on. Thumbelina sailed past towns and was swept out into the countryside. Thumbelina liked it among the fields. It was sunny and peaceful, and a pretty white butterfly fluttered down to keep her company. Suddenly a large flying beetle dive-bombed the lily pad and wrapped his legs around Thumbelina's tiny waist. In a flash, Thumbelina found herself sitting on a twig with the beetle high up in a tree, watching her lilypad drift away without her.

Hundreds of the beetle's curious friends came crawling out of the bark to peer at what he had brought home. "Urgh! Look, it's only got two legs," the beetle children squealed.

"Where are its feelers?" some of the lady beetles murmured.

"Hasn't it got a slim bottom?" other lady beetles gasped in horror, admiring their own round shiny ones.

"It is ugly," the male beetles had to admit. "Let's get rid of it." And they flew down from the tree with Thumbelina and sat her on a daisy.

Poor Thumbelina felt very like crying. But just then she noticed a little hole in the earth below her that looked very like it was a type of doorway. She jumped down from the daisy and peered into the gloom.

"Hello!" she cried. "Is anyone at home?"

After a few seconds, out popped a fieldmouse's head. She looked Thumbelina up and down, and tutted loudly. "Dear, dear!" the fieldmouse scolded. "You look exhausted and hungry. If you're as lost as you look, you're very welcome to stay here with me – in return for keeping my rooms nice and clean and tidy."

So all winter Thumbelina lived with the fieldmouse. Every day, she washed and swept and scoured and polished, and the fieldmouse was very kind to her. Although, truth to tell, Thumbelina found life rather boring. The fieldmouse wasn't at all skilled at making conversation and neither was her regular visitor, Mr Mole. He came once every week in his fine black velvet overcoat, but he didn't like to talk. He just enjoyed sitting and peering at Thumbelina through his little eyes, listening to her sing.

The fieldmouse was delighted that her friend so liked Thumbelina. "I think he's falling in love with you," she whispered to Thumbelina excitedly.

The fieldmouse was even more sure that she was right when Mr Mole invited them both to visit him in his splendid underground mansion.

"I have dug a tunnel from your house to mine," Mr Mole informed them, "so you may come and see me in comfort. Only please close your eyes when you are halfway down the passage, for I am afraid that a dead swallow is lying there."

Thumbelina wasn't at all revolted when she came across the dead bird on her first trip to Mr Mole's house. Instead, she felt pity for the poor thing, lying all stiff and still on the cold earth. While the fieldmouse ran on eagerly ahead, Thumbelina bent down and stroked the bird's feathers. "Goodbye, sweet swallow," she murmured, and she laid her head on the bird's soft breast. DUP! DUP! DUP! Thumbelina heard the swallow's heart beating – only very faintly, but Thumbelina knew that the bird was still just alive!

From then on, Thumbelina found as many excuses as possible to creep away from the fieldmouse and into the tunnel to care for the swallow.

Gradually the swallow began to recover. By the time the weather had begun to grow warmer, the swallow was well enough to stand and hop about. On the first day of spring, the swallow was totally better.

"One day, I will repay you," he twittered as he hopped up the passageway and soared off into the sky.

It was then that the fieldmouse announced to Thumbelina that she had arranged for her to be married to Mr Mole. "He is very wealthy and will take good care of you," the fieldmouse beamed.

But Thumbelina was horrified. "I cannot live my life underground!" she cried, and ran sobbing out into the fields. Just then, Thumbelina heard a familiar twittering above her head. She looked up and saw her friend the swallow swooping down towards her. "Come away with me," cried the swallow, "I know a place where you will be happy."

Joyfully, Thumbelina jumped onto his back.

The swallow flew off with Thumbelina to a land where the weather was always sunny, and where in every flower there lived a tiny person just like Thumbelina. Thumbelina was very happy in her new home. She even married a handsome prince who lived in a rosebud and who was extremely glad that she had never become Mrs Mole!

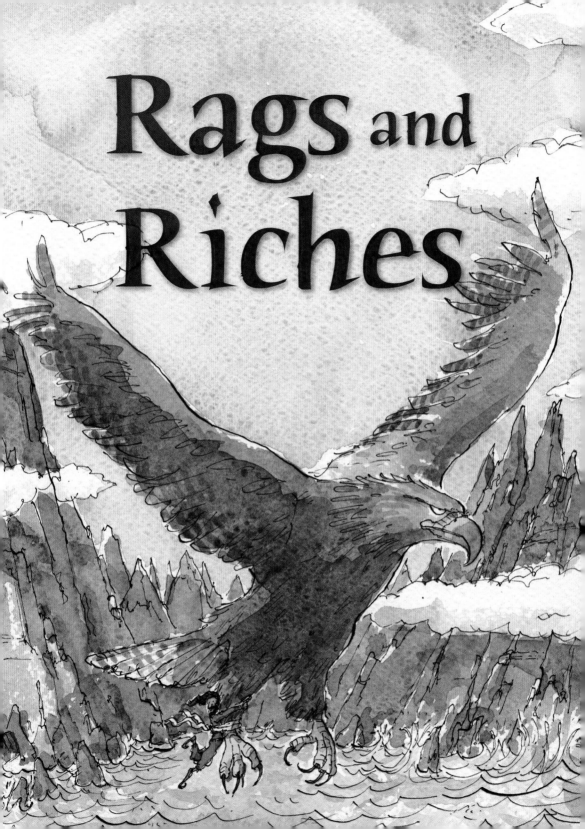

Rags and Riches

The Giant Roc

From *The Second Voyage of Sinbad the Sailor*

I DESIGNED, AFTER MY FIRST VOYAGE, to spend the rest of my days at Bagdad, but it was not long ere I grew weary of an indolent life, and I put to sea a second time, with merchants of known probity. We embarked on board a good ship, and, after recommending ourselves to God, set sail. We traded from island to island, and exchanged commodities with great profit. One day we landed on an island covered with several sorts of fruit trees, but we could see neither man nor animal. We walked in the meadows, along the streams that watered them. While some diverted themselves with gathering flowers, and others fruits, I took my wine and provisions, and sat down near a stream betwixt two high trees, which formed a thick shade. I made a good meal, and afterward fell asleep. I cannot tell how long I slept, but when I awoke the ship was gone.

In this sad condition I was ready to die with grief. I cried out in agony, beat my head and breast, and threw myself upon the ground, where I lay some time in despair. I upbraided myself a hundred times for not being content with the produce of my first voyage, that might have sufficed me all my life. But all this was in vain, and my repentance came too late. At last I resigned myself to the will of God. Not knowing what to do, I climbed to the top of a lofty tree, from whence I looked about on all sides, to see if I could discover anything that could give me hope. When I gazed toward the sea I could see nothing but sky and water; but looking over the land, I beheld something white; and coming down, I took what provision I had left and went toward it, the distance being so great that I could not distinguish what it was.

As I approached, I thought it to be a white dome, of a prodigious height and extent; and when I came up to it, I touched it, and found it to be very smooth. I went round to see if it was open on any side, but saw it was not, and that there was no climbing up to the top, as it

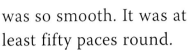

was so smooth. It was at least fifty paces round.

By this time the sun was about to set, and all of a sudden the sky became as dark as if it had been covered with a thick cloud. I was much astonished at this sudden darkness, but much more when I found it was occasioned by a bird of a monstrous size, that came flying toward me. I remembered that I had often heard mariners speak of a miraculous bird called the roc, and conceived that the great dome which I so much admired must be its egg. In short, the bird alighted, and sat over the egg. As I perceived her coming, I crept close to the egg, so that I had before me one of the legs of the bird, which

was as big as the trunk of a tree. I tied myself strongly to it with my turban, in hopes that the roc next morning would carry me with her out of this desert island. After having passed the night in this condition, the bird flew away as soon as it was daylight, and carried me so high that I could not discern the earth; she afterward descended with so much rapidity that I lost my senses. But when I found myself on the ground, I speedily untied the knot, and had scarcely done so, when the roc, having taken up a serpent of a monstrous length in her bill, flew away.

The spot where it left me was encompassed on all sides by mountains, that seemed to reach above the

clouds, and so steep that there was no possibility of getting out of the valley. This was a new perplexity; so that when I compared this place with the desert island from which the roc had brought me, I found that I had gained nothing by the change.

As I walked through this valley, I perceived it was strewn with diamonds, some of which were of surprising bigness. I took pleasure in looking upon them; but shortly I saw at a distance such objects as greatly diminished my satisfaction, and which I could not view without terror, namely, a great number of serpents, so monstrous that the least of them was capable of swallowing an elephant. They retired in the daytime to their dens, where they hid themselves from the roc, their enemy, and came out only in the night.

I spent the day in walking about in the valley, resting myself at times in such places as I thought most convenient. When night came on I went into a cave, where I thought I might repose in safety. I secured the entrance, which was low and narrow, with a great stone, to preserve me from the serpents; but not so far as to exclude the light. I supped on part of my provisions, but the serpents, which began hissing round me, put me into such extreme fear that I did not sleep. When day appeared the serpents retired, and I came out of the cave, trembling. I can justly say that I walked upon diamonds without feeling any inclination to touch them. At last I sat down, and notwithstanding my apprehensions, not having closed my eyes during the night, fell asleep, after having eaten a little more of my provisions. But I had scarcely shut my eyes when something that fell by me with a great noise awakened me. This was a large piece of raw meat; and at the same time I saw several others fall down from the rocks in different places.

I had always regarded as fabulous what I had heard sailors and others relate of the valley of diamonds, and of the stratagems employed by merchants to obtain jewels from thence; but now I found that they had stated nothing but the truth. For the fact is, that the merchants come to the neighbourhood of this valley, when the eagles have young ones, and throwing great joints of meat into the valley, the diamonds, upon whose points they fall, stick to them; the eagles, which are stronger in this country than anywhere else, pounce with great force upon those pieces of meat, and carry them to their nests on the precipices of the rocks to feed their young: the

merchants at this time run to their nests, disturb and drive off the eagles by their shouts, and take away the diamonds that stick to the meat.

I perceived in this device the means of my deliverance.

Having collected together the largest diamonds I could find, and put them into the leather bag in which I used to carry my provisions, I took the largest of the pieces of meat, tied it close round me with the cloth of my turban, and then laid myself upon the ground, with my face downward, the bag of diamonds being made fast to my girdle.

I had scarcely placed myself in this posture when one of the eagles, having taken me up with the piece of meat to which I was fastened, carried me to his nest on the top of the mountain. The merchants immediately began their shouting to frighten the eagles; and when they had obliged them to quit their prey, one of them came to the nest where I was. He was much alarmed when he saw me; but recovering himself, instead of inquiring how I came thither, began to quarrel with me, and asked why I stole his goods.

"Do not be uneasy; I have diamonds enough for you and myself, more than all the other merchants together." I had scarcely done speaking, when the other merchants came crowding about us, much astonished to see me; but they were much more surprised when I told them my story.

They conducted me to their encampment; and there, having opened my bag, they were surprised at the largeness of my diamonds, and confessed that they had never seen any of such size and perfection. I prayed the merchant who owned the nest to which I had been carried (for every merchant had his own) to take as many for his share as he pleased. He contented himself with one, and that, too, the least of them.

The merchants had thrown their pieces of meat into the valley for several days; and each of them being satisfied with the diamonds that had fallen to his lot, we left the place the next morning, and travelled near high mountains.

I pass over many things peculiar to this island, lest I should weary you. Here I exchanged some of my diamonds for merchandise. From hence we went to other islands, and at last, having touched at several trading towns of the continent, we landed at Bussorah, from whence I proceeded to Bagdad. There I immediately gave large presents to the poor, and lived honorably upon the vast riches I had brought, and gained with so much fatigue.

The Three Heads of the Well

By Flora Annie Steel

ONCE UPON A TIME there reigned a king in Colchester who was valiant, strong, wise, and famous throughout the land as a good ruler. But in the midst of his glory his dear queen died, leaving him with a daughter to look after. This maiden was renowned for her beauty, kindness and grace.

Now strange things happen – the king of Colchester heard of a lady who had immense riches, and had a mind to marry her, although she was old, ugly, hook-nosed, and ill-tempered. Furthermore, she possessed a daughter as ugly as herself. None could give the reason why, but only a few weeks after the death of his dear queen, the king married her with great pomp and festivities. Now the first thing she did was to poison the king's mind against his daughter, of whom, the ugly queen and her ugly daughter were jealous.

Now when the young princess found that even her father had turned against her, she grew weary of court life, and longed to get away from it. So, one day, she went down on her knees, and begged and prayed for the king to give her some help, and let her go out into the world to seek her fortune. To this the king agreed, and the ugly queen only gave her a canvas bag of brown bread and hard cheese, with a bottle of small-beer.

Though this was but a pitiful dowry for a king's daughter, the princess was too proud to complain, so she took it and set off on her journey.

At last she came to a cave at the mouth of which, on a stone, sat an old, old man with a white beard.

"Good day, fair damsel," he said, "where are you going?"

"Reverend father," replied she, "I'm going to seek my fortune."

"And what have you a dowry, fair damsel," said he, "in your bag and bottle?"

"Bread and cheese and small-beer, father," said she, smiling. "Will it please you to partake of either?"

"With all my heart," said he, and when she pulled out her provisions he ate them nearly all. But once again she made no complaint.

Now when he had finished he gave her many thanks, and said, "For your beauty, and your kindness, and your grace, take this wand. There is a thick thorny hedge before you that seems impassable. But strike it thrice with this wand, saying each time, 'Please, hedge, let me through,' and it will open a pathway for you. Then, when you come to a well, sit down, do not be surprised at anything you may see, but, whatever you are asked to do, please do!"

So she went on her way. After a while she came to a high, thick thorny hedge, but when she struck it three times with the wand, saying, "Please, hedge, let me through," it opened a wide pathway for her. So she came to the well, on the brink of which she sat down, and no sooner had she done so, than a golden head without any body came up through the water, singing as it came:

"Wash me and comb me, lay me on a bank to dry
Softly and prettily to watch the passers-by."

"Certainly," she said, pulling out her silver comb. Then, placing the head on her lap, she began to comb the golden hair. When she had combed it, she lifted the golden head softly, and laid it on a primrose bank to dry. No sooner had she done this than another golden head appeared, singing as it came:

"Wash me and comb me, lay me on a bank to dry
Softly and prettily to watch the passers-by."

"Certainly," said she, and after combing the golden hair, placed the golden head softly on the primrose bank, beside the first one.

Then came a third head out of the well, and it said the same thing:

"Wash me and comb me, lay me on a bank to dry
Softly and prettily to watch the passers-by."

"With all my heart," said she graciously, and after taking the head on her lap, and combing its golden hair with her silver comb, there were the three golden heads in a row on the primrose bank. She sat down to rest and cheerfully ate and drank the meagre portion

of the brown bread, hard cheese, and small-beer that the old man had left to her, for, though she was a king's daughter, she was too proud to complain.

Then the first head spoke. "What shall we 'weird' for this damsel who has been so gracious? I 'weird' her to be so beautiful that she shall charm every one she meets."

"And I," said the second head, "'weird' her a voice that shall exceed the nightingale's in sweetness."

"And I," said the third head, "'weird' her to be so fortunate that she shall marry the greatest king alive."

"Thank you with all my heart," said she, "but don't you think I had better put you back in the well before I go on? Remember you are golden, and the passers-by might steal you."

To this they agreed, so she put them back. And when they had thanked her for her kind thought and said goodbye, she went on her journey.

Now she had not travelled far before she came to a forest where the king of the country was hunting with his nobles. The king caught sight of her, and drew up his horse, amazed at her beauty. He jumped from his horse and falling on his knee begged and prayed her to marry him without delay. And he begged and prayed so well that at last she consented.

So, they returned to his palace, where the wedding festivities took place with all possible pomp and merriment. Then, ordering out the royal chariot, the happy pair departed to pay the king of Colchester a bridal visit. You may imagine the surprise and delight with which, after so short an absence, the people of Colchester saw their beloved, beautiful, kind and gracious princess return in a chariot as the bride of the most powerful king in the world. The bells rang out, flags flew, drums beat, the people cheered, and all was gladness, save for the ugly queen and her ugly daughter, who were ready to burst with envy, for the despised maiden was now above them both, and went before them at every court ceremony.

So, after the visit was ended, and the young king and his bride had gone back to their own country to live happily ever after, the ugly, ill-natured princess said to her mother, the ugly queen:

"I also will go into the world and seek my fortune. If that drab of a girl with her mincing ways got so much, what may I not get?"

So her mother agreed, and furnished her forth with silken dresses and furs, and gave her as provisions sugar, almonds, and sweetmeats of every variety, besides a large flagon of Malaga wine. Altogether a right royal dowry fit for a princess.

Armed with her plentiful package the ugly princess set forth on her journey, following the same road as her stepsister. Thus she soon came upon the same old man with a white beard, who was seated on a stone by the mouth of a cave.

"Good day" said he. "Where are you going?"

"What's that to you, old man?" she said rudely.

"And what have you for a dowry in bag and bottle?" he asked quietly.

"Good things with which you shall not be troubled," she answered pertly.

"Will you not spare an old man something to eat?" he said.

Then she laughed. "Not a bite, not a sup, lest they should choke you, though that would be small matter to me," she replied, with a toss of her head.

"Then ill luck go with you," remarked the old man as he rose and went into the cave.

So she went on her way, and after a time came to the thick, thorny hedge, and seeing what she thought was a gap in it, she tried to pass through, but no sooner had she got well into the middle of the hedge than the thorns closed in around her so that she was all scratched and torn before she won her way. Thus, streaming with blood, she went on to the well, and seeing water, sat on the brink intending to cleanse herself. But just as she dipped her hands, up came a golden head singing as it came:

"Wash me and comb me, lay me on the bank to dry
  Softly and prettily to watch the passers-by."

"A likely story," said she. "I'm going to wash myself, thank you very much." And with that she gave the head such a bang with her bottle that it bobbed below the water. But it came up again, and so did a second head, singing as it came:

"Wash me and comb me, lay me on the bank to dry
  Softly and prettily to watch the passers-by."

"Not I," scoffed she. "I'm going to wash my hands

and face and have my dinner." So she gave the second
head a cruel bang with the bottle, and both heads
ducked down in the water.

But when they came up again all draggled and
dripping, the third head came also, singing as it came:

"Wash me and comb me, lay me on the bank to dry
  Softly and prettily to watch the passers-by."

By this time the ugly princess had cleansed herself,
and, seated on the primrose bank, had her mouth full
of sugar and almonds.

"Not I," said she as well as she could. "I'm not a
washerwoman nor a barber.
So take that for your
washing and combing."

And with that, she
finished the wine, carelessly
flung the empty bottle at
the three heads floating in
the well, and carried on
greedily eating her sweets.

But this time the heads
didn't duck. They looked at
each other and said, "How
shall we 'weird' this rude girl
for her bad manners?"

"I 'weird' that to her ugliness shall be added blotches on her face," said the first head.

"And I 'weird' that she shall forever be hoarse as a crow and speak as if she had her mouth full," said the second head.

"And I 'weird' that she shall be glad to marry a cobbler," said the third head.

Then the three heads sank into the well and were no more seen, and the ugly princess went on her way. But, lo and behold! When she came to a town, the children ran from her ugly blotched face screaming with fright.

Now in the town there happened to be a cobbler who seeing the miserable, ugly princess in great distress craftily said that if she would take him for a husband he would undertake to cure her.

"Anything! Anything!" sobbed the princess.

So they were married, and the cobbler straightway set off with his bride to visit the king of Colchester. Instead of cheering, the people burst into guffaws at the cobbler in leather, and his wife in silks and satins.

As for the ugly queen, she was so enraged that she went mad with anger, and left the country. Whereupon the king, really pleased at getting rid of her so soon, gave the cobbler one hundred pounds and bade him go about his business with his ugly bride!

The Curse of Andvari's Ring

A Norse myth

IT OFTEN PLEASED ODIN, the chief of the gods, to
disguise himself with a broad-brimmed hat and
travelling cloak, and go wandering through Midgard to
see all that was happening in the world of men. For
one such journey, Odin was accompanied by his
brother, Hoenir, and the troublemaker Loki. The three
were strolling along, following the course of the river
when they saw an otter basking in
the sun, eating salmon. The quick

and cunning Loki instantly snatched up a stone and threw it at the otter, aiming perfectly and knocking it dead. "Aha!" he cried, triumphantly. "Two prizes with a single shot – and just in time for lunch!"

It wasn't long before Loki was skinning the otter, while Hoenir built a fire and Odin roasted the salmon. Before the gods had tasted even a morsel of their meal, a very small, but very furious, man appeared from over a craggy ledge and strode towards them. As he approached, he drew his gleaming sword and brandished it threateningly. "I am Hreidmar, King of the Dwarves, and I demand vengeance!" he roared, purple-faced with rage.

The gods leapt to their feet at once in alarm. "Vengeance?" Hoenir protested, "but we have done nothing to offend you."

"Nothing!" spat the king. "Nothing! You call slaughtering one of my sons nothing!" And Hreidmar pointed to the otter skin dangling from Loki's hand.

The gods looked at each other in horror. They realized at once what had happened. Dwarves knew very strong magic and some of them could even change shape and take on animal form. The gods thought that Loki had killed an otter, but in fact it was a dwarf prince.

Two burly dwarves came running up behind Hreidmar, one clutching a stone axe and the other with a dagger.

"My remaining sons, Fafnir and Regin, will have justice!" Hreidmar thundered, as the men advanced.

"You will forfeit a life for the life you have taken!" one bellowed.

"Who will pay the price for murdering our brother?" the other raged, edging closer.

"Wait a moment!" cried Odin, thinking fast. "You will gain nothing from killing any of us. However, you will profit well if we pay you compensation instead. It is true that we have grievously wronged you. Now tell us, what is the price of making amends?"

Hreidmar lifted his hand, halting Fafnir and Regin in their tracks. The dwarves turned to each other and consulted for a minute or two. With a greedy smile, Hreidmar nodded. "So be it. You shall bring enough gold to fill the skin of the otter that was once my beloved son, and to cover it entirely. Choose one of you to go and fetch the gold. The other two must remain here as our hostages." Hreidmar grinned as the otter skin grew larger and larger before their very eyes.

"I will go," Loki volunteered, relishing the chance to outdo the tricksters. "I know where there is a trove of

treasure so large, it should easily satisfy your needs –
although it will take all the cunning I possess if I am to
lay my hands on it." Without delay, he sped off, leaving
Odin and Hoenir at the mercy of the dwarves.

Loki knew that for his plan to work, he would have
to beg for the help of the giants – sworn enemies of
the gods. He needed a favour from Ran, the cold-
hearted wife of the giant who ruled the sea. Loki
wanted to borrow Ran's enchanted fishing net, which
she used to catch shipwrecked sailors and drown them
in the deeps. Fortunately, only because Loki was half-
giant, Ran grudgingly agreed.

Next, Loki journeyed to a place where a mighty
waterfall thundered over a towering cliff into a

plunging pool – the home of another dwarf, Andvari. Although Loki had had enough dealings with dwarves to last him a lifetime, he knew of no one else to turn to. Andvari was believed to have a secret treasure trove, as large as the highest mountain. Keeping his fingers crossed, Loki just hoped that the rumours were true...

Loki settled himself by the side of the pool and used his power to blend his body into the landscape. An unseeing mouse ran over his foot. An unnoticing butterfly came and settled on his nose. But not once did Loki stir. He just sat... and watched... and waited. At last he saw a trout that was bigger and shinier than all the other fish. Swifter than a darting kingfisher, he cast Ran's net, ensnared the trout, and drew it spluttering and flapping onto the bank. Grabbing it, Loki squeezed as hard as he could, until suddenly the trout changed shape – into the dwarf, Andvari!

"Stop! Stop!" Andvari gasped. "Tell me what you want and stop squashing the life out of me!"

Easing his grip a little, Loki made his demands. The dwarf was outraged, but imprisoned in Loki's clutches, he had no choice. Fuming, he directed Loki up a secret pathway behind the waterfall, to a cave that was filled from floor to ceiling with an incredible

sight – gold. Gold cups, gold crowns, gold coins, gold necklaces, gold rings, gold bracelets, gold earrings, gold weapons, gold belts, gold brooches – a million and one golden objects glistened and gleamed in the darkness. With his eyes wide, Loki said "I need it all – and I mean all."

Sulking, Andvari helped Loki to pack up all his treasure, until there was no sign that the gold had ever been there. "That's it," Andvari sighed, mournfully. "I've given you everything."

"Not quite everything," corrected Loki, taking a ring from Andvari's little finger. "Please, I've given you all the gold I have. Allow me to keep this one small ring."

"I told you," Loki insisted firmly, "I need it all."

"Then have it!" cried the devastated dwarf. "And may a curse of sorrow be on it for ever more! May wretchedness, misery and death come to whoever wears it!" Andvari would have continued, but Loki and the treasure were already gone.

When Odin and Hoenir saw Loki returning with the enormous hoard of gold, they were mightily relieved. Eagerly, King Hreidmar and his sons watched as the three gods stuffed the otter skin until it was almost bursting, and carefully covered it, bit by bit. At last, all the gold was used up and the gods were done – or so they thought.

"Not so fast!" cried Hreidmar. "There is one hair on the otter's nose still showing. Either give up more gold or give up your lives!"

Luckily, Loki remembered Andvari's ring. "Take this with my pleasure," he smirked, throwing the band of bad luck onto the pile. And the gods gladly left the dwarves admiring their newfound wealth.

This is only the start of the curse of the ring. It continued to pass from hand to hand, bringing sorrow, wretchedness, misery and death to whoever wore it – just as Andvari had desired.

The Two Sisters

By Flora Annie Steel

ONCE UPON A TIME there were two sisters who were as like each other as two peas in a pod, but one was good, and the other was bad-tempered. Now their father had no work for them, so the girls began to think of going to be servants somewhere else.

"I will go first and see what I can make of it," said the younger sister, ever so cheerfully, "then you, sis, can follow if I have good luck."

So she packed up a bundle, said goodbye, and started to find a place, but no one in the town wanted a girl, so she went farther afield into the country. And as she journeyed she came upon an oven. In the oven, a lot of loaves were baking.

Now as she passed, the loaves cried out with one voice, "Little girl! Little girl! Take us out! Take us out! Please take us out! We have been baking for seven years, and no one has come to take us out. Do take us out or we shall soon be burnt! Seven years!"

Then, being a kind, obliging little girl, she stopped, put down her bundle, took out the bread from the oven, and went on her way saying, "You will be more comfortable now."

After a time she came to a cow lowing beside an empty pail, and the cow said to her, "Little girl! Little girl! Milk me! Milk me! Please milk me! Seven years have I been waiting, but no one has come to milk me! Seven years!"

So the kind girl stopped, put down her bundle, milked the cow into the pail, and went on her way saying, "Now you will be more comfortable."

By and by she came to an apple tree so laden with fruit that its branches were nigh to break, and the apple tree called to her:

"Little girl! Little girl! Shake my branches. Please shake my branches. The fruit is so heavy I can't stand straight!"

Then the kind girl stopped, put down her bundle,

and shook the branches so that the apples fell off, and the tree could stand straight. Then she went on her way saying, "You will be more comfortable now."

So she journeyed on till she came to a house where an old witch lived. Now this witch wanted a maid, and promised good wages. Therefore the girl agreed to stop with her and try how she liked service. She had to sweep the floor, keep the house clean and tidy, the fire bright and cheery. But there was one thing the witch said she must never do, and that was look up the chimney.

"If you do," said the witch, "something will fall down on you, and you will come to a bad end."

Well, the girl swept and dusted and made up the fire, but never a penny of wages did she see. Now the girl wanted to go home as she did not like witch service, for the witch used to have boiled babies for supper and bury the bones under some stones in the garden. But she did not like to go home penniless, so she stayed on, sweeping, and dusting and doing her work, just as if she was pleased.

Then one day, as she was sweeping up the hearth, down tumbled some soot, and, without remembering she was forbidden to look up the chimney, she looked up to see where the soot came from. And, lo and behold – a big bag of gold fell plump into her lap.

Now the witch happened to be out on one of her witch errands, so the girl thought it a fine opportunity to be off home.

So she kilted up her petticoats and started to run home but she had only gone a little way when she heard the witch coming after her on her broomstick. Now the apple tree she had helped to stand straight happened to be quite close, so she ran to it and cried,

"Apple tree! Apple tree, hide me
  So the old witch can't find me,
  For if she does she'll pick my bones,
  And bury me under the garden stones."

Then the apple tree said, "Of course I will. You helped me to stand straight, and one good turn deserves another."

So the apple tree hid her finely in its green branches, and when the witch flew past saying,

"O Tree of mine! Tree of mine!
  Have you seen my naughty little maid
  With a willy willy wag and a great big bag,
  She's stolen my money – all I had?"

The apple tree answered:

"No, Mother dear,
 Not for seven year!"

So the witch flew on the wrong way, and the girl got down, thanked the tree politely, and started again. But just as she got to where the cow was standing beside the pail, she heard the witch coming again, so she ran to the cow and cried,

"Cow! Cow, please hide me
 So the witch can't find me,
 If she does she'll pick my bones,
 And bury me under the garden stones!"

"Certainly I will," answered the cow. "Didn't you milk me and make me comfortable? Hide yourself behind me and you'll be quite safe."
 And when the witch flew by and called to the cow,

"O Cow of mine! Cow of mine!
 Have you seen my naughty little maid
 With a willy willy wag and a great big bag,
 Who stole my money – all I had?"

The cow just said politely:

"No, Mother dear,
 Not for seven year!"

Then the old witch went on in the wrong direction, and the girl started fresh on her way home, but just as

she got to where the oven stood, she heard that horrid old witch coming behind her again, so she ran as fast as she could to the oven and cried,
   "O Oven! Oven! hide me
    So as the witch can't find me,
    For if she does she'll pick my bones,
    And bury them under the garden stones."

Then the oven said, "I am afraid there is no room for you, as another batch of bread is baking, but there is the baker – ask him."

So she asked the baker, and he said, "Of course I will. You saved my last batch from being burnt, so run into the bakehouse, you will be quite safe there, and I will settle the witch for you."

So she hid in the bakehouse, only just in time, for there was the old witch calling angrily,

"O Man of mine! Man of mine!
  Have you seen my naughty little maid
  With a willy willy wag and a great big bag,
  Who's stole my money – all I had?"

Then the baker replied, "Look in the oven. She may be there."

And the witch alighted from her broomstick and peered into the oven, but she could see no one.

"Creep in and look in the farthest corner," said the baker slyly, and the witch crept in. Bang! He shut the door in her face, and there she was roasting. And when she came out with the bread she was all crisp and brown, and had to go home as best she could and put cold cream all over her!

But the kind, obliging little girl got safe home with her bag of money.

Now the ill-tempered elder sister was very jealous of this good luck, and determined to get a bag of gold for herself. So she in her turn packed up a bundle and started to seek service by the same road. But when she came to the oven, and the loaves begged her to take them out because they had been baking seven years and were nigh to burning, she tossed her head and said, "A likely story indeed, that I should burn my fingers to save your crusts. No, thank you!"

And with that she went on till she came across the cow standing waiting to be milked beside the pail. But when the cow said, "Little girl! Little girl! Milk me! Please milk me, I've waited seven years to be milked."

She only laughed and replied, "You may wait another seven years for all I care. I'm not your dairymaid!"

And with that she went on till she came to the apple tree, all overburdened by its fruit. But when it begged her to shake its branches, she only giggled, and plucking one ripe apple, said, "One is enough for me, you can keep the rest yourself." And with that she went on munching the apple, till she came to the witch's house.

Now the witch, though she had got over being crisp and brown from the oven, was dreadfully angry with all little maids, and made up her mind this one should not trick her. So for a long time she never went out of the house, thus the ill-tempered sister never had a chance of looking up the chimney, as she had meant to do at once. And she had to dust and clean and brush and sweep ever so hard, until she was quite tired out.

But one day, when the witch went into the garden to bury her bones, she seized the moment, looked up the chimney, and, sure enough, a bag of gold fell plump into her lap!

Well! She was off with it in a moment, and ran and ran till she came to the apple tree, when she heard the witch behind her. So she cried as her sister had done,

"Apple tree! Apple tree, hide me
So the old witch can't find me,
For if she does she'll break my bones,
Or bury me under the garden stones."

But the apple tree said, "No room here! I've too many apples." So she had to run on, and when the witch on her broomstick came flying by and called,

"O Tree of mine! Tree of mine!
  Have you seen a naughty little maid
  With a willy willy wag and a great big bag,
  Who's stolen my money – all I had?"

The apple tree replied, "Yes, Mother dear, she's gone down there."

Then the witch went after her, caught her, gave her a thorough good beating, took the bag of money away from her, and sent her home without a penny payment for all her dusting, sweeping, brushing and cleaning.

The Enchanted Head

By Andrew Lang

ONCE UPON A TIME an old woman lived in a small cottage near the sea with her two daughters. They were very poor, and the girls seldom left the house, as they worked all day long making veils for the ladies to wear over their faces, and every morning, when the veils were finished, the mother took them over the bridge and sold them in the city. Then she bought the food that they needed for the day, and returned home to do her share of veil-making.

One morning the old woman rose even earlier than usual, and set off for the city with her wares. She was just crossing the bridge when, suddenly, she knocked against a human head, which she had never seen there before. The woman started back in horror, but what was her surprise when the head spoke, exactly as if it had a body joined on to it.

"Take me with you, good mother!" said the head imploringly. "Take me with you back to your house."

At the sound of these words the poor woman nearly went mad with terror. She turned and ran back as fast as she could, not knowing that the head was rolling after her. But when she reached her own door it bounded in before her, and stopped in front of the fire, begging and praying to be allowed to stay.

All that day there was no food in the house, for the veils had not been sold, and they had no money to buy anything with. So they all sat silent, inwardly cursing the head that was the cause of their misfortunes.

When evening came, and there was no sign of supper, the head spoke, for the first time that day:

"Good mother, does no one ever eat here?"

"No. We have no money to buy any food. Every morning I go into the city to sell my veils, and with the few shillings I get for them I buy all we want. Today I did not cross the bridge, so I had nothing for food."

"Then I am the cause of your having gone hungry all day?" asked the head.

"Yes, you are," answered the old woman.

"Well, then, I will give you money. In an hour, as the clock strikes twelve, you must be on the bridge at the place where you met me. When you get there call out 'Ahmed!' three times, as loud as you can. Then a man will appear, and you must say to him: 'The head, your master, desires you to open the trunk, and to give me the green purse which you will find in it.'"

"Very well, I will set off at once for the bridge." And wrapping her veil round her she went out. Midnight was striking as she reached the spot.

"Ahmed! Ahmed! Ahmed!" she cried, and a huge man, as tall as a giant, stood on the bridge before her.

"What do you want?" he asked.

"The head, your master, desires you to open the trunk and to give me the green purse that you will find in it."

"I will be back in a moment, good mother," said he. And three minutes later he placed a purse full of sequins in the old woman's hand. No one can imagine the joy of the whole family at the sight of all this wealth. The tiny, tumbledown cottage was rebuilt, the girls had new dresses, and their mother ceased selling veils. It was such a new

thing to them to have money to spend, that they were not as careful as they might have been, and by-and-by there was not a single coin left in the purse. When this happened their hearts sank within them, and their faces fell.

"Have you spent your fortune?" asked the head from its corner, when it saw how sad they looked. "Well, then, go at midnight, good mother, to the bridge, and call out 'Mahomet!' three times, as loud as you can. A man will appear in answer, and you must tell him to open the trunk, and to give you the red purse that he will find there."

The old woman did not need telling twice, but set off at once for the bridge.

"Mahomet! Mahomet! Mahomet!" cried she, with all her might, and in an instant a man, still larger than the last, stood before her.

"What do you want?" asked he.

"The head, your master, bids you open the trunk, and to give me the red purse that you will find in it."

"Very well, good mother, I will do so," answered the man, and, the moment after he had vanished, he reappeared with the purse in his hand.

This time the money seemed so endless that the old woman built herself a new house, and filled it with the

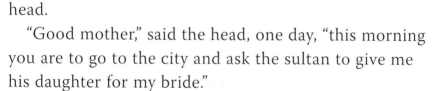

most beautiful things that were to be found in the shops. Her daughters were always wrapped in veils that looked as if they were woven out of sunbeams, and their dresses shone with precious stones. The neighbours wondered where all this sudden wealth had sprung from, but nobody knew about the head.

"Good mother," said the head, one day, "this morning you are to go to the city and ask the sultan to give me his daughter for my bride."

"Do what?" asked the old woman in amazement. "How can I tell the sultan that a head without a body wishes to become his son-in-law? They will think that I am mad, and I shall be laughed from the palace and stoned by the children."

"Do as I bid you," replied the head, "it is my will."

The old woman was afraid to say anything more,

and, putting on her richest clothes, started for the palace. The sultan granted her an audience at once, and, in a trembling voice, she made her request.

"Are you mad, old woman?" said the sultan, staring at her in amazement.

"The wooer is powerful, oh sultan, and nothing is impossible to him."

"Is that true?"

"It is, oh sultan, I swear it," she answered.

"Then let him show his power by doing three things, and I will give him my daughter."

"Command, oh gracious prince," said she.

"Do you see that hill in front of the palace?" asked the sultan.

"I see it," answered she.

"Well, in forty days the man who has sent you must make that hill vanish, and plant a beautiful garden in its place. That is the first thing. Now go, and tell him what I say."

So the old woman returned and told the head the sultan's first condition.

"It is well," he replied, and said no more about it.

For thirty-nine days the head remained in his favourite corner. The old woman thought that the task set before him was beyond his powers, and that no more would be heard about the sultan's daughter. But on the thirty-ninth evening after her visit to the palace, the head suddenly spoke.

"Good mother," he said, "you must go tonight to the bridge, and when you are there cry 'Ali! Ali! Ali!' as loud as you can. A man will appear before you, and you will tell him that he is to level the hill, and to make, in its place, the most beautiful garden that ever was seen."

"I will go at once," answered she.

It did not take her long to reach the bridge that led to the city, and she took up her position on the spot where she had first seen the head, and called loudly "Ali! Ali! Ali." In an instant a man appeared before her, of such a huge size that the old woman was half frightened, but his voice was mild and gentle as he said, "What is it that you want?"

"Your master bids you level the hill that stands in front of the sultan's palace and in its place to make the most beautiful garden in the world."

"Tell my master he shall be obeyed," replied Ali, "it shall be done this moment." And the old woman went home and gave Ali's message to the head.

Meanwhile the sultan was in his palace waiting till the fortieth day should dawn, wondering that not one spadeful of earth should have been dug out of the hill.

"If that old woman has been playing me a trick," thought he, "I will hang her! And I will put up a gallows tomorrow on the hill itself."

But when tomorrow came there was no hill – when the sultan opened his eyes he could not imagine why the room was so much lighter than usual, or why a sweet smell of flowers had filled the air.

"Can there be a fire?" he said to himself, "the sun never came in at this window before. I must get up and see." So he rose and looked out, and underneath him flowers from every part of the world were blooming, and creepers of every colour hung in chains.

Then he remembered. "Certainly that old woman's son is a clever magician!" cried he, "I never met anyone as clever as that. What shall I give him to do next? Let me think. Ah! I know." And he sent for the old woman, who was waiting below.

"Your son has carried out my wishes very nicely," he said. "The garden is larger and better than that of any other king. But when I walk across it I shall need some place to rest on the other side. In forty days he must build me a palace, in which every room shall be filled with different furniture from a different country, and each more magnificent than any room ever seen."

'Oh! He will never be able to do that,' thought she, 'it is much more difficult than the hill.' And she walked home slowly, with her head bent.

"Well, what am I to do next?" asked the head cheerfully. And the old woman told her story.

"Dear me! Is that all? Why it is child's play," answered the head, and troubled no more about the palace for thirty-nine days. Then he told the old woman to go to the bridge and call for Hassan.

"What do you want, old woman?" asked Hassan, when he appeared, for he was not as polite as the others had been.

"Your master commands you to build the most magnificent palace that ever was seen," she replied, "and you are to place it on the borders of the new garden."

"He shall be obeyed," answered Hassan. And when the sultan woke he saw, in the distance, a palace built of soft blue marble, with slender pillars of pure gold.

"That old woman's son is certainly powerful," he cried, "what shall I bid him do now?" And after thinking for some time he sent for the old woman, who was expecting the summons.

"The garden is wonderful, and the palace the finest in the world," said he. "Let your son fill it with forty servants whose beauty shall be unequalled."

This time the king thought he had invented something totally impossible. Thirty-nine days passed, and at midnight on the night of the last the old woman was standing on the bridge.

"Bekir! Bekir! Bekir!" cried she. And a man appeared, and inquired what she wanted.

"The head, your master, bids you find forty servants of unequalled beauty and place them in the sultan's palace on the other side of the garden."

And when, on the morning of the fortieth day, the sultan went to the blue palace, and was received by the forty servants, he nearly lost his wits from surprise.

"I will give my daughter to the old woman's son," thought he. "If I were to search all the world through I could never find a more powerful son-in-law."

And when the old woman entered, he informed her that he was ready to fulfil his promise, and she was to bid her son appear at the palace without delay.

This command did not at all please the old woman, though she made no objections to the sultan.

"All has gone well so far," she grumbled, when she told her story to the head, "but what do you suppose the sultan will say, when he sees you?"

"Never mind what he will say! Put me on a silver dish and carry me to the palace."

So it was done, though the old woman's heart beat as she laid down the dish with the head upon it.

At the sight before him the king flew into a rage.

"I will never marry my daughter to such a monster," he cried. But the princess said, "You have given your word, my father, and you cannot break it," said she.

"But, my child, it is impossible for you to marry such a being," exclaimed the sultan.

"Yes, I will marry him. He has a beautiful head, and I love him already."

So the marriage was celebrated. When the merry-making was done, and the young couple were alone, the head suddenly disappeared, or, rather, a body was added to it, and one of the handsomest young men that ever was seen stood before the princess.

"A wicked fairy enchanted me at birth," he said, "and for the rest of the world I must always be a head only. But for you, and you only, I am a man."

Love and Friendship

The Magic Tinderbox

Retold from the original tale by Hans Christian Andersen

A SOLDIER CAME marching down the road – left, right! left, right! left, right! "Good morning, sir," croaked an ugly witch sitting at the roadside. "If you do as I say, I will make you very rich. You see that huge tree there –" the witch pointed over to an old oak – "it is quite hollow." You must climb to the top, wriggle through a hole and then lower yourself down the inside of the trunk all the way to the bottom. You will see three doors. Open the first one and you will find yourself inside a room where a frightening dog sits on a box full of money. Spread my blue-and-white checked apron on the floor, put the dog onto it, and he won't bother you at all. Then you can open the box and take out as much money as you can carry. In this first room, the money will be copper. If you'd rather have silver, you must face the even scarier dog in the second room. If you'd prefer gold, you must go into the third room – but there the dog is yet more terrifying."

"What do you want for yourself?" the soldier grinned.

"I don't want a single coin of the money," the witch cackled. "Just bring me a rusty old tinderbox that my granny forgot last time she was in there."

"Very well," agreed the soldier, and the witch gave him her apron. Then the soldier shimmied up the outside of the old oak tree, wriggled through the hole, and lowered himself down the inside. He found himself in a corridor lit by one hundred burning lanterns, and sure enough, there were three doors in front of him. The soldier bravely put his hand on the first doorknob and turned it.

"Great Scott!" he cried, springing back in alarm. There in the middle of the room was a dog with eyes the size of teacups. The soldier tore his eyes away from its staring gaze, lay the witch's apron on the floor and lifted the dog on to it. Then he unlocked the box the dog had been sitting on. Amazing! It was filled to the brim with copper coins. The soldier gleefully grabbed huge handfuls and stuffed them into his knapsack, his pockets and even his boots.

The second dog couldn't possibly have eyes bigger than that first one, the soldier thought. Boldly, he walked to the second doorknob and turned it...

"Good lord!" he yelled. There in the middle of the room was a dog with eyes the size of mill-wheels. Round and round and round they churned – it made you dizzy just to look at them. Once again, the soldier forced himself to look away. He laid the witch's apron down, heaved the dog onto it, and unlocked the box on which it had been sitting. Fantastic! There before him was a treasure trove of silver! The soldier got rid of all the copper coins and filled his knapsack and pockets.

"Surely the third dog's eyes can't be any bigger than that!" the soldier said to himself, laughing at his good

luck. He went to the third doorknob and turned it...

"Heavens above!" he cried. The third dog had eyes the size of the Round Tower of the city of Copenhagen. Not only that, but they whizzed round and round in his head like Catherine Wheels. It was several minutes before the soldier found he could look at something other than the dog's enormous spinning eyeballs. Then he laid down the witch's apron, hauled the dog onto it, and unlocked the box it had been sitting on. Unbelievable! There was enough gold to buy the palace of the King of Denmark himself! Chortling with joy, the soldier emptied his knapsack and pockets again and crammed them with gold instead. He hurried off down the corridor, found the tinderbox, and then climbed up and out of the tree.

"Where's my tinderbox then?" the witch cackled.

"Tell me why you want it so badly and I'll give it to you," replied the soldier, firmly.

"Where IS IT?" the witch shrieked in annoyance.

"If you don't tell me why you want it, I'll cut off your head," insisted the soldier.

"GIVE ME MY TINDERBOX!" the witch howled.

"Very well," said the soldier, and he drew his sword and cut off the witch's head. Then he went on his merry way down the road, with his knapsack and pockets weighed down with gold, and the witch's tinderbox tucked safely inside his jacket.

At the very next town, the soldier booked into the best hotel, ate in the most expensive restaurant, and went to the most exclusive shop to buy himself new clothes. At once the soldier found he had a lot of new friends and they told him of all the wonders to be seen in the town – particularly the beautiful princess, who lived in the castle on top of the hill.

"How can I get to see her?" the soldier asked.

"You can't," his new friends explained, "no one can. For it has been prophesied that she will one day marry a common soldier, and the king and queen keep the princess locked up so this can never happen."

Day after day, the soldier spent his gold on the finest things money could buy for himself and his friends. It was a horrible shock when he went one morning to fill his pockets and found that all the gold was gone. Suddenly, the soldier's friends disappeared. The soldier had to move out of the grand hotel and into a dingy attic at the top of fourteen flights of stairs. He didn't even have enough money for a candle to cheer things up with a bit of light. Then the soldier remembered the witch's tinderbox. Surely he could use that to give him a few sparks to start a warming fire? No sooner had

the soldier struck the tinderbox once with the flint than there was a flash of lightning and the dog with eyes the size of teacups appeared.

"What is your command, sir?" the dog growled.

Once the soldier had got over the shock, he stammered, "Well, I suppose I'd like some money."

The dog immediately vanished – but reappeared with a purse of money clamped between its jaws.

The soldier whooped with delight. Suddenly he understood the secret of the tinderbox. Strike it once, twice or three times, and the dog from the first, second or third room appeared to grant his wishes!

Soon the soldier was richer than ever and he moved back into the grand hotel. He had everything he could wish for – except for a wife. That princess must be very bored locked up there in the castle, the soldier thought to himself.

The soldier waited till it was dark, then struck the tinderbox once. In a flash, the dog with the eyes like teacups appeared. "I would like to see the beautiful princess," the soldier said. Before he could blink, the dog ran off and then reappeared with the princess, fast asleep. She was indeed very beautiful and the soldier couldn't resist bending over to give her a kiss. The dog then disappeared and the princess was gone.

Next morning,
up in the castle on the hill,
the princess remembered what had
happened as if it had been a strange dream,
and she told her mother and father all about it. The
king and queen were deeply worried. The clever queen
filled a pretty silk bag with flour and tied it around her
daughter's neck when she went to bed. Then the queen
pierced a tiny hole in the bag, tucked the princess in
and kissed her goodnight.

Once again, the soldier sent the dog to fetch the
princess. Neither the dog nor the soldier noticed the
thin line of flour that ran down from the silk bag and
left a tell-tale trail all the way from the castle to his
door. And in the morning, the soldier was woken by
royal officers breaking down his door. They grabbed

him and dragged him away to be hanged.

A huge crowd of townspeople had gathered to watch. Opposite the gallows sat the king and queen and all the members of the town council. Just as the hangman put the noose around the soldier's neck, the desperate man had an idea. "Will you grant me one last wish?" he yelled out to the king. "I would like to smoke a pipe of tobacco before I die."

The king thought for a moment. "Very well," he said. To the soldier's great delight, the hangman untied his hands and offered him a pipe and some matches.

"Don't worry," the soldier grinned, "I have my own light," and he pulled out his tinderbox and struck it three times.

At once, the dog with the eyes as big as teacups, the dog with the eyes as big as mill-wheels, and the dog with the eyes as big as the Round Tower of the city of Copenhagen stood before him. "Save me," the soldier cried, "or I will surely die!" The dogs growled like rumbling thunder and sprang among the crowd, scattering them everywhere in terror. They made straight for the king and queen and the table of town councillors. One by one, the dogs picked them up in their jaws and hurled them far, far away over the most distant hills. "Hooray!" the townspeople cried. "We never liked them anyway. We'd much prefer the brave soldier to be our king and the beautiful princess to be our queen!" And that's exactly what happened. They were married straight away – and the three dogs were guests of honour at the wedding feast.

Beauty and the Beast

Retold from the original tale by Madame Leprince de Beaumont

THERE WAS ONCE a businessman who had made a fortune by trading overseas. He lived in a magnificent mansion staffed by servants and with a TV in every room – including the indoor swimming pool. The businessman's wife had died, so he had brought up their three beautiful daughters on his own.

Unfortunately, the two eldest girls, Bianca and Bettina, lazed about all day watching chat shows, flicking through magazines and day-dreaming of marrying professional footballers. But Belle, the youngest daughter, was a great help to her father in running his business. She also enjoyed reading books on engineering and space exploration, for she was as intelligent as she was beautiful, and she had an avid interest in rocket science.

The businessman once had to go away on an important trip for work.

"Don't forget to bring us back some jewellery!" yelled Bianca.

"And some perfume!" bellowed Bettina.

"Is there nothing you would like, darling?" the businessman asked Belle.

Belle thought for a while. "Just a beautiful rose, please Daddy," she smiled.

"That's my girl!" the businessman said, and gave a cheery wave as he drove away.

But when the businessman finally returned, he was downcast and empty-handed.

"I'm afraid your dear old Dad has had it," the businessman explained. "I was on my way back last night, but it was dark and raining and somehow I got completely lost in the middle of nowhere. The only house for miles around was a spooky old mansion, and I

went to ask for help. The lights were on, the front door was open, but nobody seemed to be at home. I thought it was very strange, but I was so desperate that I crept inside and stayed the night. Early this morning, as I was hurrying off through the grounds, I stopped to pick a rose for Belle. 'STOP THIEF!' someone roared. 'This is my house and those are my roses! Is this how you repay my hospitality? I am going to kill you!' The man who came striding towards me was uglier than a monster in a film. He had a hairy face and bloodshot eyes, a snout for a nose and teeth like fangs. His hands were clawed and his body huge and hulking. I realised that the beast was deadly serious, so I fell on my knees in terror and begged for mercy. 'I will give you three months to say goodbye to everyone,' he growled. 'After that, you must return here to die... unless you have a daughter who is willing to come in your place and live here with me forever.'"

Bianca and Bettina stood gawping in horror. "Oh Daddy," they wailed, "who is going to look after us when you're gone?"

"Don't worry, Daddy," Belle comforted her father. "I can't let you die. I will go instead of you."

"Belle, you will do nothing of the kind!" her father protested. "You haven't seen this guy!"

"I don't care!" said Belle, resolutely sticking out her chin. And nothing Belle's father could say would make her change her mind. "If you sneak off without me, I shall just follow you," was her final word on the subject. So three months later, the broken-hearted businessman accompanied his brave daughter to the door of the huge, lonely mansion and kissed her for the last time. He could hardly see through his tears as he turned and walked away...

"Right," Belle said to herself firmly, though her bottom lip was trembling. "Let's find the library. Maybe it has a good science section." She set off through the stone corridors and oak-panelled halls, exploring. It was an eerie feeling to be all alone in such an enormous old place. Suddenly, Belle stopped in surprise. There, right in front of her was a door marked 'Belle's room'. She put her hand on the iron handle and gently pushed. It swung open with a creak. Belle gasped with delight. Inside, was everything she could possibly have wished for. There was a soft, white bed. Wardrobes full of beautiful clothes. But best of all, lining the walls was shelf after shelf of books.

"The owner of this place can't be all bad," Belle murmured to herself. She drew down the nearest book. It was bound in ancient leather and had gold-edging.

She read the first page:

     Belle, you have a heart of gold

     Like girls in fairytales of old.

     Whatever you wish, it will come true

     There's magic waiting here for you.

  "Hmmm," wondered Belle. "Well, the only thing I really wish is that I could see if my Dad is okay."

At that very moment, Belle noticed a mirror on the bedroom wall begin to cloud over. Mists swirled across the glass, and when they cleared, instead of her own

reflection, she saw a picture of her father, sitting at home sadly without her. After a few moments the picture vanished, but Belle was very grateful to have been able to see her father at all. The owner of this place is actually very kind, Belle thought to herself.

Just then, Belle heard the dinner bell ringing from the great hall. She hurried along and found a delicious meal laid out for one. No sooner had she swallowed three mouthfuls than she heard a shuffling and a snuffling. The food stuck in her throat and her heartbeat quickened. Belle forced herself to turn round and face her host.

Her father had been right. He was truly hideous.

"I'm Belle," she whispered, remembering her manners, like the well-brought up girl she was. "My room is wonderful – thank you."

"Call me Beast," said the monster, a look of pleasure lighting up his sad eyes. "Did you really like everything?"

"Yes, of course," said Belle. "Particularly the books. I love books, especially those on rocket science."

"They are your books now," said Beast. "Everything here is yours. I give it all to you. You can do with everything just what you wish. That goes for me, too. If I'm bothering you just tell me to go away and I will."

The Beast looked down at his huge, flat feet. "I know I'm exceedingly ugly. I might put you off your food." He sighed. "And not only am I ugly, I'm very stupid too."

"Now, now," comforted Belle. "I'm sure that's not the case. Anyone who is ready to say they are stupid can't possibly be stupid. The only people who really are stupid are those who won't admit that they're stupid!"

"Do you really think so?" sighed the Beast.

"Yes, of course!" laughed Belle. "And if you're really worried about being stupid, I can teach you all about rocket science. Let me get my books..."

A sheepish smile came over the Beast's ugly face as he listened to Belle read. After a while, he suddenly interrupted her.

"Belle, will you marry me?" he asked.

Belle was extremely taken aback. She looked at the monster as he crouched adoringly in front of her. "I'm sorry," she said. "I wish I could, but I really don't want to."

And so the time passed. Each day, Belle read in her room and walked in the beautiful grounds, admiring the roses. And each evening, the Beast came to visit her. As the weeks went on, Belle began to enjoy his company and looked forward to seeing him. But each night the Beast asked her to marry him, and even though Belle liked him more and more as a friend, she simply couldn't – well, fancy him.

Belle's only other worry was her Dad. Each day she saw in the mirror that he was pining more and more without her. Her sisters were selfish, unkind and thoughtless, and her father had grown quiet and pale and thin.

"Dear Beast," Belle begged one night, "allow me to go back to see my dad. I am afraid that he is dying of a broken heart."

Much to Belle's surprise, the Beast nodded his agreement. "Of course, Belle," he said, "if that is what will make you happy. Only I don't know what I'll do without you..."

"Darling Beast," whispered Belle, stroking his matted, shaggy hair, "I promise I'll be back in a week."

"Then I promise you that when you wake up tomorrow morning, you'll be at home with your father," sighed the Beast. "Take this ring. When you're ready to leave, just put it by the side of your bed at night. As you sleep, it will bring you back here."

Sure enough, next morning Belle woke up back in her old bed. Her dad couldn't believe his eyes! He and Belle hugged and laughed and spent a wonderful holiday doing all the things they used to enjoy doing

together – going through his accounts, visiting the science museum, watching old musicals on TV... The week flew by in the twinkling of an eye. "Please, Belle, don't go," begged her dad, and Belle didn't have the heart to leave.

But several nights later, Belle had a terrible dream. She saw the Beast lying in the garden of his mansion, under the rose bushes that he loved so much.

Belle knew that he was dying.

"Daddy," she sobbed the next morning. "I'm worried that something dreadful has happened to the Beast. He's my best and truest friend – and it's all my fault!"

That night, Belle put the Beast's ring by her bedside. It didn't seem as if she'd been asleep for five minutes when she woke up in her beautiful white room in the mansion. Belle sped off into the moonlit garden and there, lying under the rose bushes just as in her dream, lay the Beast. She flung herself down by his side and heaved his big, heavy head into her lap. Her tears plopped one by one onto his hairy face.

Weakly, the Beast opened his eyes and smiled. "I thought you had forgotten your promise," he whispered. "Now I have seen you once again, I can die happily."

"No!" Belle cried. "You can't die! You mustn't leave me! I love you!" And she kissed him.

At that very moment, the night sky was lit up by a million rainbow-coloured fireworks. Belle gazed upwards in surprise – she thought things like that only happened in films. When she looked back down at the Beast again, the monster was gone. Lying in her lap was a handsome, happy prince. He sprang up and lifted

Belle to her feet with joy in his eyes.

"My darling Belle," he told her, "Thank you for setting me free! I have lived under a wicked enchantment for years which forced me to appear as the Beast – not only ugly but stupid, too – until a beautiful girl willingly fell in love with me. You are the only person in the world who saw through my ugly appearance and sensed what I was really like inside. Now we will live together happily forever."

And that's exactly what they did. But this is a real tale, not a fairytale, and real tales don't have entirely happy endings. The prince took

Belle to live at his palace – and her dad went to live with them too. But Belle's selfish sisters got what they deserved. They were turned into statues and set at the palace gates until such time as they began to think about other people rather than themselves. As far as I know, they're both there still...

Cinderella

Retold from the original tale
by Charles Perrault

ONCE UPON A TIME, when there were still fairy
godmothers, there was a girl called Cinderella.
She lived with her father and his new wife, and her two
new step-sisters. The step-mother did not like
Cinderella very much, mostly because she was so much
nicer than her own two daughters. Cinderella was also
much prettier. Oh, but the step-sisters were ugly!

Cinderella had to do all the work in the house as the
ugly sisters were also very lazy. They spent all the
father's money on new clothes and endless pairs of
shoes, and then went off to parties leaving poor
Cinderella with piles of stockings to mend.

One day a very grand invitation arrived. The prince

was looking for a wife, and had decided to give a ball
in three days time for all the young ladies in the land.
The ugly sisters could talk about nothing else. They
bought lots of new dresses and many pairs of matching
shoes, and then spent
every hour trying
them all on.

They made Cinderella curl their hair and iron their ribbons and powder their noses. Cinderella was so exhausted running around after them that she had no time to look into her own wardrobe to choose what she should wear.

In a waft of perfume, the ugly sisters swept out of the door into the carriage without as much as a thank you to Cinderella. She closed the door sadly, and went to sit by the fire in the kitchen.

"I wish I could have gone to the ball, too," she sighed.

There was a sudden swirl of stars, and there in front of Cinderella stood an old lady with a twinkle in her eye, and a wand in her hand.

"You shall go to the ball, my dear Cinderella. I am your fairy godmother," she said, smiling. "Now, we must be quick, there is much to do! Please bring me a large pumpkin from the vegetable patch. Oh, and six mice from the barn, and you will find four lizards by the water butt."

Cinderella did as she was bid. With a wave of the wand, the pumpkin was turned into a glittering golden coach and the mice into six pure white horses. The lizards became elegant footmen, dressed in green velvet.

"Now you, my dear," said the fairy godmother, turning to Cinderella. A wave of the wand, and Cinderella's old apron disappeared and there she stood in a white dress, glittering with golden stars. Her hair was piled on top of her head and it too was sprinkled with stars. On her feet were tiny glass slippers with diamonds in the heels.

"Enjoy yourself, my dear," said the fairy godmother, "but you must leave before midnight for then my magic ends and you will be back in your old apron with some mice and lizards at your feet!"

When Cinderella arrived at the ball everyone turned to look and stare at this unknown beauty who had arrived so unexpectedly. The prince hurried over to

ask her to dance and then would not dance with anyone else all evening. The ugly sisters were beside themselves with rage, which of course made them look even uglier.

Cinderella was enjoying herself so much that she forgot the fairy godmother's warning, so she had a terrible fright when the clock began to strike midnight. She turned from the prince with a cry and ran down the stairs of the palace into her carriage, and disappeared as suddenly as she had arrived. One of the tiny glass slippers with diamonds sparkling in the heels had slipped from her foot as she ran. The prince picked it up and turning to the crowded ballroom declared, "I shall marry the girl whose foot fits this slipper!"

Cinderella, meanwhile, had just managed to reach her garden gate when all her finery disappeared, and by the time the ugly sisters arrived home, both in a towering rage, she was sitting quietly by the fire.

The next morning, the prince went from house to house looking for the mystery girl whose foot would fit the glass slipper. But no one had feet that small. He reached Cinderella's house where first one ugly sister

and then the next tried to squash her big feet into the slipper.

"Please let me try," said a quiet voice from the corner, and Cinderella stepped forward. The sisters just laughed in scorn but they soon stopped when they saw that the tiny slipper fitted Cinderella perfectly. There was a sudden swirl of stars, and there in front of Cinderella stood her fairy godmother with a twinkle in her eye, and a wand in her hand. In an instant, Cinderella was clothed in a gorgeous dress of cornflower blue silk decorated with pearls. On her feet she wore white boots with blue tassels.

The prince whisked Cinderella off to the palace to meet the king and queen, and the wedding took place the very next day. Cinderella forgave the ugly sisters, she was that sort of girl. But the prince insisted the sisters spent one day a week working in the palace kitchens just to remind them how horrid they had been to Cinderella.

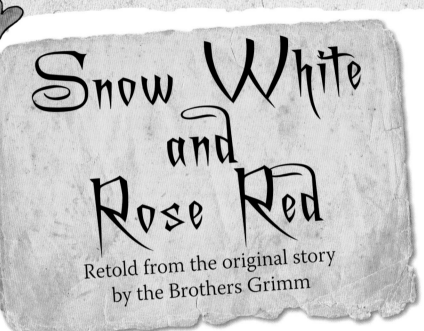

Snow White and Rose Red

Retold from the original story by the Brothers Grimm

ONCE UPON A TIME there was a widow who had two daughters, Snow White and Rose Red. Snow White was quiet and gentle, Rose Red was wild as the hills, but they loved each other, and their mother, so the little house in the woods was a happy one.

One winter evening as they all sat round the fire there was a knock at the door. Rose Red opened it and gave a scream. There stood a great big brown bear! But in a deep rumbly voice the bear said, "Please do not be afraid. All I ask is that you let me sleep by your fire tonight. It is so cold outside."

"Of course you may shelter with us," said the mother. And she called the girls to set the soup on the stove and to put another log on the fire.

"Would you brush the snow from my fur, please?" asked the bear. Rose Red fetched the big broom and carefully brushed the bear's great shaggy coat. Snow White gave him a great bowl of hot soup and the bear gulped it down in one. Then he stretched out in front of the fire and was soon fast asleep.

In the morning, Snow White let him out of the

cottage and he padded off into the forest through the deep snow. But in the evening, he returned and once again Snow White and Rose Red and their mother looked after him. After that the bear came every night all through the winter, and they grew very fond of him. But when spring came, the bear told them he would not be returning any more.

"I have to guard my treasure. Once the snows have melted all kinds of wicked people try to steal it," he said and giving them all a hug he set off through the forest. Just as he passed through the garden gate, his fur caught on a nail. For a fleeting moment Snow White thought she saw a glint of gold, but the bear hurried off and was soon out of sight.

A few days later, Rose Red and Snow White were out gathering berries to make jam when they came alongside a fallen tree. Then they saw a very cross dwarf, tugging at his beard which was trapped by the great tree trunk.

"Well, don't stand there like a pair of silly geese! Come and help me!" he shrieked.

Well, no matter how hard they tugged, Rose Red and Snow White were not strong enough

to lift the tree, so Rose Red took her scissors out and snipped off the end of the dwarf's beard. He was absolutely furious, and snatched up a big bag of gold from the tree roots and disappeared without a word of thanks.

Some days later the girls' mother said she really fancied a piece of fish for supper, so they went down to the river to see what they could catch. But instead of a fish, there on the bank they found the cross dwarf again. This time his beard was caught up in his fishing line.

"Don't just stand there gawping," he yelled, "help me get free!"

Snow White tried to untangle it but it was impossible, so she too snipped a piece off his beard. He was quite white with rage, but just grasped a casket of jewels that lay at the water's edge and turned away without a word of thanks.

It was the Spring Fair a few days later. The girls

decided to go and buy some new ribbons for their hats, and their mother wanted needles for her embroidery, so they set off early in the morning. They had not gone far when they heard a terrible shrieking and crying. They ran towards the sound, and there once more was the cross dwarf, this time struggling in the huge talons of an eagle. They tugged and tugged and the eagle had to let go.

"You have torn my coat," muttered the ungrateful dwarf and picked up a basket of pearls and hobbled off as fast as possible. The girls just laughed and continued on their way to the fair.

They had a wonderful time, and it was quite late when they walked slowly home. The sun was just sinking behind a big rock when, to their astonishment, they came across the dwarf again. There, spread out on the ground in front of him, was a great pile of gold, precious jewels and pearls.

Suddenly the dwarf saw Snow White and Rose Red.

"Go away! Go away! You horrid girls are always in my way," he shouted. But just then there was a huge growl and the great brown bear stood by their side. With one huge paw he swiped the dwarf up, up into the sky and no one ever saw where he fell to earth again. The bear turned towards Snow White and Rose Red and as they looked, his great shaggy coat fell away. There stood a handsome young man, dressed in a golden suit of the richest velvet.

"Do not be afraid, Snow White and Rose Red," he said smiling. "Now you can see who I really am. That wicked dwarf put a spell on me so he could steal all my treasure, but you have broken the spell by your kindness."

They all went home, laden with the treasure. They talked long into the night, and it was all still true the next morning! Snow White married the handsome young man who, by great good fortune, had a younger brother who married Rose Red, so they all lived happily ever after.

So if you ever find a dwarf with half his beard missing, I would be very careful if I were you.

The Fish and the Ring

By Flora Annie Steel

ONCE UPON A TIME there lived a baron who was a great magician, and could tell by his arts and charms everything that was going to happen at any time.

Now this great lord had a little son born to him as heir to all his castles and lands. So, when the little lad was about four years old, wishing to know what his fortune would be, the baron looked in his Book of Fate to see what it foretold.

And, lo and behold! It was written that this much-loved, much-prized heir to all the great lands and castles was to marry a low-born maiden. So the baron was dismayed, and set to work by more arts and charms to discover if this maiden were already born, and if so, where she lived.

And he found out that she had just been born in a very poor house, where the poor parents already had five children.

So he called for his horse and rode far away, until he came to the poor man's house, and there he found the poor man sitting at his doorstep very sad and doleful.

"What is the matter, my friend?" asked he, and the poor man replied:

"May it please your honour, a little lass has just been born to our house, and we have five children already, and where the bread is to come from to fill the sixth mouth, we know not."

"If that be all your trouble," said the baron readily, "maybe I can help you. So don't be downhearted. I am just looking for such a little lass to be a companion to my son, so, if you will, I will give you ten crowns for her."

Well! The man he nigh jumped for joy, since he was to get good money, and his daughter, so he thought, a good home. Therefore he brought out the child then and there, and the baron, wrapping the babe in his cloak, rode away. But when he got to the river he flung the little thing into the swollen stream, and said to himself as he galloped back to his castle:

"There goes Fate!"

But, you see, he was just sore mistaken. For the little lass didn't sink. The stream was very swift, and her long clothes kept her up till she caught in a snag just opposite a fisherman, who was mending his nets.

Now the fisherman and his wife had no children, and they were just longing for a baby, so when the

good man saw the little lass he was overcome with joy, and took her home to his wife, who received her with open arms.

And there she grew up, the apple of their eyes, into the most beautiful maiden that ever was seen.

Now, when she was about fifteen years of age, it so happened that the baron and his friends went a-hunting along the banks of the river and stopped to get a drink of water at the fisherman's hut. And who should bring the water out but, as they thought, the fisherman's daughter.

The young men of the party noticed her beauty, and one of them said to the baron, "She should marry well, read us her fate, since you are so learned in the art."

Then the baron, scarce looking at her, said carelessly, "I could guess her fate! Some wretched yokel or other. But, to please you, I will cast her horoscope by the stars, so tell me, girl, what day you were born?"

"That I cannot tell, sir," replied the girl, "for I was picked up in the river about fifteen years ago."

Then the baron grew pale, for he guessed at once that she was the little lass he had flung into the stream, and that Fate had been stronger than he was. But he kept his own counsel and said nothing at the time. Afterwards, however, he thought out a plan, so he rode

back and gave the girl a letter.

"See you!" he said. "I will make your fortune. Take this letter to my brother, who needs a good girl, and you will be settled for life."

Now the fisherman and his wife were growing old and needed help, so the girl said she would go, and took the letter.

And the baron rode back to his castle saying to himself once more:

"There goes Fate!"

For what he had written in the letter was this:

Dear Brother, take the bearer and put her to death immediately.

But once again he was sore mistaken, since on the way to the town where his brother lived, the girl had to stop the night in a little inn. And it so happened that that very night a gang of thieves broke into the inn, and not content with carrying off all that the innkeeper possessed, they searched the pockets of the guests, and found the letter which the girl carried. And when they read it, they agreed that it was a mean trick and a shame. So their captain sat down and, taking pen and paper, wrote instead:

> Dear Brother, take the bearer and marry her to my son without delay.

Then, after putting the note into an envelope and sealing it up, they gave it to the girl and bade her go on her way. So when she arrived at the brother's castle, though rather surprised, he gave orders for a wedding feast to be prepared. And the baron's son, who was staying with his uncle, seeing the girl's great beauty, was not unwilling, so they were fast wedded.

Well! When the news was brought to the baron, he was beside himself, but he was determined not to be outdone by Fate. So he rode quickly to his brother's and pretended to be quite pleased. And then one day, when no one was near, he asked the young bride to come for a walk with him, and when they were close to some cliffs, seized hold of her, and was for throwing her over into the sea. But she begged hard for her life.

"It is not my fault," she said. "I have done nothing. It is Fate. But if you will spare my life I promise that I

will fight against Fate also. I will never see you or your son again until you desire it. That will be safer for you, since, see you, the sea may preserve me, as the river did."

Well! The baron agreed to this. So he took off his gold ring from his finger and flung it over the cliffs into the sea and said:

"Never dare to show me your face again till you can show me that ring likewise."

And with that he let her go.

Well! The girl wandered on, and she wandered on, until she came to a nobleman's castle, and there, as they needed a kitchen girl, she took work.

Now one day, as she was cleaning a big fish, she looked out of the kitchen window, and who should she see driving up to dinner but the baron and his young son, her husband. At first she thought that, to keep her promise, she must run away, but afterwards she remembered they would not see her in the kitchen, so she went on with her cleaning of the big fish.

And, lo and behold! She saw something shine in its inside, and there, sure enough, was the baron's ring! She was glad enough to see it, I can tell you, so she slipped it on to her thumb. But she went on with her work, and dressed the fish as nicely as ever she could,

and served it up as pretty
as may be, with parsley
sauce and butter.

Well! When it came
to table the guests
liked it so well that
they asked the host
who cooked it.
And he called to
his servants, "Send
up the cook who
cooked that fine
fish, that she may
get her reward."

Well! When the
girl heard she was
wanted she made
herself ready, and with the gold ring on her thumb,
went boldly into the dining hall. And all the guests
when they saw her were struck dumb by her wonderful
beauty. And the young husband started up gladly, but
the baron, recognizing her, jumped up angrily and
looked as if he would kill her. So, without one word,
the girl held up her hand before his face, and the gold
ring shone and glittered on it, and she went straight up

to the baron, and laid her hand with the ring on it before him on the table.

Then the baron understood that Fate had been too strong for him, so he took her by the hand, and, placing her beside him, turned to the guests and said:

"This is my son's wife. Let us drink a toast in her honour."

And after dinner he took her and his son home to his castle, where they all lived as happy as could be forever afterwards.

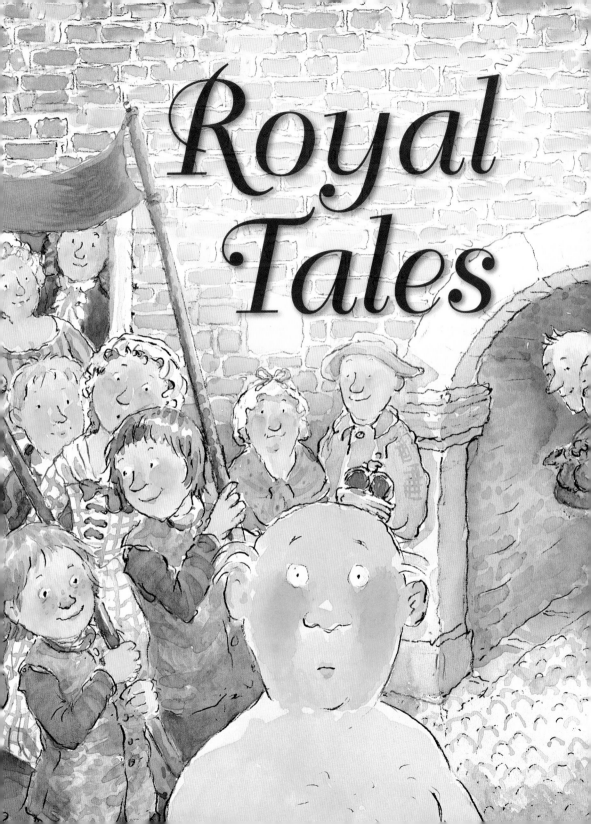

Royal Tales

The Emperor's New Clothes

Retold from the original tale by Hans Christian Andersen

*T*HERE WAS ONCE an emperor who loved new clothes above everything else. Designers, tailors, clothmakers, dyers, and specialists in all sorts of needlework travelled to his city from all over the world. Anyone who could suggest flashy, fancy new outfits for the emperor was always very welcome at the palace.

One day, it was the turn of two weavers to be quickly ushered into the emperor's dressing room. The emperor, his butler and all his Officers of the Royal Wardrobe, gasped with amazement as they listened to them describe their work.

"We have created a special fabric that is so light and airy the wearer cannot feel it," the first weaver announced.

"Our samples are top secret, which is why we have not been able to bring any to show you," the second weaver explained.

"However we can assure you that not only are our designs and patterns exquisitely beautiful," said the first weaver, "but the fabric has the unique advantage that it is completely invisible to anyone not worthy of his job."

"Or who is just plain stupid!" laughed the second weaver, and the emperor and all his courtiers gasped and chuckled along.

"We would be honoured if you would like to order the first suit made out of this extraordinary fabric, your majesty," said the first weaver, bowing low.

The emperor clapped his hands with delight.

"I'd like to place an order right away!" he commanded, and he gave the two weavers a large sum of money so that they could buy the rare, expensive materials they needed and begin their work without delay.

The weavers set up their looms in the palace studio and got going right away. News of the strange cloth spread round the city like wildfire and soon everyone was talking about it. But the weavers worked behind closed doors and no one got even a glimpse of what they were doing. Still, day and night everyone heard the looms clicking and the shuttles flying, and work on the magical cloth seemed to be progressing well.

As the days went on, the emperor began to feel rather uneasy about seeing the cloth for the first time. Imagine if I can't see the fabric myself! he thought to himself. How dreadfully embarrassing that would be! The worried emperor decided to send his trusted old butler to see how the weavers were getting on. He was sure that his butler was both fit for his job and very wise, and would be sure to see the wonderful material.

The weavers bowed low and ushered the butler into the studio. But the butler couldn't see anything at all. Heavens above! the butler thought to himself. Those looms look totally bare to me! I must either be a bad butler, or else I'm an idiot. No one must find out…

So he praised the material that he could not see, told the king that the weavers' work was indeed magnificent, and everyone in the city heard that the cloth was truly unbelievable!

Soon afterwards, the weavers sent word to the emperor that they needed more money to buy essential items for the work. The emperor had been so delighted with the butler's report that he sent them twice as much money as before. The emperor was more excited than ever. "I'm going to have the most amazing suit of clothes in the world!" he giggled to himself.

Eventually, just as the impatient emperor thought he was going to explode with waiting, the weavers announced their work was finished. They went to the dressing room to present the material to the emperor amid fanfares of trumpets. "Is the cloth not beautiful beyond all imagining?" the weavers sighed.

The emperor smiled a wide smile, trying to hide his horror. All that the weavers appeared to be holding up before him was thin air. The emperor's worst fear had come true – to him the cloth was invisible! I cannot be thought to be a fool or not worthy to be ruler, the despairing emperor thought. So he beamed and leant forwards and inspected the air. "Wonderful! Splendid! Magnificent!" he cried, and his butler and all the Officers of the Royal Wardrobe nodded and cried out compliments. None of them could see anything either, but they weren't about to risk losing their jobs by admitting it.

So the weavers got out their tape measures and their scissors and they set about cutting the thin air (or so it seemed) into a pattern. All night long they sewed with needles that appeared to have no thread, and in the morning they announced that the emperor's new clothes were ready. "If your majesty would care to disrobe, we will dress you in the amazing garments."

The emperor swallowed hard and took off all his clothes. The weavers helped him on with the underpants and trousers and shirt and jacket that he couldn't see. "Aren't they lighter than cobwebs?" they sighed. The emperor spluttered his agreement. He couldn't feel that he had any clothes on at all.

The emperor stood back and looked at himself in the mirror. According to what he saw, he didn't have a stitch on! But he turned this way and that, pretending to admire himself. And the butler and all the Officers of the Royal Wardrobe cried out, "How wonderfully the new clothes fit you, sire!" and "We have never seen the like of the amazing colours!" and "The design is a work of genius!" – even though it looked to them as if the emperor was as naked as the day he was born.

Everyone else can see my new suit except me, the emperor thought to himself glumly. And he walked out of the palace to parade before the people

in his marvellous new clothes.

The streets were lined with hundreds of people who ooohed! and aaaahed! over the emperor's invisible new clothes – for none of them wanted to admit that they couldn't see them.

Suddenly, a little boy's shrill voice rose over the applause of the crowd.

"But the emperor has nothing on!" the child shouted. "Nothing on at all!" Suddenly there was a stunned silence and the little boy found that hundreds of pairs of eyes were staring at him. Then someone sniggered... someone else tried to stifle a giggle... another person guffawed and snorted... and the whole

crowd burst out into uncontrollable peals of laughter.

The emperor's face turned as red as a ripe tomato. "I am indeed a fool!" he murmured. "I have been swindled by two tricksters!" He ran back to the palace as fast as his short, naked legs could carry him – but the clever (and now very rich) weavers were long gone!

Rumpelstiltskin

Retold from the original tale by the Brothers Grimm

ONCE UPON A TIME there was a miller. He was a foolish man who was always boasting. Then he went too far.

The king was riding past the mill with his huntsmen one day. The miller's daughter was sitting in the doorway, spinning. The king noticed that she was a pretty girl so he began talking to her. Her father came bustling up and began to tell the king what a splendid daughter she was.

"Why, your Majesty, she can even spin straw into gold!" boasted the ridiculous miller.

Needless to say, the poor girl could do nothing of the sort but the king thought this was an excellent way

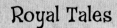

to refill the palace treasure house which was rather empty, so he took her back to the palace. He put her in a room with a great pile of straw and told her he wanted to see it all spun into gold the next morning, or else it would be the worse for her.

As soon as the door was locked she began to cry. The task was impossible. Then she heard a thin little voice.

"Do stop crying! You will make the straw all wet, and then we will have no chance of turning it into gold!"

There in front of her stood a strange little man. He had a tiny round body with long skinny legs and huge feet. His clothes looked as if they had seen better days, and on his head he wore a tall battered-looking hat.

"If you give me your necklace, I will do what the king has asked of you," he snapped.

The miller's daughter unclasped her necklace and handed it to the little man. He hid it deep in one of his pockets, and sat down by the spinning wheel.

The spinning wheel turned in a blur. The pile of straw grew smaller, and the mound of shining gold grew higher. As the first light of day shone in through the window it was all done.

The strange little man disappeared as suddenly as he had appeared. The king was delighted with the great pile of gold, and asked the miller's daughter to marry him. She was too shy to reply so the king just took her silence as

421

her agreement and married her anyway that afternoon.

For a while all was well. But then the treasure house grew empty again so once more the poor girl, now the queen, was locked in a room with a pile of straw and a spinning wheel.

As the queen wept, once more the strange little man appeared. The queen asked him to help her again, and offered him all the rich jewels she was wearing. But the strange little man was not interested in jewels.

"You must promise to give me your first born child," he whispered.

The queen was desperate. But she promised and the little man sat down at the spinning wheel. A great pile of gold appeared by the side of the spinning wheel, and by dawn the straw had all gone. The king was delighted and for a while all was well. Then the queen gave birth to a beautiful baby, and she remembered with dread her promise to the strange little man. Seven days after the baby was born, he appeared by the side of the cradle. The queen wept.

"There you go again," said the little man crossly, "always crying!"

"I will do anything but let you have my baby," cried the queen.

"Very well then, anything to make you stop crying,"

said the little man, who by now was dripping wet from all the queen's tears. "If you can guess my name in three days, I will let you keep your baby," he said and disappeared as suddenly as he had appeared.

The next morning the little man appeared by the side of the cradle. The queen had sent messengers out

far and wide to see if anyone knew the strange little man's name.

"Is it Lacelegs?" she asked.

"No!"

"Is it Wimbleshanks?"

"No!"

"Is it Bandyknees?"

"No!"

And the little man disappeared as suddenly as he had appeared. The queen sent out even more messengers to the lands far beyond the borders of the kingdom. The second morning the strange little man appeared by the side of the cradle.

"Is it Bluenose?" the queen asked.

"No!"

"Is it Longtooth?"

"No!"

"Is it Skinnyribs?"

"No!" and the little man disappeared with a nasty laugh.

The queen waited up all night as her messengers came in one by one, and just as she was giving up all hope of saving her precious baby, in came the very last one. He was utterly exhausted but he brought the queen the best of news. In a deep, deep, dark forest he

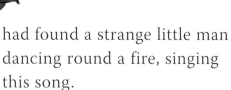

had found a strange little man dancing round a fire, singing this song.

"Today I brew, today I bake,
    Tomorrow I will the baby take.
    The queen will lose the game,
    Rumpelstiltskin is my name!"

When the strange little man appeared again by the cradle, the queen pretended she still did not know his name.

"Is it Gingerteeth?" she asked.

"No!" said the little man, and he picked the baby up.

"Is is Silverhair?" asked the queen.

"No!" said the little man, and he started to walk towards the door, with a wicked smile.

"Is it Rumpelstiltskin?" asked the queen, and she ran up to the strange little man.

"Some witch told you that!" shrieked the little man, and he stamped his foot so hard that he fell through the floor and was never seen again. The queen told the king the whole story and he was so pleased his baby and his queen were safe that he forgot to be cross with the miller who had told such a terrible fib in the first place!

Snow White and the Seven Dwarfs

Retold from the original tale
by the Brothers Grimm

THE QUEEN WAS sitting at the window sewing, and thinking about her baby who would be born soon. As she sewed she pricked her finger, and red blood fell on the snow by the ebony window ledge.

"I wish that my daughter be as white as snow, as black as ebony and as red as blood," she said to herself, and so it happened. Her tiny daughter had snow-white skin, lips as red as blood and hair as black as ebony, so she was called Snow White. But the queen died and the king married again. His new wife was very beautiful but she had a cold heart, and she did not love Snow White.

Every morning the new queen would look into her magic mirror and say,

"Mirror, mirror on the wall
 Who is fairest in the land?"

and the mirror would always reply, "Thou, oh queen, Thou art fairest in the land."

So the queen was content. Seven years passed and Snow White grew into a lovely young girl, with her mother's gentle nature.

One morning the queen looked into her mirror as usual, but the mirror's reply filled her with a deep envy.

"Thou, oh queen,
 Thou art indeed fair

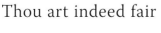

But Snow White is the fairest in the land."

She ordered her woodsman to kill Snow White. But he could not bear to do such a wicked deed so he hid Snow White deep in the forest. Poor Snow White wandered about until she was utterly weary.

Suddenly, she caught sight of a light through the trees in the distance. It came from a little house with a lantern glowing in one small window. The door swung open at her touch, so she stepped inside. Everything was as neat as a new pin. A scrubbed wooden table was set, with seven plates and seven cups. Seven little chairs were ranged round the table, and along the back wall there were seven little beds, each with a brightly

coloured blanket.

There was a basket of logs beside the fireplace, and Snow White soon had a cheerful fire going. She sat in one of the little chairs and before long was fast asleep.

Now the cottage belonged to seven dwarfs and when they came home that evening, they were very worried to discover Snow White fast asleep. They tiptoed round preparing their supper, but as the wonderful smell of stew filled the room, Snow White awoke with a start. She was very surprised to see seven little faces looking at her, but soon she was telling them how she came to be in the forest. They were very angry when they heard about the wicked queen.

"Might I stay with you?" asked Snow White. "I could look after you, and have supper ready every night."

The dwarfs were just delighted with this suggestion, and immediately set about making Snow White her own chair by the fireside and her own bed.

Back in the castle, the queen looked into her mirror in the morning, and asked,

"Mirror, mirror on the wall,

Who is fairest in the land?"

But you can imagine her rage when the mirror replied,

"Thou, oh queen, Thou art indeed fair,

But Snow White with the seven dwarfs does dwell

and she is fairest in the land."

So the wicked queen disguised herself as an old pedlar, and searched out the dwarfs' cottage. Snow White did not recognize the queen.

"Goodness me, you need new laces for your dress," said the old woman, and she pulled the new laces so tightly that Snow White was unable to breathe.

When the dwarfs came home that evening, they were horrified to discover Snow White lying on the floor as if dead. They lifted her up and, of course, saw the laces. They quickly cut the tight cord and the colour came back to Snow White's cheeks.

"Now you know the queen will stop at nothing," they

cried. "You must not let anyone indoors again."

The queen looked in her mirror the next morning, and went white with rage when it told her Snow White was still the fairest in the land. She disguised herself as a gypsy, selling wooden pegs and combs. Snow White remembered what the dwarfs had said and would not open the door. But the gypsy passed one of the combs through the window, and the minute it touched her hair, Snow White fell down in a faint for the comb was poisoned.

When the dwarfs came home and found Snow White, they immediately suspected the queen. They found the comb and pulled it out, and Snow White sat up, quite recovered. They pleaded with her to be more careful the next morning when they set off for work.

So when a farmer's wife appeared trying to sell apples, Snow White would not even open the window.

"Why, anyone would think I was trying to poison you," said the farmer's wife, who was, of course, the

wicked queen in disguise.

"I only want to give you some apples. Look how juicy they are!" and she took a big bite out of one.

So Snow White thought it must be all right and she took the apple. But the queen had poisoned it on one side only, and the minute Snow White took a bite she fell down dead.

This time when the dwarfs came home, there was nothing they could do. Snow White was indeed dead. They could not bear to bury her in the cold earth so they placed her in a glass coffin. They wrote her name on the side in silver and put the coffin in a sheltered part of the forest, and planted wild flowers all round about.

When the queen looked into her mirror the next morning, it gave her the answer she wanted.

"Thou, oh queen,
Thou art fairest in the land."

Years and years passed. Snow White lay in her coffin, looking as beautiful as ever. The dwarfs watched over her day and night, and one day they found a young prince kneeling by the side of the glass coffin. He had fallen in love with Snow White the moment he had set eyes on her. When the dwarfs saw how deeply the prince felt about their beloved Snow White, they agreed that he take the glass coffin to his palace where he wished to set it in his rose gardens.

As the prince lifted the glass coffin, the piece of poisoned apple flew from her lips, and Snow White opened her eyes. She saw the prince, she saw her faithful dwarfs and she cried, "Where am I? What has happened?"

There was huge excitement as everyone tried to talk at once. The prince wasted no time and asked Snow White to marry him. She agreed as long as the dwarfs could come and live at the palace as well, and they all lived happily ever after.

But what of the queen? She looked in her mirror the morning Snow White and the prince were to be married.

"Mirror, mirror on the wall
Who is fairest in the land?"
The mirror replied,
"Snow White, oh queen,
Snow White who marries her prince today,
She is fairest in the land."

The queen was so ugly in her rage that the mirror cracked from side to side. And she was never able to look in a mirror ever again as long as she lived.

The Little Mermaid

Retold from the original tale by Hans Christian Andersen

FAR, FAR OUT in the ocean, the water is as blue as cornflowers and deeper than the tallest mountain. It is there that the sea-people live, and in the very deepest waters lies the Sea King's palace of coral and mother-of-pearl. The Sea King's beloved wife had died, so his mother, the old queen, took care of his six beautiful mermaid daughters. All day long, the princesses sang and danced, swimming in and out of the pillars and halls of the palace. Sometimes shy, brightly coloured fish swam up to eat out of their hands. And at other times, each would tend the little garden that she cared for in the royal grounds. Each mermaid princess gave her garden its own particular

style and design: one was shaped like a whale; another had a rockery of shells; yet another had flowerbeds where the sea-horses came to graze. But the youngest mermaid's garden was shaped like the sun that shone on the world above the sea, and the flowers that grew there blazed red and orange and yellow like the sunlight.

The little mermaid had never been up to the ocean's surface and seen the upper world, for the princesses were only allowed to do so when they reached fifteen years old. But the little mermaid longed for that day to come. She loved to hear the stories her grandmother told of people and ships and cities and animals and meadows and forests and the like. And many a night the little mermaid stood at her open chamber window, peering up at the watery reflections of the moon and the stars and the dark shapes of ships as they passed like clouds above her.

When each of her sisters came of age, the little mermaid begged them eagerly to tell her everything they had seen. Then at last, she turned fifteen and it was her turn to see the upper world for herself.

The little mermaid thought it was more beautiful than she had ever imagined. Her head broke through the foam when the sun had just gone down and the clouds looked as if they were on fire with red and gold. The sound of music and singing was coming from a tall-masted ship bedecked all about with coloured flags and banners. Suddenly rockets zoomed up from it into the sky which exploded into stars that fell glittering all around her – the little mermaid had never seen fireworks before. When she was lifted up on the swell of the sea, she saw onto the ship's magnificent deck and understood the reason for the wonderful celebrations: it was the birthday party of a prince, more handsome than any merman she had ever seen.

As the little mermaid gazed with delight at the prince and his ship, she heard a familiar rumbling stirring deep within the sea. A storm was coming! All at once the sky darkened. Sheets of rain lashed the ship. The waves towered into mountains that hurled

the ship upwards and sent it crashing down towards the depths. The little mermaid saw with alarm that the ship wouldn't be able to hold out against the might of the weather and the ocean, and she ducked under the waves as wooden planks and other pieces of the ship came flying out of the darkness at her head. Through the murky waters, the little mermaid was horrified to see human bodies come floating down around her – and among them was her beautiful prince, choking and gasping for air.

The little mermaid shot through the water and clutched him close to her, and began swimming up to the light until his head was above water. The little mermaid hauled the exhausted prince to the shore and let the waves wash him onto the sand, and she stayed in the foam and watched him until the storm had died away and the morning sunlight came streaming warmly through the clouds. Then she saw the green hills for the first time and heard the peal of bells, and she saw a group of young girls come skipping out of a white building with a cross on the top. One of the girls noticed the prince where he lay. She ran to him and laid his head in her lap, and slowly the prince opened his eyes. He looked up at the girl and smiled, and the little mermaid turned away sadly, for she knew the prince thought it was that girl who had rescued him.

From that moment on, the little mermaid was thoughtful and sad. She longed to see her handsome prince again, to tell him that she loved him and wanted to be with him forever. She wanted to be human more than anything else in the whole world. There was only one thing she could do: make the dangerous journey to the cold, dark depths of the ocean to see the Water-Witch.

The Water-Witch's lair was set about with the skeletons of humans she had drowned and the remains of ships she had wrecked. The little mermaid

trembled with fear as she explained why she had come.

"What you long for is extremely difficult to give," the Water-Witch cackled.

"I can make your tail disappear and give you legs so that you can walk about with the humans in the world above. But every step you take will be as painful as if you are treading on knives. And I cannot make your prince fall in love with you. It is up to you, and you alone, to do that. If your prince marries another, the morning afterwards your heart will break and you will turn to foam on the water."

The little mermaid shuddered, but she bade the Water-Witch continue.

"The price for such strong magic is very high," spat the witch. "Once I have given you legs, there is no changing your mind. You will never be able to return to the sea as a mermaid to see your family... And there is one more thing. I cannot mix the potion you need unless you give me your voice."

The little mermaid longed for her prince and for a human soul that she whispered, "So be it." The words were the last sounds she ever uttered. For then the Water-Witch took the little mermaid's voice and brewed up an evil-smelling potion for her in exchange.

The little mermaid felt as if her heart would break

with grief as she swam back past her father's palace, leaving her sleeping family for the world above. She splashed onto the sand, half-choking through her tears and half-gasping for air, and looked at her beautiful silvery fishtail for the last time. Then the little mermaid raised the witch's brew to her lips and drank deeply. At once pain wracked her body and she fell into a dead faint…

The little mermaid awoke to find her handsome prince standing over her, looking worried. "Are you all right?" he asked, but the little mermaid couldn't reply. Instead, she smiled as she looked down at her body and saw that she had the prettiest pair of legs she could have wished for. Falteringly, she stood up for the very first time. The little mermaid put out her foot – and it was true, each step was like treading on knives. But soon she was dancing and running and skipping along the beach for joy, and the prince was utterly enchanted.

The prince took his new little friend back to the palace and dressed her in fine robes of silk and satin. He didn't seem to mind that she was dumb, and kept her by his side at all times, calling her "my beautiful little foundling".

Yet although the little mermaid was happier than she

had ever dreamed was possible, there was a sadness in her eyes and a heaviness in her heart. Each night, she would creep out of the palace and go down to the seashore. Sometimes she saw her sisters way out among the surf, and they would sing to her sadly as they floated on the waves. Once, she even thought she glimpsed the golden crowns of her father and grandmother – but perhaps it was just the moonlight glinting on the water.

Eventually a day came when the prince led the little mermaid onto a fine ship just like the one from which she had rescued him. They sailed for a night and a day, and all the time the little mermaid longed to leap into the waves and dive down to see her family. The ship finally arrived in the harbour of a neighbouring kingdom, and the people lined the streets to meet them, cheering. "See how they welcome me," the prince whispered to the little mermaid. "For today I am going to marry their princess."

The little mermaid felt as if someone had grabbed

her heart with icy fingers. Surely it couldn't be true? But when the prince's bride came running down the palace steps to meet him, the little mermaid understood. It was the girl who had found him on the beach; the girl whom the prince thought had saved him from the sea; the girl whom the prince thought was the little mermaid.

That afternoon, the little mermaid stood in church dressed in silk and gold, holding the bride's train. And all the way back to the ship, she cried silent, dry tears.

That night, as the splendid ship floated on the waves, there were flags and fireworks and music and dancing – and the little mermaid felt no more a part of the celebrations than she had when she had watched the prince's birthday party from afar.

The little mermaid stood on the deck all night and listened to the sighing of the sea. She felt the warm night wind on her face and her hair floated in the damp sea mists. When the first rays of the dawn lit

up the horizon, the little mermaid prepared herself to dissolve into foam on the waves. But instead, she saw transparent beings of light flying to her through the air. They lifted her up on their wings and soared off into

the sky, and the little mermaid found that she was one of them. "We are the daughters of the air. We do not have an immortal soul, but if we perform enough acts of goodness, we will win one for ourselves. And this is your reward for the suffering you have endured."

The little mermaid raised her hands towards the sun and the tears in her eyes were tears of joy. She looked down upon the prince and his bride on their ship. They were searching for her in the water, thinking she had fallen overboard. But the little mermaid didn't stay to watch them for long. She blew them a kiss and flew onwards with the daughters of the air.

The Dragons of Peking

A Chinese folk tale

ONCE THERE WAS a poor prince who ruled over a group of peasants, living in a cluster of wooden huts in some dry, dusty fields. This sad little place was called Peking. However, the prince was good-hearted and determined, and had grand dreams of building Peking into a splendid city. The first thing he did was work hard with the men, women and children to build a high, solid wall with broad gates to keep enemies out.

The people were delighted. Little did they know that with all their digging, clearing, carrying and building, they'd disturbed two dragons who'd been asleep in an underground cave for thousands of years. You can imagine how grumpy the dragons felt when they were woken from their lovely long nap! "Who does this prince think he is," the first dragon growled, "getting his people to come banging around our cave like that!"

"Let's teach them all a lesson," the second dragon snorted.

That night, the two dragons wove a spell, turning themselves into an old man and an old woman. They stole away to the prince's house and, using magic, they crept past the royal guards, through several locked doors, into the very room where the prince lay, snoring soundly. The wrinkled couple asked, "O wise and gracious lord, we have come to ask your permission to leave your city of Peking and to take two baskets of water with us."

The prince stirred and murmured, "Why, of course you may," before falling back into a deep sleep.

The old man and woman hurried off to the river excitedly. It was narrow and muddy, but it was Peking's main source of water. They dipped their baskets into the stream and in minutes the river dwindled to a trickle, then dried up completely. Unbeknown to the prince, the disguised dragons' water baskets were enchanted – even if an entire ocean were poured into them, they would never be filled.

Next, the old man and woman took their water

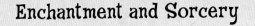

baskets, which were no heavier than before, off to the village spring. Soon, instead of a bubbling gush of water, there was just a muddy puddle. Then they visited every house in the village, draining all the water baskets of every last drop. Finally, the stooped pair hobbled off with their water baskets down the road that led out of Peking.

By the time the sun rose, the wicked old couple were far away. Shouts of horror could be heard from all over Peking as the people woke and discovered that there was no water. Before long, there was a clamouring crowd outside the prince's house. "What shall we do?"

they shouted. "Our lips are parched. We can't boil any rice for breakfast. Our crops are withering in the sun before our very eyes!"

A stale smell wafted under the prince's nostrils. "Oh dear," he sighed, "has anyone been able to have a bath this morning?" The people shuffled about and looked down, red-faced.

Then the prince remembered his dream about the two old people and their water baskets. Being a wise person who believed in magic, he was very suspicious and dashed off to see his faithful old advisor straight away.

"Aha!" his advisor nodded with a knowing smile. Mumbling under his breath, he took the prince straight off to the dragons' cave outside the city. When the faithful old advisor saw the cave was empty, he said,

452

"Well, there you are then."

"Well, there I am then – what?" said the prince, rather frustrated.

"My father was told about this cave by his father, who was told by his father, who was told by–"

"Yes, yes!" cried the prince impatiently. "Please get on with it!"

"Two dragons were asleep here, who obviously weren't very impressed with your plans to improve the city. They've taken your water and gone!"

At once the prince called for his spear and his horse, and shot down the road in a cloud of dust. He thundered past many travellers until, after hours of hard riding, he recognized the old couple from his dream and reined in his panting horse. "I gave my permission for an old man and woman to take two baskets of water," the prince yelled, "not the two dragons that you really are!" He plunged his spear into each of their baskets and water immediately began to gush out in a cascading torrent.

With a spine-chilling roar, the old couple began to change back into dragons before the prince's horrified eyes. But before the fire-breathing creatures could pounce on him, they were swept off in one direction by the swirling waters, while the prince on his horse was carried off in the other. Everywhere was submerged under water, and the prince's horse scrambled onto a jutting crag that poked up out of the water. It had once been the peak of a gigantic mountain.

"Now what am I to do?" frowned the prince, dripping from head to foot.

"I shall pray to heaven for help," came a voice. The prince looked round in surprise and saw a Buddhist monk, who had been sitting there so silently that the prince hadn't even noticed him. The monk shut his eyes and bowed his head – and as he prayed, the waters vanished. The prince thanked the Buddhist monk earnestly and began galloping back to Peking.

As soon as the prince neared the city, the people came pouring out of the gates with happy faces. "You'll never believe it!" they cried. "All our water has come back. But best of all, a brand new fountain has sprung up. It has swelled the river with water more sweet and crystal clear than any we have ever seen!"

Thanks to the magical fountain, the land around Peking changed from being a dry, dusty wasteland to a beautiful, lusciously green paradise. The prince fulfilled his plans of making the city one of the most splendid in the world and, as far as the people know, the dragons have never come back.

Fairy Ointment

By Joseph Jacobs

DAME GOODY WAS a nurse that looked after sick people, and minded babies. One night she was woke up at midnight, and when she went downstairs, she saw a strange, little old fellow, who asked her to come to his wife who was too ill to mind her baby. Dame Goody didn't like the look of the old fellow, but business is business, so she popped on her things, and went down to him. And when she got down to him, he whisked her up on to a large coal-black horse with fiery eyes, that stood at the door, and soon they were going at a rare pace, Dame Goody holding on to the old fellow like grim death.

They rode and they rode, till at last they stopped before a cottage door. So they got down and went in and found the good woman in bed with the children playing about, and the babe, a fine bouncing boy, beside her.

Dame Goody took the babe, which was as fine a baby boy as you'd wish to see. The mother, when she handed the baby to Dame Goody to mind, gave her a box of ointment, and told her to stroke the baby's eyes with it as soon as it opened them.

After a while it began to open its eyes. Dame Goody saw that it had eyes just like its father. So she took the box of ointment and stroked its two eyelids with it. But she couldn't help wondering what it was for, as she had never seen such a thing done before. So she looked to see if the others were looking, and, when they were not noticing, she stroked her own right eyelid with the ointment.

No sooner had she done so, than everything seemed changed about her. The cottage became elegantly furnished. The mother in the bed was a beautiful lady, dressed up in white silk. The little baby was still more beautiful than before, and its clothes were made of a sort of silvery gauze.

Its little brothers and sisters around the bed were flat-nosed imps with pointed ears, who made faces at one another, and scratched their heads. In fact, they were up to all kinds of mischief, and Dame Goody knew that she had got into a house of fairies. But she said nothing to nobody, and as soon as the lady was well enough to mind the baby, she asked the old fellow to take her back home. So he came round to the door with the coal-black horse with eyes of fire, and off they went as fast as before till they came to Dame Goody's cottage, where the strange fellow lifted her down and left her, thanking her civilly enough, and paying her more than she had ever been paid before for such service.

Now next day happened to be market day, and as Dame Goody had been away from home, she wanted many things in the house, and trudged off to get them at the market. As she was buying the things she wanted, who should she see but the strange fellow who had taken her on the coal-black horse. And what do you think he was doing? Why he went about from stall to stall taking things from each – here some fruit, and there some eggs, and so on – and no one seemed to take any notice.

Now Dame Goody did not think it her business to interfere, but she thought she ought not to let so good a customer pass without speaking. So she went up to him, bobbed a curtsey and said:

"Good day, sir, I hope your good lady and the little one are as well as—"

But she couldn't finish what she was saying, for the

funny old fellow started back in surprise, and he said to her, "What! Do you see me today?"

"See you," said she, "why, of course I do, as plain as the sun in the skies, and what's more," said she, "I see you are busy, too, into the bargain."

"Ah, you see too much," said he, "now, pray, with which eye do you see all this?"

"With the right eye to be sure," said she, as proud as can be to find him out.

"The ointment! The ointment!" cried the old fairy thief. "Take that for meddling with what don't concern you – you shall see me no more." And with that he struck her on the right eye, and she couldn't see him anymore, and, what was worse, she was blind on the right side from that hour till the day of her death.

The Prince with the Nose

By Dinah Maria Mulock Craik

THERE WAS ONCE A KING who was passionately in love with a beautiful princess, but she could not be married because a magician had enchanted her. The king went to a good fairy to inquire what he should do. Said the fairy, after receiving him graciously:

"Sir, I will tell you a secret. The princess has a great cat whom she loves so well that she cares for nothing else; but she will be obliged to marry any person who is adroit enough to walk upon the cat's tail."

"That will not be very difficult," thought the king to himself, and departed, resolving to trample the cat's tail to pieces rather than not succeed in walking upon it. He went immediately to the palace of his fair mistress and the cat; the animal came in front of him, arching its back in anger as it was wont to do. The king lifted up his foot, thinking nothing would be so easy as to tread on the tail, but he found himself mistaken. Minon – that was the creature's name – twisted itself round so sharply that the king only hurt his own foot by stamping on the floor. For eight days did he pursue the cat everywhere: up and down the palace he was after it from morning till night, but with no better success; the tail seemed made of quicksilver, so very lively was it. At last the king had the good fortune to catch Minon sleeping, when – tramp, tramp – he trod on the tail with all his force.

Minon woke up, mewed horribly, and immediately changed from a cat into a large, fierce-looking man, who regarded the king with flashing eyes.

"You must marry the princess," cried he, "because you have broken the enchantment in which I held her, but I will be revenged on you. You shall have a son with a nose as long as this," – he made in the air a curve of half a foot – "yet he shall believe it is just like all other noses, and shall be always unfortunate till he has found out it is not. And if you ever tell anybody of this threat, you shall die on the spot."

The king, who was at first much terrified, soon began to laugh at this adventure. 'My son might have a worse misfortune than too long a nose,' thought he. 'At least it will hinder him neither in seeing nor hearing. I will go and find the princess, and marry her at once.'

He did so, but he only lived a few months after, and died before his little son was born, so that nobody knew anything about the secret of the nose.

The little prince was so much wished for that when he came into the world they agreed to call him Prince Wish. He had beautiful blue eyes, and a sweet little mouth, but his nose was so big that it covered half his face. The queen, his mother, was inconsolable. But, with time, she grew so used to the prince's nose that it did not seem to her any larger than ordinary noses of the court, where, in process of time, everybody with a long nose was very much admired, and the unfortunate people who had only snubs were taken little notice of.

Great care was observed in the education of the prince, and as soon as he could speak they told him all sorts of amusing tales, in which all the bad people had short noses, and all the good people had long ones. When he was old enough his tutor taught him history, and whenever any great king or lovely princess was referred to, the tutor always took care to mention that he or she had a long nose. All the royal apartments were filled with pictures and portraits having this peculiarity, so that at last Prince Wish began to regard the length of his nose as his greatest perfection.

When he was twenty years old his mother and his people wished him to marry. They procured for him the portraits of many princesses, but the one he preferred was Princess Darling, daughter of a powerful monarch and heiress to several kingdoms. Alas! With all her beauty, this princess had one great misfortune, a little turned-up nose. However, one clever person struck out a bright idea. He said that though it was necessary for a man to have a great nose, women were different, and that a learned man had discovered in a very old manuscript that the celebrated Cleopatra, queen of Egypt, the beauty of the ancient world, had a turned-up nose. At this information Prince Wish was so delighted that he immediately sent off ambassadors to demand Princess Darling in marriage.

She accepted his offer at once, and returned with the ambassadors. He made all haste to meet and welcome her, but when she was only three leagues distant from his capital, before he had time even to kiss her hand, the magician who had once assumed the shape of his mother's cat, Minon, appeared in the air and carried her off before the lover's very eyes.

Prince Wish, almost beside himself with grief, declared that nothing should induce him to return to his kingdom till he had found Princess Darling. He mounted a good horse, laid the reins on the animal's neck, and let him take him wherever he would.

The horse entered a wide, extended plain, and trotted on steadily the whole day without finding a single house. Master and beast began almost to faint

with hunger, and Prince Wish might have wished himself safe at home again, had he not discovered, just at dusk, a cavern, where sat a little woman who might have been more than a hundred years old.

She put on her spectacles the better to look at the stranger, and he noticed that her nose was so small that the spectacles would hardly stay on. Then the prince and the fairy – for it was a fairy – burst into a mutual fit of laughter.

"What a funny nose!" cried the one.

"Not so funny as yours, madam," returned the other. "But pray let us leave our noses alone, and be good enough to give me something to eat, for I am dying with hunger, and so is my poor horse."

"With all my heart," answered the fairy. "Although your nose is ridiculously long, you are no less the son of one of my best friends. I loved your father like a brother. He had a very handsome nose."

"What is wanting to my nose?" asked Wish.

"Oh! Nothing at all. On the contrary, there is a great deal too much of it, but never mind, one may be a very honest man, and yet have too big a nose.

"I will give you some supper directly, and while you eat it I will tell you my history in six words, for I hate much talking. A long tongue is as insupportable as a long nose; and I remember when I was young how much I used to be admired because I was not a talker, indeed, my mother, for poor as you see me now, I am the daughter of a great king, who always—"

'Hang the king your father!' Prince Wish was about to exclaim, but he stopped himself, and only observed that however the pleasure of her conversation might

make him forget his hunger, it could not have the same effect upon his horse, who was really starving.

The fairy, pleased at his civility, called her servants and bade them supply him at once with all he needed. "And," added she, "I must say you are very polite and very good-tempered, in spite of your nose."

"What has the old woman to do with my nose?" thought the prince. "If I were not so very hungry I would soon show her what she is – a regular old gossip and chatterbox. She fancies she talks little, indeed! One must be very foolish not to know one's own defects. This comes of being born a princess. Flatterers have spoiled her, and persuaded her that she talks little."

While the prince thus meditated, the servants were laying the table, the fairy asking them a hundred questions, simply for the pleasure of hearing herself talk. 'Well,' thought Wish, 'I am delighted that I came hither, if only to learn how wise I have been in never listening to flatterers, who hide from us our faults, or make us believe they are perfections. But they could never deceive me. I know all my own weak points, I trust.' And truly he believed he did.

So he went on eating contentedly, nor stopped till the old fairy began to address him.

"Prince," said she, "will you be kind enough to turn a

little? Your nose casts such a shadow that I cannot see what is on my plate. And, as I was saying, your father admired me and always made me welcome at court. What is the court etiquette there now? Do the ladies still go to assemblies, promenades, balls? I beg your pardon for laughing, but how very long your nose is."

"I wish you would cease to speak of my nose," said the prince, becoming annoyed. "It is what it is, and I do not desire it any shorter."

"Oh! I see that I have vexed you," returned the fairy. "Nevertheless, I am one of your best friends, and so I shall take the liberty of always—"

She would doubtless have gone on talking till midnight, but the prince, unable to bear it any longer, here interrupted her, thanked her for her hospitality, bade her a hasty adieu, and rode away.

He travelled for a long time, half over the world, but he heard no news of Princess Darling. However, in each place he went to, he heard one remarkable fact – the great length of his own nose. The little boys in the streets jeered at him, the peasants stared at him, and the more polite ladies and gentlemen whom he met in society used to try in vain to keep from laughing, and to get out of his way as soon as they could. So the poor prince became gradually quite forlorn and solitary. He thought all the world was mad, but still he never thought of there being anything queer about his nose.

At last the old fairy, who, though she was a chatterbox, was very good-natured, saw that he was almost breaking his heart. She felt sorry for him, and wished to help, for she knew the enchantment, which hid from him the Princess Darling, could not be broken till he discovered his own defect. So she went in search of the princess, and being more powerful than the magician, she took her away from him, and shut her up in a palace of crystal, which she placed on the road which Prince Wish had to pass.

He was riding along, very melancholy, when he saw the palace, and at its entrance was a room made of glass, in which sat his beloved princess, smiling and beautiful as ever. He leaped from his horse, and ran towards her. She held out her hand for him to kiss, but he could not get at it for the glass. Transported with eagerness and delight, he dashed his sword through the crystal, and succeeded in breaking a small opening, to which she put up her beautiful rosy mouth. But it was in vain, Prince Wish could not approach it. He twisted his neck about, and turned his head on all sides, till at length, putting up his hand to his face, he discovered the impediment.

"It must be confessed," exclaimed he, "that my nose is too long."

That moment the glass walls all split asunder, and the old fairy appeared, leading Princess Darling.

"Admit, prince," said she, "that you are very much obliged to me, for now the enchantment is ended. You may marry the object of your choice. But," added she, smiling, "I fear I might have talked to you forever on the subject of your nose, and you would not have believed me in its length, till it became an obstacle to your own inclinations. Now behold it!" and she held up a crystal mirror. Are you satisfied to be no different from other people?"

"Perfectly," said Prince Wish, who found his nose had shrunk to an ordinary length. And, taking the Princess Darling by the hand, he kissed her, courteously, affectionately, and satisfactorily. Then they departed to their own country, and lived very happy all their days.

Persephone and the Pomegranate Seed

An ancient Greek myth

OF ALL THE GODS and goddesses on Mount Olympus, Demeter loved the earth and its mortals the most. The great goddess of the harvest, she taught people how to plant, raise and reap grain, fruits and vegetables. In return, mortals loved Demeter dearly. Each mealtime, farmers' wives would set an extra place at the table, hoping that the goddess would grace them with her presence.

Demeter and the mighty father of the gods, Zeus, had a daughter, Persephone, who was their greatest joy. A beautiful girl, she cherished the earth, just like her mother. Persephone delighted in roaming the world, picking wild flowers in sunny meadows, and appreciating the splendour and beauty all around her.

One day, the goddess of love and beauty, Aphrodite, looked down from Mount Olympus. She smiled, catching sight of Persephone and her two best friends, the goddesses Athene and Artemis, enjoying themselves. Out of the corner of her eye, she also noticed the ruler of the underworld, Hades, riding through the sky in his black chariot.

Hades often left his dark kingdom to survey the earth above. The Titans, who had been imprisoned deep inside the world, were forever writhing about, trying to shake off their chains, and breathing fire in their fury. Hades had to watch that the earthquakes and volcanoes they caused were not tearing asunder the roof of his kingdom.

A sudden idea came to Aphrodite. She smiled mischeviously. None of the three goddesses, nor Hades, had ever been in love. But she could change all that. She quickly worked some magic, then sat back to watch the fun...

Sure enough, it wasn't long before Hades marched into Zeus' throne room. "Brother," the king of the underworld announced, "I am in torment. I have fallen deeply in love with your daughter, Persephone, and cannot rest for longing. I have come to ask for her hand in marriage. I swear that I will love her for eternity and do everything in my power to make her happy."

Zeus was pleased. The mighty king of a vast kingdom, Hades was a wise and fair ruler. He owned all the wealth of the earth, including diamonds and emeralds.

"I can think of no one better as a husband for Persephone," Zeus assured his brother. "However, I fear that Demeter will not allow it. She will never see her daughter taken from the sunshine that she loves to live underground – no matter how excellent a husband you are."

Hades groaned. "Brother, believe me, I know this too well – and I have tried my hardest to forget Persephone. My thoughts are filled with her, day and night. I can admire no other. If I cannot have Persephone as my wife, I fear my heart will break and I will never recover from such sorrow."

Zeus thought for a moment. "If asking Demeter will bring certain rejection, do not ask her. Seize Persephone and sweep her away. By the time Demeter finds out, it will be too late for her to do anything." Hades embraced his brother, then strode away, determinedly.

The very next day, Persephone, Athene and Artemis were laughing and playing in the woods, when in a clearing, Persephone spotted a flower she had never seen before. Delighted at its shimmering colours and delicate petals, she stooped to breathe in its sweet fragrance.

Suddenly, a thunderous rumble shook the earth and the ground opened wide. Out of underworld came a gleaming, black chariot pulled by two wild-eyed horses. Persephone tried to run but she was quickly seized by a strong arm and swept up into the arms of

the dark lord himself. Hades had come to collect his love. Galloping faster than the wind, the horses sprang away across the earth.

Athene and Artemis fell to their knees in the quake, and didn't see Hades take Persephone. On hearing her scream, they span round to find that she had vanished.

The bunch of flowers she had been picking were strewn around a gaping fissure in the earth. The panicked goddesses ran back and forth, desperately calling her name – but the only reply was the agitated bowing of the plants in the breeze and the alarmed rustling of the leaves.

Meanwhile, Persephone was held tightly in Hades' grasp as the chariot sped across fields valleys. Beside herself with terror, Persephone cried out, "Mother! Father! Help me! Someone, please help me!" But the lord of the dead simply cracked his whip, and they galloped through the sky, far away from the gods and goddesses of Mount Olympus. Persephone's voice simply faded and died on the wind.

Fortunately, the lord of the sun Helios was journeying in his own chariot high in the sky. For one brief moment, Helios saw the frothing horses, the grim-faced lord of darkness, and the horrified, screaming girl. Suddenly, the ground split in two, the horses and the chariot plunged down into the depths, and the earth sealed over them. Persephone was gone.

When Athene and Artemis told Demeter that Persephone had disappeared, the great goddess was beside herself with grief. Demeter set off across the whole world, desperately looking everywhere for her beloved child – but no one could tell her anything.

Demeter's sorrow soon turned to rage, and her anger turned on the earth and all the mortals it fed. The goddess commanded every seed to shrivel, every plant to droop, and every tree to wither. She ordered cold winds to blow, drying the soil. Then she told heavy rains to fall, washing away the earth's goodness. She prevented animals from giving birth to young. She ordered bushes not to bear fruit and vegetables not to sprout. She commanded leaves to fall from trees.

Helios saw what was happening from his chariot, high in the heavens. Deeply concerned, he hurried to Demeter at once to explain what he had seen. Demeter was not reassured or relieved at the news, and took out her fury on the entire world. Boiling with rage, she was determined to make all mortals suffer as she was suffering. She would leave them to die of starvation. Then the gods would be sorry.

Zeus was indeed alarmed as he beheld his dying world. He had underestimated Demeter's grief and wrath and immediately sent his messenger, Hermes, to the underworld. "Find Persephone and bring her back to her mother," Zeus ordered Hermes. "But hurry, for if she has eaten any of the food of the dead, she must remain in the underworld forever!"

Hermes sped into the kingdom of darkness. Kneeling before the thrones of Hades and his new queen, he explained that Demeter would destroy all creation if Persephone were not returned to the light at once. The sorrowful girl's heart was filled with hope at the messenger's words – until Hermes looked sternly at her and said, "Tell me, Persephone, that you have not yet eaten the food of the dead."

Persephone's heart began to flutter. "I have," she gasped, "but only one pomegranate seed – that's all."

The king of the underworld took Persephone's hand. "You now belong to me and my kingdom, but I will not force you to stay here forever," he said gently. "You must keep me company here for only half of every year. Now, go to your mother. But remember I love you."

Soon Persephone and Demeter were joyfully reunited. Touched by Hades' kindness, Persephone found herself thinking fondly of the sad king sitting alone in the underworld without her. She would be glad to return to him when the time came.

Every spring and summer, Demeter rejoices that Persephone is with her and the earth flourishes. But every autumn and winter, Demeter mourns her daughter's descent into the underworld, and the earth becomes barren once more.

Rip Van Winkle

An American legend

I N A VILLAGE in the foothills of the Catskill Mountains of America lived a man called Rip Van Winkle. Everybody liked Rip. He was a generous, easy-going man who was always glad to lend a hand to his neighbours. In fact, Rip Van Winkle was always to be found doing anybody else's work except his own. And didn't his wife remind him about it all the time! Nag, nag, nag it was, all day long. "Rip, if you're not too busy varnishing Mrs Green's fence today, you can mend the holes in the shed. Instead of helping to burn the farmer's rubbish, you can feed the chickens and milk the cows. Then if you can stop yourself from building Arne Jacob's wall for him, there's our potatoes

to dig up and the wagon to be washed down and the gutters to be cleared out and the yard to be swept and..." And so it was every day, on and on and on and on.

Every now and again, Rip Van Winkle whistled for his faithful dog Wolf, shouldered his gun, and strode away from his wife without a word. Off he would stroll up the mountainside, along the river and through the pine forests until his wife's screeching voice had grown so faint that he could no longer hear it, and he was surrounded only by the twittering of the birds, the rustling of the trees in the breeze and the panting of his companion by his side. Rip always knew there would be heck to pay when he got home. But a day off in the peaceful sunshine was well worth it!

One day when Rip had disappeared on one of these rambles, he was taking a rest under a shady tree, when he heard a voice calling his name. "Rip Van Winkle! Rip Van Winkle! Rip Van Winkle!" came the high, shrill cry.

Wolf's ears flattened against his skull and he gave a long, low growl. Rip looked in the direction Wolf was snarling and there among the long grass was a nodding green feather. The nodding green feather was tucked into a bright red cap. The cap was on the head of a bearded man no higher than his own boot, struggling under the weight of a big beer barrel.

"Rip Van Winkle! Rip Van Winkle! Rip Van Winkle!" shouted the dwarf, crossly.

"Will you get yourself over here and give me a hand with this barrel before it squashes me!"

Rip was so used to doing what he was told that he jumped up to help at once.

"That's better," wheezed the dwarf, as Rip took one end of the heavy barrel. "Now up we go!" Rip nearly tripped over as the dwarf stomped away up the mountain, pulling the barrel and Rip Van Winkle with him.

After at least an hour's tramping and much huffing and puffing, the dwarf led Rip Van Winkle straight behind a thundering waterfall, through a hidden door and into an enormous cavern.

Dwarfs were swarming everywhere. Some were dressed in aprons, pouring endless tankards of beer out of big kegs just like the one Rip was helping to carry. Others were playing nine pins, rolling smooth round black rocks at copper skittles and cheering loudly. Yet more dwarfs were drinking and clinking their tankards together, singing noisy songs.

"Pull up a chair," Rip's new friend invited him, lowering the barrel to the floor and passing him a tankard. "Help yourself to a drink. You must be gasping thirsty after that climb – I know I am!"

The stunned Rip Van Winkle did just that. "My,

that's mighty powerful stuff!" he spluttered, as he swallowed down a huge gulp of the dwarf beer. "But whatever it is, it's very good!" He licked his lips and poured himself another tankardful. None of the dwarfs was taking a blind bit of notice of him, so Rip Van Winkle sat back and began to watch the nine pins competition. "Well, this is a most pleasant way to spend the afternoon," he thought, helping himself to another beer... and another... and another... and another. And before Rip Van Winkle even realized he was drunk, he had slumped forwards onto a huge flat rock and was snoring loudly.

When Rip woke up, the dwarfs were gone and the cavern was empty. "Come on, Wolf," he yawned, and they both stood up and stretched. "We'd better hurry back or we'll never hear the last of it." Through the little door they strode and out from behind the waterfall and off down the mountain. "Wait for it," he murmured to his dog as he climbed the porch steps to his house. "Any minute now, that wife of mine will start screeching fit to wake the dead." Rip put his hand on the doorknob and turned. He nearly walked smack-bang into the door as it failed to open. "Well, this needs a bit of oil," he murmured to himself. He rattled the knob and twisted it about. "Funny," Rip remarked, "I think it's locked. She never locks the door, never."

At that very moment, the front door opened and there stood a woman with an angry face. "Who are you?" the woman snapped. "What are you up to, trying to get in my front door?" She was not his wife. In fact, Rip Van Winkle had never seen her before.

"Who are you?" gasped Rip. "What are you doing in my house?"

"Your house!" the woman scoffed. "I've lived here for over nineteen years!"

Rip Van Winkle backed off the porch and looked around him. He scratched his head and stared. The woman was right – it wasn't his house. Well, it looked similar to his house, but the curtains at the window were different. There were strange chairs on the verandah. The wagon in the yard was not his wagon.

"But – I – How –" stuttered Rip. "Where's Mrs Van Winkle?"

"Mrs Van Winkle?" the puzzled woman gawped.

"She left here nearly twenty years ago, just after her husband wandered off and disappeared. Now, be off with you or I'll call the police!"

"Twenty years!" marvelled Rip Van Winkle, as he wandered away stroking his beard. His beard! Suddenly Rip realized that his beard hung down to his knees. The woman's words had to be true! He had been asleep for twenty years!

Rip Van Winkle's hands trembled with the shock as he reached down and patted the bemused Wolf comfortingly. Then his mouth began to curve upwards in a small smile. "Just imagine, Wolf," he murmured. "No more nagging – ever!" Rip Van Winkle turned and strode across the street, whistling a merry tune. Happily, the inn was in the same place it always had been – and when the townspeople heard his story, he never had to buy himself another pint of beer again.

The Man who would not Scold

By Norman Hinsdale Pitman

OLD WANG LIVED in a village near Nanking. He cared for nothing in the world but to eat good food and plenty of it. His greatest pleasure was to eat at someone else's table when he knew that the food would cost him nothing, and you may be sure that at such times he always licked his chopsticks clean. But when he was spending his own money, he tightened his belt and drank a great deal of water, eating very little but scraps such as his friends would have thrown to the dogs.

One day while Wang was lying half asleep on the bank of a stream that flowed near his house he saw a flock of ducks swimming in the river. He knew that

485

they belonged to a rich man named Lin who lived in the village. They were fat ducks, so plump and tempting that it made him hungry to look at them. 'Oh, for a boiled duck!' he said to himself with a sigh. 'Why is it that the gods have not given me a taste of duck during the past year? What have I done to be thus denied?'

Then the thought flashed into his mind: 'Here am I asking why the gods have not given me ducks to eat. Who knows but that they have sent this flock thinking I would have sense enough to grab one? Friend Lin, many thanks for your kindness. I think I shall accept your offer and take one of these fowls for my dinner.' Of course Mr Lin was nowhere near to hear old Wang thanking him.

By this time the flock had come to shore. The miser picked himself up lazily from the ground, and, after tiring himself out, he at last managed to pick one of the ducks up, too. Once in his own yard, he lost no time in killing and preparing it for dinner. He ate it, laughing to himself all the time at his own slyness, and wondering what his friend Lin would think if he chanced to count his ducks that night. 'No doubt he will believe it was a hawk that carried off that bird. I think I will repeat the dose tomorrow. It would be a pity to leave the first one to pine away in lonely grief. I could never be so cruel.'

So old Wang went to bed happy. For several hours he snored away noisily. At midnight, however, he was wakened from his sleep by an unpleasant itching. His whole body seemed to be on fire, and the pain was more than he could bear. He got up and paced the floor. At early dawn he stepped outside his shanty. Lo, and behold, he found little red spots all over his body. Before his very eyes he saw tiny duck feathers sprouting from these spots. As the morning went by, the feathers grew larger and larger, until his whole body was covered with them from head to foot. Only his face and hands were free of the strange growth.

With a cry of horror, Wang began to pull the feathers out by handfuls, flinging them in the dirt and stamping on them. "The gods have fooled me!" he yelled. "They made me take the duck and eat it, and now they are punishing me for stealing." But the faster he jerked the feathers out, the faster they grew in again, longer and more glossy than before. Then, too, the pain was so great that he could scarcely keep from rolling on the ground. At last, completely worn out by his useless labour, and moaning with despair, he took to his bed. He tossed about and fell into a troubled sleep, and, sleeping, had a dream.

A fairy came to his bedside, it was Fairy Old Boy, the friend of the people. "Ah, my poor Wang," said the fairy, "all this trouble you have brought upon yourself by your shiftless, lazy habits. When others work, why do you lie down and sleep your time away?."

"I know you are telling the truth," wailed Wang, "but how, oh, how can I ever work with all these feathers sticking out of me? They will kill me!"

"Hear the man!" laughed Old Boy. "Now, if you were a hopeful, happy fellow, you would say, 'What a stroke of luck! No need to buy garments.' You are a pretty fellow to be complaining, aren't you?"

After joking in this way for a little while, the good fairy changed his tone of voice and said, "Now, Wang, are you really sorry for the way you have lived? I hear your parents died of hunger because you would not help them."

Wang, seeing that Old Boy knew all about his past life, and, feeling his pain growing worse and worse every minute, cried out at last: "Yes! I will do anything you say. Only, I pray you, free me of these feathers!"

"I wouldn't have your feathers," said Old Boy, "and I cannot free you of them. Only you can. What you need is to hear a good scolding. Go and get Mr Lin, the owner of the stolen duck, to scold freely. The harder he scolds, the sooner will your feathers drop out."

Mr Wang meant all right when he started out from his shanty. From his little hoard of money he took enough cash to pay Mr Lin for the stolen duck. He would do everything the fairy had told him and even more. But this doing more was just where he got into trouble. As he walked along the road jingling the string of cash, and thinking that he must soon give it up to his neighbour, he grew very sad. He loved every copper of his money and he disliked to part with it. After all, Old Boy had not told him he must confess to the owner of the duck – he had said he must go to Lin and get Lin to give a good scolding. "Old Boy did not say that Lin must scold me," thought the miser. "All that I need do is to get him to scold, and then my feathers will drop off and I shall be happy. Why not tell him that old Sen stole his duck, and get him to give Sen a scolding? That will surely do just as well, and I shall save my money as well as my face."

The longer Wang talked to himself, the surer he became that it was useless to tell Lin that he had stolen the duck. By the time he had reached the duck man's house he had fully made up his mind to deceive him. Mr Lin invited him to come in and sit down.

"Well, what's your business, Wang? You have come out early, and it's a long walk from your place to mine."

"Oh, I had something important I wanted to talk to you about," began Wang slyly. "That's a fine flock of ducks you have over in the meadow."

"Yes," said Mr Lin smiling, "a fine flock indeed." But he said nothing of the stolen fowl.

"How many have you?" questioned Wang more boldly.

"I counted them yesterday morning and there were fifteen."

"But did you count them again last night?"

"Yes, I did," answered Lin slowly.

"And there were only fourteen then?"

"Quite right, Wang, one of them was missing, but one duck is of little importance. Why do you speak of it?"

"What, no importance! Losing a duck? How can you

say so? A duck's a duck, isn't it, and surely you would like to know how you lost it?"

"A hawk most likely."

"No, it wasn't a hawk, but if you would go and look in old Sen's duck yard, you would likely find feathers."

"Nothing more natural, I am sure, in a duck yard."

"Yes, but your duck's feathers," persisted Wang.

"What! You think old Sen is a thief, do you, and that he has been stealing from me?"

"Exactly! You have it now."

"Well, well, that is too bad! I am sorry the old fellow is having such a hard time. He is a good worker and deserves better luck. I should willingly have given him the duck if he had only asked for it. Too bad that he had to steal it."

Wang waited to see how Mr Lin planned to punish the thief, feeling sure that the least he could do, would be to go and give him a good scolding.

But nothing of the kind happened. Instead of growing angry, Mr Lin seemed to be sorry for Sen.

"Aren't you even going to give him a scolding?" asked Wang in disgust.

"What use, what use? Hurt a neighbour's feelings just for a duck? That would be foolish indeed."

By this time the Miser King had begun to feel an

itching all over his body. The feathers had begun hurting again. He became excited and threw himself on the floor in front of Mr Lin.

"Hey! What's the matter, man?" cried Lin, thinking Wang was in a fit. "What's the matter? Are you ill?"

"Yes, very ill," wailed Wang. "Mr Lin, I'm a bad man, and I may as well own it at once and be done with it. There is no use trying to dodge the truth or hide a fault. I stole your duck last night, and today I came sneaking over here and tried to blame old Sen."

"Yes, I knew it," answered Lin. "I saw you carrying the duck off. Why did you come to see me if you thought I did not know you were guilty?"

"Only wait, and I'll tell you everything," said Wang, bowing still lower. "After I had boiled your duck and eaten it, I went to bed. Pretty soon I felt an itching all over my body. I could not sleep and in the morning I found that I had a thick growth of duck's feathers from head to foot. The more I pulled them out, the thicker they grew in. I could hardly keep from screaming. I took to my bed, and after I had tossed about for hours a fairy came and told me that I could never get rid of my trouble unless I got you to give me a thorough scolding. Here is the money for your duck. Now for the love of mercy, scold, and do it quickly, for I can't stand the pain much longer."

Wang was grovelling in the dirt at Lin's feet, but Lin answered him only with a loud laugh which finally burst into a roar. "Duck feathers! All over your body? Why, that's too good a story to believe!"

"Scold me! Scold me!" begged Wang.

But Lin only laughed the louder. "Pray let me see this wonderful growth of feathers first, and then we'll talk about the scolding."

Wang willingly opened his garment and showed the doubting Lin that he had been speaking the truth.

"They must be warm," said Lin, laughing. "Winter is soon coming and you are not over fond of work. Won't they save you the trouble of wearing clothing?"

"But they make me itch so I can scarcely stand it! I feel like screaming out, the pain is so great,"

"Be calm, my friend, and give me time to think of some good scold-words," said Lin at last. "I am not in the habit of using strong language, and very seldom lose my temper. Really you must give me time to think of what to say."

Mr Lin was now out of patience with his visitor. He could hold his tongue no longer:

"You lazy hound! You whelp! You turtle! You lazy, good-for-nothing creature! I wish you would hurry up and roll out of this!"

Now, in China, this is very strong language, and, with a cry of joy, Wang leaped from the ground, for he knew that Lin had scolded him. No sooner had the first hasty words been spoken than the feathers began falling from the lazy man's body, and, at last, the dreadful itching had entirely stopped. On the floor in front of Lin lay a great pile of feathers, and Wang, freed from his trouble, said, "Thank you kindly, my dear friend, for the pretty names you have called me. You have saved my life, I have learned my lesson well, I hope, and I shall go out from here a better man. Fairy Old Boy told me that I was lazy. You agree with the fairy. From this day, however, you shall see that I can bend my back like a good fellow. Goodbye, and many thanks for your kindness."

So saying, with many low bows and polite words, Wang left the duck owner's house, a happier and a wiser man.

Mrs Bedonebyasyoudid and Mrs Doasyouwouldbedoneby

From *The Water Babies* by Charles Kingsley

AND NOW HAPPENED to Tom a most wonderful thing – he came upon a water baby. A real live water baby, sitting on the white sand, very busy about a little point of rock. And when it saw Tom it looked up for a moment, and then cried, "Why, you are not one of us. You are a new baby! Oh, how delightful!"

Tom looked at the baby again, and then he said: "Well, this is wonderful! I have seen things just like you, but I thought you were shells, or sea creatures. I never took you for water babies like myself."

"Now," said the baby, "come and help me, or I shall not have finished before my brothers and sisters come, and it is time to go home."

"What shall I help you at?"

"In the last storm, the rock garden was ruined. And now I must plant it again with seaweeds, coral and anemones."

So they worked away at the rock, and planted it, and smoothed the sand down round it, and capital fun they had. Then, in came dozens of babies, and when they found that he was a new baby, they hugged him and kissed him, and there was no one ever so happy as poor little Tom.

"Now then," they cried, "we must come away home, or the tide will leave us dry. We have mended all the broken seaweed, and put all the rock-pools in order, and planted all the shells again in the sand."

And this is the reason why the rock-pools are always so neat and clean – because the water babies come inshore after every storm to sweep them out, and comb them down, and put them all to rights again. They leave sea anemones and the crabs to clear away everything, till the good tidy sea has covered up all the dirt in soft mud and clean sand.

Now when Tom got home, he found that the isle stood all on pillars, and that its roots were full of caves all curtained and draped with seaweeds, purple and crimson, green and brown, and strewn with soft white sand, on which the water babies sleep every night. But, to keep the place clean and sweet, the crabs picked up all the scraps off the floor and ate them like so many monkeys, while the rocks were covered with ten thousand sea anemones, and corals, who scavenged the water all day long, and kept it nice and pure.

But I wish Tom had given up all his naughty tricks. Instead, he frightened the crabs, to make them hide in the sand and peep out at him with the tips of their eyes, and put stones into the anemones' mouths, to make them fancy that their dinner was coming.

The other children warned him, and said, "Take care what you are at. Mrs Bedonebyasyoudid is coming." But Tom never listened, and, one Friday morning early, Mrs Bedonebyasyoudid came indeed.

A tremendous lady she was, and when the children saw her they all stood in a row, smoothed down their bathing dresses, and put their hands behind them, just as if they were going to be examined by the inspector.

And she had on a black bonnet, and a black shawl, and a pair of large green spectacles, and a great hooked nose, hooked so much that the bridge of it stood quite up above her eyebrows, and under her arm she carried a great birch-rod. Indeed, she was so ugly that Tom was tempted to make faces at her – but did not, for he did not admire the look of the birch-rod under her arm.

And she looked at the children one by one, and seemed very much pleased with them, though she never asked them one question about how they were behaving, and then began giving them nice sea-cakes.

Now little Tom watched all these sweet things given away, till his mouth watered, and his eyes grew as round as an owl's. For he hoped that his turn would come at last, and so it did. For the lady called him up, and held out her fingers with something in them, and popped it into his mouth – and, lo and behold, it was a cold hard pebble.

"You are a very cruel woman," said he, and began to whimper.

"And you are a very cruel boy, who puts pebbles into the sea anemones' mouths, to take them in, and make them fancy that they had caught a good dinner! As you did to them, so I must do to you."

"Who told you that?" said Tom.

"You did yourself, this very minute."

Tom had never opened his lips, so he was very much taken aback indeed.

"Yes, everyone tells me exactly what they have done wrong, and that without knowing it themselves. So there is no use trying to hide anything from me. Now go, and be a good boy, and I will put no more pebbles in your mouth, if you put none in other creatures."

"I did not know there was any harm in it," said Tom.

"Then you know now."

"Well, you are a little hard on a poor lad," said Tom.

"Not at all – I am the best friend you ever had. But I will tell you, I cannot help punishing people when they do wrong. I like it no more than they do."

"Was it long ago since they wound you up?" asked Tom. For he thought, the cunning little fellow, 'She will run down some day, or they may forget to wind her up.'

"I was wound up once and for all, so long ago, that I forget all about it."

"You must have been made a long time!" said Tom.

"I never was made, my child, and I shall go forever and ever, for I am as old as Eternity, and yet as young as Time."

And there came over the lady's face a very curious expression – very solemn, and very sad, and yet very, very sweet. And she looked up and away, as if she were gazing through the sea, and through the sky, at something far, far off, and as she did so, there came such a quiet, tender, patient, hopeful smile over her face that Tom thought for the moment that she did not look ugly at all.

And Tom smiled in her face, she looked so pleasant for the moment. And the strange fairy smiled too, and said:"Yes. You thought me very ugly just now, did you not?"

Tom hung down his head, and got very red about the ears.

"And I am very ugly. I am the ugliest fairy in the world, and I shall be, till people behave themselves as they ought to do. And then I shall grow as handsome as my sister, who is the loveliest fairy in the world. Her name is Mrs Doasyouwouldbedoneby. So she begins where I end, and I begin where she ends, and those who will not listen to her must listen to me, as you will see."

Poor old Mrs Bedonebyasyoudid! She has a great deal of hard work before her, and had better have been born a washerwoman, and stood over a tub all day. But, you see, people cannot always choose their own profession.

Tom determined to be a very good boy all Saturday, and he was, for he never frightened one crab, nor tickled any live corals, nor put stones into the sea anemones' mouths, to make them fancy they had got a dinner. And when Sunday morning came, sure enough, Mrs Doasyouwouldbedoneby came too. Whereat all the little children began dancing and clapping their hands and Tom danced too with all his might.

And as for the pretty lady, I cannot tell you what the colour of her hair was, or, of her eyes. No more could Tom, for, when anyone looks at her, all they can think of is that she has the sweetest, kindest, tenderest, funniest, merriest face they ever saw, or want to see. But Tom saw that she was a very tall woman, as tall as her sister. But instead of being gnarly and horny, and scaly, and prickly, like her, she was the most nice, soft, fat, smooth, pussy, cuddly, delicious creature who ever nursed a baby, and she understood babies thoroughly, for she had plenty of her own, whole rows and regiments of them, and has to this day. And all her

delight was, whenever she had a spare moment, to play with babies, in which she showed herself a woman of sense, for babies are the best company, and the pleasantest playfellows, in the world, at least, so all the wise people in the world think. And therefore when the children saw her, they naturally all caught hold of her, and pulled her till she sat down on a stone, and climbed into her lap, and clung round her neck, and caught hold of her hands. And then they all put their thumbs into their mouths, and began cuddling and purring like so many kittens, as they ought to have done. While those who could get nowhere else sat down on the sand, and cuddled her feet – for no one, you know, wear shoes in the water. And Tom stood staring at them, for he could not understand what it was all about.

"And who are you, you little darling?" she said.

"Oh, that is the new baby!" they all cried, pulling their thumbs out of their mouths, "And he never had any mother," and they all put their thumbs back again, for they did not wish to lose any time.

"Then I will be his mother, and he shall have the very best place, so get out, all of you, this moment."

And she took up two great armfuls of babies – nine hundred under one arm, and thirteen hundred under

the other – and threw them away, right and left, into the water. But they did not even take their thumbs out of their mouths, but came paddling and wriggling back to her like so many tadpoles, till you could see nothing of her from head to foot for the swarm of little babies.

But she took Tom in her arms, and laid him in the softest place of all, and kissed him, and patted him, and talked to him, tenderly and low, such things as he had never heard before in his life, and Tom looked up into her eyes, and loved her, and loved, till he fell fast asleep from pure love.

And when he woke she was telling the children a story. And what story did she tell them? One story she told them, which begins every Christmas Eve, and yet never ends at all forever and ever. And, as she went on, the children took their thumbs out of their mouths and listened quite seriously, but not sadly at all, for she never told them anything sad, and Tom listened too, and never grew tired of listening. And he listened so long that he fell fast asleep again, and, when he woke, the lady was nursing him still.

"Don't go away," said little Tom. "This is so nice. I never had any one to cuddle me before."

"Now," said the fairy to Tom, "will you be a good boy for my sake, and torment no more sea beasts till I come back?"

"And you will cuddle me again?" said poor little Tom.

"Of course I will, you little duck. I should like to take you with me and cuddle you all the way, only I must not," and away she went.

So Tom really tried to be a good boy, and tormented no sea beasts after that as long as he lived, and he is quite alive, I assure you, still.

Freya and the Brising Necklace

A Norse myth

THE BEAUTIFUL GODDESS Freya wandered through the halls of her palace, counting her blessings. She had a wonderful husband, the god Odur, and two lovely daughters, as fair as flowers. They had an elegant home and splendid garden in the heavenly realm of Asgard, surrounded by their friends. Still, Freya's heart was restless, yearning for excitement.

Preparing her carriage pulled by cats, she decided to go on a journey. First, she travelled through Midgard to see the world of humans. Then she journeyed through the land of the light elves, Alfheim, home of her dear brother, Frey. Finally, she found herself at Svartalfheim, the realm of the black dwarves.

A wicked dwarf called Dvalin and his three equally wicked brothers learned that the beautiful goddess was coming and set a trap for her. Deep inside a dark cave, they built a workshop and busied themselves with an anvil, hammer and a fiery furnace. As Freya wandered along, the noise of the dwarves sparked her curiosity and she drew closer.

Lit only by a raging furnace, Freya found four dwarves hard at work. They pretended not to notice her arrival. Looking around, she gasped in astonishment at the most beautiful necklace she had ever seen. Unbeknown to the unfortunate Freya, the necklace was enchanted. From the moment the goddess laid her eyes on it, the charms began to take effect and she felt an uncontrollable need to possess it.

"You have surely crafted the most exquisite necklace in the universe," Freya breathed, her heart pounding. "How much silver do you ask for it?"

"The Brising Necklace is indeed the most desirable adornment in all creation," Dvalin replied, "but we could not sell it for all the silver in the world."

Freya's pulse raced. She could not take her eyes off it. "Then how much gold do you ask for it?" she said.

"The Brising Necklace is not for sale for any treasure of gold," Dvalin countered.

Freya began to feel desperate. She could not walk away without it. "There must be some treasure you will take for the necklace," she implored. "Please tell me, what is your price? I am willing to pay!"

The dwarf brothers exchanged evil glances. "The only treasure we will exchange for the necklace is you," Dvalin stated firmly. "You must be married to each of us for one day and one night, and in return, the necklace will be yours."

Freya was so enchanted that she did not hesitate. "So be it," she agreed, and the deal was done.

As soon as Freya held the Brising Necklace as her prize, she came to her senses and felt ashamed. How she regretted betraying her beloved Odur. Hurrying home to Asgard, she stowed the necklace safely in her chamber, setting strong magic onto the door. Her secret was safe forever...

However, the mischievous god Loki made it his unofficial business to find out about everything that went on in the universe. He soon discovered all about Freya's misdemeanour and, being the troublemaker he was, he delighted in telling all to Odur.

Odur was furious, not at Freya, but at Loki. "How dare you enter my home and accuse my wife of such unfaithfulness, without a shred of evidence!" Odur roared. "I utterly refuse to believe it. Unless you can bring me this Brising Necklace as proof, I shall tear you limb from limb if you cross my path again!"

Fuming, Loki slunk away. He was determined to make Odur eat his words by somehow stealing the necklace. Loki knew that Freya had sealed the chamber with magic, so he turned himself into a fly and zipped around the door and windows, searching for a tiny hole to squeeze through. At last he found one – it was no bigger than the eye of a needle, but it was enough.

Holding his breath, Loki wriggled through, and found himself inside Freya's chamber. There she was, asleep, wearing the cursed Brising Necklace. Even Loki had to admit that it truly was a priceless work. Silently, he turned himself back into human form, and gently slid the necklace from around her throat. Quietly unlocking the door, he stole away into the night.

When Freya awoke the next morning, she knew that her secret had been discovered. Beside herself with anguish, she hurried to find her husband to confess everything. However, Odur was nowhere to be seen.

Distraught, Freya dashed to the mighty Odin and threw herself at his feet. Weeping bitterly, she told all. "I shall never rest until I find my husband and beg his forgiveness," she sobbed.

Odin looked grave. The all-seeing father of the gods knew all about Freya's sin, and how her estranged husband had stridden away, heartbroken. He also knew where Odur was … but he decided the goddess had to learn a bitter lesson. "Wander the universe until you find Odur and win his pardon," Odin announced. "But you must wear the necklace forever more, as a permanent reminder of your mistake."

Odin sent the messenger, Heimdall, to retrieve the necklace from Loki, and soon it was clasped around Freya's neck once more.

With a heavy heart, Freya wandered away from Asgard, searching for her husband. Wise Odin watched her go with fondness, knowing that all would soon be well again between them.

Index of Stories